Light of the Ark

Book I of Light the Ark Series - A Christian Fiction
Thriller

James Bonk

Anthony James Bonk

Books By James Bonk

Light of the Ark Series

1. Light of the Ark

2. Shadows of the Ark

3. Light of the World

- Isaiah and the Sea of Darkness (standalone prequel)

More Fiction

- Christian's Look Back at Life

Stay up to date on new releases and email exclusive content: https://sendfox.com/jamesbonkwrites

Dedication

To my girls,
You are my foundation.

Note to Reader – Thank You!

T hank you so much for reading. I hope you enjoy this book as much as I enjoyed writing it.

Want to be updated on release dates and other books in the series?

Sign up here to join and receive infrequent updates: https://sendfox.com/jamesbonkwrites

Table of Contents

Chapter One

Coffee with Dad

T he steam from the coffee rose before his face as he stared, lost in thought. He was inches away from taking a sip, but his mind was captured before he could. "Dad."

He wasn't here; his mind was somewhere else.

"Dad..."

His eyes were locked on the Bible on the end table next to him. It was an old Bible but had held up well. The thick green covers were tattered from wear, but it was handled with care for the decades or more it had been in the family's possession. Even with the wear, it always had sort of a glow to it, a welcoming and unique nature. Recent events added deep cuts into the hard green backing, and the spine of the book was half torn off, now held by a strip of grey duct tape. Matthew knew more about the story and the book, but far from all of it. That would take a lifetime.

"Dad. You okay?"

The funeral was yesterday. All of the boys, along with their wives and kids, had packed into the old home they grew up in. Zechariah had three boys: Luke, Mark, and Matthew. Each of them had two kids. The extra twelve in Zech and Mary's home was a strain, but a welcome one to the heads of the Light family. Each son had offered to put his family in a hotel, or in Matthew's case, drive the hour and stay in their own home, but their mother wouldn't hear of it. Secretly, all of the boys liked being back in their old home. The sons, wives, and grandparents could all have breakfast together, play games in the backyard, and stay up late playing cards after the kids went down. That sort of family time does not happen when part of the family wakes up in a hotel twenty minutes away.

Back when the boys were young, the house was busy, loud, and all-around hectic. Now that their kids were here, it brought back those chaotic memories. The grandkids ranged from diapers to high school and thankfully all got along and played well with each other.

"Hey, Grandpa!"

Matthew's oldest daughter's voice snapped Zech out of his trance before Matthew's words could. The aged patriarch smiled at the five-year-old to acknowledge her. She thanked him for the bacon but now was eager for her grandfather's famous pancakes. He loved making his grandkids bacon, especially the real pork kind, as well as blueberry pancakes. Zech's wife Mary made nearly every meal in that house since they were married, but once a week and on special occasions, Zech made bacon and pancakes. Mary would talk with the kids and grandkids while sipping on her coffee, and Zech worked away in the kitchen, usually singing along to various country songs. The house picked up the wonderful smell of bacon. The smell rolled through the house and Zech's ear-to-ear grin was nearly as contagious as the hunger.

This morning was different, though. The funeral lingered in the air while recent events weighed on Matthew's and Zech's minds.

The artifact, as they had come to call it, was paramount, but for different reasons.

The crate.

Jeremiah.

Terrence.

Isaiah.

Even Micah loomed in their thoughts. That was new for Matthew, but not for Zech, as Micah had been a daily thought for nearly three decades.

As more grandkids ran past, Zech looked to his son, finally acknowledging him.

"Paul stopped by last night while you and Liz were out. He asked for us to come by the yard today. He and I both want to talk with you about the other night. The situation with Terrence."

"Dad, I already told the cops everything, and honestly, I am sick of talking about Terrence," Matthew replied. His voice echoed his frustration, but he kept it low with the kids nearby.

"You have learned more about your family and our responsibilities than I ever thought you would. There is much more to this than you know. And, honestly, I'm glad it is you that will be taking over."

Matthew stared at his dad, trying to get a read on him. Zech was not a huge man, but strong in his days, and he still carried a presence with him. The sort of presence that you respected, physically and spiritually. Matthew did not know what his father meant, but given the past two months, he knew it was serious.

***

Zech had pastored the church for decades, just as his father Isaiah did before him, as did his father... and his. None of his three sons were going to be the next pastor. Mark, the middle son, worked with the church, but as a missionary, currently based in Eastern Europe. Zech had flown Mark, his wife, and two kids in for the funeral. Zech still mentored Mark and saw the kids on video calls weekly. Mark never saw himself as a pastor, and while he always attended, he did not work in the church for most of his twenties. He made his own path in finance and eventually tech investing, advising on IPOs and amassing a small fortune in his mid-twenties. However, he gave it all up, sold his shares in numerous companies that became tech giants, and moved into ministry. His small fortune could have been quite a large one if he had held on for only a few short years longer, but nope. Mark cashed out and never looked back. He never told Matthew the full reason, but his brothers knew. The week before Mark quit, he was on a trip with a few young and soon-to-be billionaires. He was being courted to help with their next IPO. The trip took a few detours, though, and Mark realized the slippery slope he was tip-toeing. His clients convinced the pilots of the private flight to divert the plane towards Vegas. Mark spent two nights trying to deal with the events, to just get through, but on the third day, enough was enough. He did not reboard the original flight and never looked back.

Luke was the oldest and lived a few hundred miles away in Atlanta. He loved the church and was a member at a sister location in Atlanta, but never showed interest in leading the church his father spent his life growing. Luke had had a rebellious childhood, mixing in with the wrong crowd and keeping his mother up many late nights during his teenage years. He took the long road, but eventually, after moving out and no longer getting financial support from his parents, Luke started building a new life. He rose up in the ranks at a local car shop from part-time work to becoming the right-hand man of the owner. Within a few years, Luke opened his own shop, and within another ten years, he owned a successful regional chain based in Atlanta. Matthew could see his father's work ethic and his mother's kindness in both of his brothers, and it served them well in their professional and personal lives.

The family torch to lead the church would have fallen onto Matthew, if it had not been for Jeremiah, Matthew's best friend who was practically a fourth son. Zech had been childhood friends with Jeremiah's father, Micah. When Micah passed away in his thirties, Jeremiah was only six years old, and Zech took it on himself to be Jeremiah's father-figure.

"J," as he had been called since he was a kid, fit in perfectly with the family. He and Matthew had been best friends their whole lives. The three Light boys were all above average height and played sports growing up, and J fit right in. J fit right in with the older boys as well, as he always seemed to be an inch or two taller and ten to twenty pounds heavier than Matthew. He could join one of Mark's teams without friends knowing he was younger, whereas Matt was obviously the youngest.

J took more to reading and noticed when Zech always had the Bible out. While Matthew took a love of math into the engineering field, and J took a love of reading into scripture. The time in scripture at such a young age led him to become a Bible competition finalist and champion numerous times throughout grade school. By the time he was sixteen, he was filling in for the youth pastor and giving guest sermons to his peers in the youth groups.

***

Childhood memories of J and himself flashed in Matthew's mind as he took his turn getting lost in thought. The steam from his coffee began to fade in the cool morning air.

The thoughts of long-ago good times with his friend began to fade, and the past two months came into focus. Matthew could see J talking with Terrence after the Christmas Eve service.

Why did he not insist on finding out more?

He saw the look on J's face as he walked away from Terrence.

There were plenty of chances, but he figured his friend was fine. "He would say something. He's fine." Matthew heard his past self say it, over and over.

If he had only known then all the damage and the subsequent death that would come.

He could have helped.

He should have helped.

He would have helped! If he only knew...

Zech brought him back from his spiraling thoughts.

"We'll head to Paul's after breakfast. He said he'll be at the yard all morning working on repairs from last week's damage. For now, it's time we get these kids some pancakes before they mutiny on us."

***

Matthew and his wife Elizabeth, who went by Liz, had always been close to his parents. They enjoyed visiting for their own sake but mostly for their two girls. Grandma was their best friend and the only person Matthew knew who could out-energy a five-year-old. From a tea party, to freeze tag, into the pool, out of the pool, to another tea party, to story time, and on and on. Those kids slept great at their grandparents' house.

The adults would stay up late playing Euchre or Sequence or just talking, but soon would pass into a deep sleep just like the girls. The peacefulness of the house always took over.

Matthew and Liz had been married over ten years now. Liz's father, Paul Stollard, ran the Storage Yard just outside of town near the river. Paul was a little older than Zech and was almost like an older brother to him. They had been family friends for as long as Zech could remember. The Stollards regularly came to church, but being an hour away from the grounds, they did not always attend all the functions and events. That was a reason Matthew and Liz joked they should have met sooner.

Liz was a couple of years younger than Matthew. They could have met at a younger age but had a different circle of friends, attended different service times, and were in different youth groups. They had "known of" each other for years but went to different schools as kids. But then, at a mutual friend's party in college, they both delighted in seeing an old face from home and struck up a conversation. The friendship quickly turned into more, and from then on, they were inseparable and married less than two years later. Liz was a beautiful woman with amber-brown hair, bright brown eyes, and a picture-perfect smile. Matthew joked that she could grace the covers of any risqué men's magazine, yet he loved how she could dress conservatively and still be more desirable than any model in a low-cut shirt.

Liz was not only beautiful, but she was also Matthew's spiritual anchor. Without her, he likely would have drifted away from the church. With two young kids and living an hour away, it was easy to justify watching the message online or not at all. However, it was Liz who corralled the family and insisted they attend in person. It was so much easier to watch online, or better yet, simply listen to the audio version later in the week, but Liz would not have it, especially being the daughter-in-law to Pastor Zech and Mary. Liz knew they needed to be in person.

Matthew had been in church his whole life, but more out of habit than a burning desire. Once he moved out of his parent's house, the Sunday morning habit took a slight hit that snowballed into a low attendance rate, only attending during holidays or special events before dating Liz. He always felt like he was in the public eye as he passed through the rotunda and into the sanctuary each Sunday. His passive nature toward church bled into his professional life even after marrying Liz, more doing what he was told instead of proactively trying to help the company. His boss saw his potential—it flashed at times on big contracts where all of the company's leadership could not ignore it—however, it was few and far between. His boss gradually gave him more responsibility to flush out that potential, but the results were not reliable. Only in the past couple of months did his boss notice a change.

Being the youngest of three boys and having a best friend the size of his older brother, Matthew learned how to survive more than learning how to thrive. Unless he tried his absolute hardest, he did not have a shot in the backyard sports and games. Given the extra effort, he could hang with the larger boys, and it helped him best the majority of his peers; however, it also led to a fear of failure. Most new things he could succeed at, but eventually, there came a time when the effort waned and he stopped caring. It was all or nothing, and too often lately, he felt like nothing was winning, never putting in the work to carry his skills into mastery. Granted, his breadth in many sports and professional topics was immense, but he kept hitting the ceiling of his own burnout. Once he figured something out, he moved on. He feared his job at the engineering consulting company was coming to the same head. He was a licensed Professional Engineer for a private consulting company. He was brought in to help design manufacturing areas, warehouses, and office spaces, and then provide the simulations to show what tweaks could be made during build or later life to customize the space for optimum efficiency. He learned all the coding and visualization required to complete a seven-figure contract himself. However, where he really shined was when he put himself in the shoes of the workers who would one day inhabit the space. When that happened, he was a magnitude better than his old self. He would delegate the drawings and simulations, then critique and communicate with the team with ease as the project vastly improved from what he could do on his own. This was the potential his bosses saw, but unfortunately, Matthew seemed to randomly flash upward potential as opposed to consistently growing into the promotion he recently received.

But that all changed at the start of the new year. Two months ago, Matthew gradually showed the consistency his bosses desired. There was something growing in him. Something all the mentoring and training had not flushed out.

***

The family cleaned up the pancake breakfast, or what was left of it after the kids inhaled their meals. Matthew and his brothers decided to postpone their five-mile run into the woods, given Zech and Matthew's trip to see Paul and their now full bellies nearly putting them to sleep. Luke and Mark, along with their wives and Mary, moved into the backyard with the kids on the crisp morning. The ladies were planning a girls' trip to a few stores capped with lunch at the local Greek restaurant while the dads gathered the kids for a mix of football and tag. It looked more like Calvinball to Matthew as he turned from the back porch toward his father.

Matthew was glad the recent events, especially the funeral, were not weighing too hard on anyone as the day went on. Everyone except himself and his father. Both men took on a somber tone as the rest of the family moved away from breakfast. They quietly cleaned up the plates and silverware together. Zech's Bible now loomed heavy on Matthew's mind. It was one room away, but in his mind's eye, he could see it glowing.

The worn green Bible.

Decades old or more.

How it glowed bright in his mind.

As he began to ask his dad a question, Matthew paused when his cat, a fluffy grey Chartreux named Porkchop, jumped onto the front window seat. Recently, Matthew found himself talking to the cat more and more in the early morning hours. The cat, now ten years old, had been his confidant these past couple months. Matthew had a new appreciation for the feline and decided to bring him with them during the short stay at Zech and Mary's home.

He watched the cat as it stared back at him; with a slow blink, it moved its gaze to the front yard, seemingly directing Matthew to look. As Matthew looked through the front window, his grip on the used forks and knives turned white knuckle as his vision focused on what was outside on the front curb.

It was Terrence.

And he was holding a sledgehammer.

Terrence stared through the front window and his eyes met Matthew's. How long had he been out there? Did he watch them all eat breakfast or had he just pulled up?

Before Matthew could finish his thought, Terrence raised the sledgehammer, and with one smooth motion, brought it down like a meteor on the Lights' mailbox.

Matthew did not even notice the shotgun-like boom of the impact. He stared and thanked God the kids were in the backyard. Terrence then shot a look back at Matthew after the destruction, holding the gaze just as they locked eyes in the Storage Yard only days before when the muzzle of Terrence's shotgun was pointed into Matthew's chest.

Terrence then moved back into his car and was gone without another sound.

Matthew looked at the mailbox as his father came around from the kitchen. Zech asked what the noise was. The iron pole and box slouched, hunched over and pitiful after the blow, half as tall as it once was.

The family name "Light" now appeared scratched and shattered, hardly legible in the shadows of the bent iron.

Chapter Two

Months Ago

Matthew and Liz struggled to get the girls dressed and in the car in time for the drive to church. If traffic was light, they could make it to church in forty-five minutes, but other times, it took over an hour.

The church had grown over the years, and for the past five years, it offered three Christmas Eve services: an afternoon service geared toward the more elderly "sages" age group of the church, an evening service targeting families, and a night service that targeted singles and younger members.

The three services were J's idea and helped immensely. At first, Zech was unsure of going to three services. A typical Sunday was two services and the required volunteers and church staff were large enough. Now if there were three services for the holiday, Zech would be asking all his staff and most of the volunteers to give up their Christmas Eve. However, he had faith in J's idea, and it proved to be a shot in the arm to the church's Christmas efforts. Not only did it alleviate the overflow problems and "standing room only" issues, but the targeted services encouraged more interactions amongst similar members, regular attenders, and first-timers.

The sages could get in before the large crowds, and most decided to stick around to watch the youngsters enjoy the cookies and events in between services. The youth group led a live nativity in the entrance way as well as Christmas carols at key spots in the rotunda. There was always something to watch and discuss as people funneled in and out of the sanctuary. Both the nativity and carols were J's suggestions, but this time, they came via two of the high school students he mentored. Many of the high school youth group members and young professionals in the church looked up to J. He held himself with confidence and was comfortable in his own skin. His confidence being a Christian was in stark contrast to what the young church goers were living through in daily life, many at secular high schools and colleges. Many times, they felt the need to shy away from their religion while away from church.

Act like you like the normal music and shows.

Don't talk about Casting Crowns.

Don't talk about the Bible, especially the latest Bible Study on Romans.

Don't be a weirdo.

But J gave them the confidence to show their true colors. It was still hard as a young person in school or early work life, but now J had built a few young leaders to follow in his footsteps and lead major portions of the youth group. In comparison to the older Zech, J was the "Cool Pastor" that all the kids looked up to.

The second service in the evening was for families. In addition to the music, coffee, and cookies, there was a kids' church that kicked off in parallel to the regular service. Some parents kept their children for worship and then led them over to kids' church during announcements but before the sermon started. This one was Isaiah's idea from decades before in order to get parents more focused on the message, instead of being paranoid that their child was going to be the one to scream in the middle of service.

As the second service funneled out, the music moved from live carolers to recordings, in part to give the singers a break, but also to have a more contemporary feel. This fit the younger crowd and singles in the third and final service. Zech was a strong believer in cultural influence. He ensured there were popular artists singing songs about Jesus's birth. He weaved this into the message to show not all of pop culture was anti-church. However, the meat of the message was a strong warning that many people, especially celebrities, were not Christ followers, and the young crowd would always contend with temptation in the world. Zech spoke to this crowd, telling them they must be unique in the world and learn to discern right from wrong, to rebuke when necessary, yet to show love and treat your neighbor as you would yourself.

Matthew and Liz arrived later than expected but with enough time to enjoy a cup of coffee and a cookie for each girl while they hummed along to the carolers.

The winters in North Florida were usually mild, but this one was colder than normal, and a sign to come for the entire season. The highs were in the forties this week, when high fifties or sixties were the norm in late December. The warm church was a welcome sight as cars pulled in under overcast skies and a setting sun.

The Light family found seats just off the main portion of the rotunda and looked around for friends as they talked and sipped coffee. The girls enjoyed their Christmas cookies. Matthew caught a glimpse of his friend J through the crowd. He was on the other side of a large group, greeting people as they came in from the cold. Matthew decided not to interrupt but would keep an eye out in order to say hi before service started.

They mostly people-watched and sang along with the girls and carolers as they said hello to those they knew. As service time approached, they began making their way into the sanctuary, but Matthew could not find J. He was usually in the rotunda, helping to herd people into the service as worship started, before taking his front row seat next to Zech and Mary.

Matthew and Liz had a handful trying to shepherd the girls in for worship. Apparently, cookies and juice right before asking them to sit still was not the best idea. They looked at each other with a sarcastic "who knew" look and both were thankful for the kids' church starting shortly.

Finally, right before entering service, Matthew saw J, now on the other side of the rotunda and talking to someone Matthew did not know. He was older than J and Matthew but maybe ten years younger than Zech, with dark tan skin and a short but quite full beard. The man had a half-smile on his face as the conversation progressed while J's typical smile was a somber straight line across his face under tightly squinted eyes. Matthew knew this look on J, and he had not seen it in years. It was from their younger days of playing sports together. Back then, it was precursor to J exploding on someone. J was always one of the larger kids for his age, and always had confidence in his game, but surprisingly, his talents were more of a finesse game. He could weave through the defense with ease. His finesse combined with his size surprised most opponents and got under their skin, which J would just laugh about and kick his own game up a notch. It was not easy to get under J's skin, but it did happen, and when an opponent did, the entire game would be derailed.

Matthew was more a grinder on those teams, a hard work ethic he learned from playing against older brothers. He learned that if he could hold his own with the bigger kids, he could excel against his peers.

When J was derailed, it was because the opponent went after Matthew, J's closest friend and practically brother. The events played themselves out in nearly the same manner every time. It drove their coaches crazy and J was usually benched because of it. The scenario would go like this: Matthew would pester the opposition all game, eventually causing a turnover or drawing a penalty. The opposition would let Matthew know how they felt about it, usually with a stick to the back of Matthew's knee. Matthew was good at drawing penalties, but if the hit was particularly bad and J saw it, the offending player found himself buried into the boards or sliding across the ice. J would end up in the penalty box and arguing with the refs. The old story replayed more often their last couple years of competitive hockey as smarter teams figured this out. It was an easy way to get under J's skin, and thus take the leading scorer out of the game.

As Matthew followed his girls into service, he made a note to talk to J later. Flashes of a younger J smashing an opponent across the ice were bright in his mind.

***

Worship was incredible. The band led the audience through a series of favorites, starting with "Silent Night" and gradually building to an energetic and emotional rendition of "Mary did you know." Matthew helped the girls back through the rotunda towards sign-in for kids' church. As he left the sanctuary, he once again saw J and the man he had been speaking to before worship. Now they were parting ways, the man leaving the church and J heading into service. Matthew was able to catch his eye and wave as he guided the girls, but J only gave a slight nod, mostly keeping his head down. Not a Christmas Eve greeting you typically gave your best friend of thirty-plus years. The sanctuary doors closed behind J and Matthew felt a tug on his arm. The girls were eager to get into their own version of service, where they would play games and laugh without being shushed for every noise they made.

As Matthew dropped them off and made his way back to Liz, his mind could not shake J. The look on J's face concerned him. It was now slightly different than the same look he saw so many times before as kids, the one that inevitably led to an opposing player being tossed across the ice like a frustrated child throws their stuffed animal.

No... No. This look was now different. There was still the hint of anger, but now frustration and confusion crept over his friend's distant expression. Matthew knew his friend well, but what troubled him the most was not recognizing that look, not understanding what was going on in his friend's mind.

Matthew's mind snapped back to the present as his father took the pulpit in the center of the wide stage. Growing up, he had heard every one of his dad's Christmas sermons, and in most cases, way more than once, as Zech would practice them at home leading up to the holiday service.

This one did not disappoint the crowd, as Pastor Zechariah started light-hearted to warm the crowd up, and then got deep into the word, even challenging the audience on deep introspection at times. That was Zech's typical style, and it was a good one with long-time members and first-timers alike.

Zech started by speaking of children's faces on Christmas morning. Those bright smiles that make all the buying, wrapping, and other chaotic events of the season worth it. He spoke of taking long walks with his wife, Mary, through neighborhoods that went overboard with brilliant lights.

The seasoned pastor then transitioned into how God must look down on us, just like we look upon our children on Christmas. How he imagined God smiling, full of love for even the smallest gifts he gives us, but also trying to lift our spirits as we grow frustrated and drift from him, as a child may pout for not being able to receive a present early. Zech transitioned to a soft voice, as if he was talking to one of his grandchildren but as God speaking to an adult.

"It's okay, child. I love you. You are not ready for that gift yet, but come, be with me, and you will have love. You will have peace. You will have gifts that make your worries melt away. Seek me. Look inside yourself and you will find me. I never left. Talk to me in prayer. My love is in you. You have the greatest gift already. I gave you my son. The blood of life was spilled for you. Do not forget that gift. I gave it to you because I love you."

As Zech wrapped up the message, he asked the crowd about their gifts.

"Are you giving gifts just to give them, or out of love?"

"Are you hanging lights to keep up with your neighbors, or to celebrate Jesus' birth?"

Zech let those questions sink in for a moment. Then he allowed a slight smirk across his face. Those who knew him, knew what that smirk meant and what was coming next.

"Oh, and speaking of lights. Who here has a Nativity scene up in their yard?!?!"

First-timers, and even some regular attenders, were caught off guard by the question and change in the pastor's tone. It was a "did you do your homework" type tone that a parent might give to a procrastinating child.

"For those who have a Nativity scene up, thank you. And to those who don't..."

He let the comment linger in the air... before breaking it like a sudden bass drum in a quiet room.

"GO GET ONE!

"PUT IT UP!

"And I don't care that tomorrow is Christmas. That means you'll probably get a great deal on the bigger, more expensive ones. Get it, display it, and leave it up until New Year's."

His voice settled back to his normal volume and tone.

"Because how can we make Jesus the center of our lives if we are not going to make him the center of the season?"

He dropped his volume again but added a brightness to it, as if talking to a child.

"Show the world how happy you are to receive his gift of life, like a child on Christmas morning."

***

Christmas night was always spent at Zech and Mary's home. With Mark's family traveling for missionary work, and Luke in Atlanta, the whole family hadn't been together in years. With Mark's family flying in, Luke happily came in from Atlanta, while the closest son, Matthew, was the last to arrive. He, Liz, and the two young girls pulled up to a full house as the Christmas lights blazed across the house and yard, adding brightness to the cloudy afternoon.

Of course, the Nativity scene was front and center in the lawn. Matthew laughed with his brothers about the reoccurring Nativity message their dad inserted every December.

The three Light boys enjoyed being back together at their parents' house. They did not expect it would happen under much more somber events in only two months.

J pulled up soon after while dinner, laughter, and anticipation of presents began to fill the house. J was not married and had no kids. He had seriously dated a few women over the years, one they had hoped worked out, and two others they were extremely glad did not. The one-that-got-away had moved for her career, relocating to the New England area and a few years later opened her own OB/GYN office. She attended the Lights' church while completing her residency in the area. She and J hit it off right away, but six months later, the offer from Boston Medical Center came, and the relationship ended rather uneventfully. She lingered in J's mind frequently, as she did in his hopeful friends' minds as well.

J had spent Christmas morning with his mother and stepfather. They lived in the Central Florida area, nearly two hours away, and he made the drive the night before, after the Christmas Eve services. His mother, Ruth, remarried about fifteen years after her late husband, J's father Micah, passed away. She was close with the Lights but never quite the same after Micah died. Thankfully, she married a good man and moving away from town to start her later years fresh was a breath of fresh air for her. J admitted a few times that he never saw her so happy, only vaguely remembering the joyous times when Micah was still alive.

Isaiah, the oldest member of the family and Zech's father, also arrived in time for dinner. He was approaching ninety years old, but he still drove and was free to leave the assisted living home at will. His late wife, Zech's mother Rebecca, had passed away over ten years ago. Her passing felt like mercy after a series of three strokes in two years. She held on for a few more tough years, but the pancreatic cancer in her final year brought her home. Isaiah took it rough, not leaving the house much. Zech and Mary did his grocery shopping, cleaned up the house, and hired a company to maintain the lawn. The family thought he might pass soon after the devastation, but after about a year, he turned a corner. He began carrying his Bible more often, taking long walks with his friend Jimmy, and had even suggested selling the home and moving into assisted living, a suggestion that shocked Zech. Isaiah could be quite stubborn at times, but now he seemed twenty years younger as he remembered his wife with a smile instead of a tear.

In assisted living, Isaiah seemed to take another leap forward when residents started playing cards in their rec room. Just as he passed on to Zech and the entire family, Isaiah was a skillful card player. The quick wit that helped him become a great preacher and church leader served him well at the card table.

Isaiah had many friends at the home now, and his best friend Jimmy came by to see him often. Every Sunday, Isaiah and Jimmy would drive over to the church and walk around the lake behind the main building. Since Rebecca's passing, they added a walk and a meal together each holiday. Isaiah also did not want to infringe on the family's Christmas morning time. He remembered Zech's bright smile on Christmas morning and knew each parent deserved a cozy Christmas morning with their children. Still, no one was going to stop him from enjoying Christmas dinner and watching those kids opening up presents.

As dinner concluded and the wrapping paper came off all the presents, the kids broke off to play with their toys and watch *Elf* for seemingly the hundredth time. The adults broke out the cards and picked teams. Euchre was their family's game and a tradition on the holidays. Games typically went quickly with another pair always ready to take on the winner. A playoff-style bracket emerged as the night went on, with Mark and Matthew taking on Luke and J. The winners would play Mary and Isaiah in the humorously titled "Grand Master World Universe Championship."

Luke and J won a close game, but with much debate. Depending on who you asked, the losers claimed the winners cheated repeatedly or as the winners put it, "You're just mad you lost." Luke had pushed the rules of games since he was a kid, falling back on the "it's not cheating unless you get caught" tagline for years. He was a little rebel who loved breaking rules when he was younger. He matured as he got older, and went off on his own, but back at the card table, he was back to being his adolescent breaking-the-rules self. The added winning edge was a welcome byproduct of knowing he could agitate his brothers.

J had learned from Luke the same tricks. Matthew could usually catch him as J threw off-suit and held back the strong card that should have been sucked out, but he had not been able to catch him this time. Matthew knew something was up, however the argument ended as the kids, the Christmas cookies, and other discussions pulled away his attention. He high-fived Mark and they agreed they would get them next time.

While the semi-finals were close, the championship game was a blowout. Luke and J's tricks were no match for Isaiah and Mary. The few times they tried to throw off, Mary instantly spotted it and quickly took the points. She knew her son's tricks better than he did. Isaiah then went "alone" twice in the match and both times took all five books. It seemed over before it started and the game ended 10-1. Isaiah's body may have been eighty-eight, but his mind was as young and sharp as ever.

***

As the game wrapped up, Matthew finally asked J about the night before, the conversation he noticed across the rotunda. J was taken aback for a moment and shrugged it off, but Matthew knew something was up. He guided J to the back patio to enjoy the cold evening and asked again. Now, in private, J shared more.

"Weird guy... I welcomed him to the church as I do everyone. He seemed so familiar as he approached. We talked about traveling and overseas trips, I mentioned how I always wanted to retrace Paul's journeys. He used to live in town but had been in the Middle East, between Israel and Iran, for most of the last thirty years. He asked about the church missionaries and where we were planting new churches. He wanted to offer to help make connections for new folks in the area."

J paused for a moment. His words were positive, but his expression foretold something wasn't right.

"All was good. He complimented the church and how much it has grown since he last saw it. But then he said he knew Dad. And not Zech, I mean my real dad, Micah."

"Wow..." Matthew commented. "Really? Who was this guy?"

"Said his name was Terrence. He also said if I ever wanted to talk about Dad, to give him a call."

Matthew's eye caught the cracked window to the kitchen. Isaiah and Zech were talking, but now both were looking at J.

After a few quiet moments, Zech said Luke, Mark, and their families were preparing to leave.

Zech poked his head out. "Come on in and say bye."

Isaiah also said his goodbyes and headed back to the home, but not without a quick soft-spoken word to Zech. Matthew's curiosity wished that he could over-hear it.

Before he could ask his dad, Liz said they were ready to go as well. The girls were falling asleep on the couch while cozied up to their grandmother. However, Zech stepped in and stopped the wake-up. He asked Liz to let them lie for a while. No harm in letting them sleep. "How often does Grandma get to enjoy them being this quiet?" he said with a warm smile.

Liz agreed and took a blanket and cozied up as well.

Zech turned to Matthew and J. He ushered them outside quietly.

"What was it you boys were just talking about back here?"

"Oh, not much, just Christmas Eve service, and how one day the entire town will have a Nativity scene in their yard," J responded quickly.

Zech laughed slightly.

"Well, if I have anything to say about it, they certainly will."

Zech's face then turned solid and serious quickly.

"Did I hear you say you met a man named Terrence last night?"

"Yeah."

Zech took a deep breath.

"Isaiah saw him too. It's been a long time since I have seen him. And honestly, I should not be surprised he's back."

The two men stared at Zech, waiting for him to continue.

"Many years ago, he was a close friend of your dad and me. We mentored him...brought him into the church... but..."

He paused for a moment and looked out over the backyard.

"But I'm afraid he has been on a dark path ever since."

Chapter Three

The History of Shade

Thirty years ago, Terrence Shade was a teenager and looked up to the preacher's son and his best friend. Terrence's father was not around, and the few times he did see his father, the man was usually a combination of drunk and angry. His mother wanted to help the boy and even prayed a few times for him, but she was apathetic and distant more often than not. Years ago, on a particularly bad day, in an attempt to get away from Terrence's father, she had driven around with the toddler for hours and eventually came across a Saturday evening service. Nearly out of gas, she stopped and took the boy inside. She prayed and felt hope for the first time since she could remember. However, the steps were slippery that night. As the two left, Terrence ran out of service smiling brightly, but too close to cars leaving the parking lot. His mother stepped quickly to grab him and rolled her ankle on the sidewalk steps, falling harshly in the process. Her limp was noticeable for at least two years after the injury and the deep purple bruise seemed to last just as long.

But it was overshadowed by what Terrence's father put on her face that night.

When mother and son returned home, not only was Terrence's father angry they had left, but there was another eruption over the gas in the car. The drive took the often-empty tank from half-full to nearly bone dry. With the pain of her ankle, and the added bruises from her husband, Terrence's mother removed herself emotionally after that night. She decided to never return to church, or to run away again, not even putting up much of a defense that night. Two blows struck her, the first a backhand smack that glanced off the top of her head, but the second was a hard swung open palm that caught her nose. A blood-soaked shirt and two black eyes was how Terrence remembered that night. Not even in Kindergarten yet, he had vague memories of his mother not responding to his father's attacks. She didn't respond to much anymore, eventually getting addicted to pain medicine. Terrence's father had since moved out, but he returned periodically, and brought with him a heavy hand. The pills helped.

***

As the years passed and Terrence entered high school, his mother showed flashes of her love for her son. It was few and far between, but dropping him off at a local youth group changed the trajectory of his life. She had yet to attend a single service, but when she saw a boy similar to Terrence's age set up a roadside sign pointing to the church, her heart was touched and she started dropping him off weekly. However, Terrence lied about attending. He was scared to go in, simply watching his mother drive away and hiding in the backwoods behind the small church, then resurfacing as her car approached. He was good at hiding, watching, and waiting.

Who knows how long he would have kept up the lie, if it wasn't for Micah.

One day, Micah saw the youngster being dropped off. He did not recognize the boy and waved from across the small parking lot. The boy's head was down, but Micah made a mental note to introduce himself. The newly appointed youth pastor finished unloading extra chairs and snacks, bringing them around for the waiting kids. As he said hi to all the youth, he could not find that boy amongst the others.

He nearly forgot about it, but moments later as he kicked off their small dinner with a prayer, something through the back window caught his eye.

It was that boy!

He was in the woods, cutting through the back of the property. In his avoidance, Terrence had figured out a trail behind the church. He could walk home in thirty minutes, leaving him an hour to do whatever he wanted. This had the added benefit of not having to worry if his mom forgot to pick him up. One day, he waited two hours past, into the cool evening, and once she arrived, she did not even seem to realize she was late. He knew it was the pills, and he decided to take the trail every night after.

The following week, Micah was ready for him. He stood on the curb welcoming in everyone that night, and he certainly surprised an unsuspecting Terrence. Micah had even waved to Terrence's mother and shouted what a great boy the youngster had been lately.

"Good to see you, ma'am! You have a great boy here!"

Terrence was dumbfounded and held a "caught red-handed" look on his face. Micah was a large man, not only tall but held a strong frame to match. He stood six-five and about two hundred and seventy-five pounds, dwarfing the youth. Terrence was just under six feet and appeared much smaller next to Micah.

As the guilty look on Terrence's face deepened, Micah smiled wider.

"Relax, kid. You are welcome here. You can choose to walk through the woods again and I won't stop you or rat you out."

Micah pointed to the side of the building.

"But I think it's time you gave walking through that front door a chance."

Micah motioned to the main entrance of the church as he spoke.

"It may not look like much, but there is a lot inside."

The church was only a fraction of the size it would become decades later. The same church was easily confused with an old house, because that was exactly what it was. Built in the 1940s, the structure was abandoned in the 1960s when the county began consolidating land and redefining the city limits. Isaiah had purchased the land, stretching the miniscule church budget to its limit, but he saw the future potential. The small house only scratched the surface of the property. Over 100 acres of woodlands, a lake, and more importantly, room to expand. Regardless, it helped move the church from the stuffy high school gym they were meeting at when Isaiah purchased it.

Terrence looked up at Micah, still with a guilty look on his face. Then he looked ahead toward the entrance and went inside.

***

Zech and Micah were in their late twenties. They led the church's youth group and would soon be taking over more church operations and ministries. Micah took the lead on interactions with the kids, as he had a knack for communicating and connecting with the youth. Zech led the operations and finances. It was a learning and development step for both of them as Isaiah was grooming them both in multiple overlapping areas of church leadership.

Zech had not noticed Terrence the way Micah had, but after a month of regularly attending the weekly meetings, everyone in the church knew Terrence.

Terrence had been shy at first. A few kids had introduced themselves and made small talk, but Terrence was reserved and had not carried on many conversations. It was a good group of kids, and none were picking on him or singling him out, but they certainly did not extend themselves to make him feel welcome. Terrence felt alone. He tried to tag along with Micah every chance he got. Helping cleanup, sitting by him at dinner, and even trying to awkwardly stand next to him while Micah gave the Youth Group sermon one night. That night was embarrassing, and some kids laughed under their breath at him. Terrence heard and shot them a hard stare.

It was team game night and broomball was the activity. Micah and Zech were team captains, and to Terrence's horror, Zech had picked him. It was bad enough that he was not on Micah's team, but he was the sixth pick. Micah had chosen three other kids before him!

Terrence stewed over this as the game kicked off.

Laughter filled the air as the kids tried directing the mini-playground ball with the brooms and their tiny plastic ends. The hard-to-use sticks evened the playing field nicely between the athletic and unathletic kids. They cleared the sanctuary chairs and had a large room to work with. As they ran back and forth, many of the boys dreamed of hitting that perfect shot, while most of the girls just wanted to avoid being hit in the face by these crazy sticks the boys were waving around.

When Micah's team took a 4-1 lead, Terrence had started fuming. He pouted from not being chosen for Micah's team and now he was being humiliated.

"Come on!" a teammate shouted toward Terrence in a relatively innocent way, as the boy pushed up court and was eager for a pass. However, Terrence had not taken it as teamwork. Terrence had drifted back to defense and was responsible to restart play after the previous goal. After his teammate's comment, Terrence took a wild golf swing and sent the ball hard into the ceiling, nearly hitting a female teammate with his backswing.

As Micah's team gathered the ball back in play, Zech quietly asked Terrence if he was okay.

"Hey pal, are you doing al..."

But he was quickly cut off.

"I'M FINE!"

Zech caught Micah's eye and hinted at the upset Terrence. They both kept their eye on him more and tried to include him more in the play. But it backfired.

One of Micah's better players caught on to Zech passing more often to Terrence. He stepped up to intercept a pass and the two young males bumped shoulders. Terrence kept his balance and the other boy had dropped to one knee. Rising from his knee, he reached his stick for the ball, but Terrence had stopped paying attention to the ball. In a flash, Terrence pivoted in front of the boy, grabbing the slack of his shirt near the shoulder with one hand. The other hand swung with all the young adolescence could muster. The clenched fist missed, but

the forearm caught the boy on the cheek. The unsuspecting boy went down hard. The half punch, half push
that Terrence landed ultimately did little damage, but
the boy's head hitting the thin, hard carpet did.

Zech and Micah, along with most of the kids, rushed
to the boy. Micah asked one of the older girls to call the
boy's parents as Zech pulled the car around. The boy
had gone limp after his head bounced off the ground.
Twenty-five minutes later, he came to while in the ER,
not remembering where he was or what year it was.

During the commotion after the injury, Terrence
looked on. When Micah looked his way, he thought he
saw the troubled boy smile.

***

The injured boy made a full recovery but was never
back at youth group again. Later that year, his parents
started attending another local church. Zech and Micah
had each reached out to them repeatedly, to offer their
apologies and talk through the situation. The father had
joked with Micah that it might toughen the kid up and
help him in next year's football tryouts, but the mother
of the boy would have none of it.

She called Isaiah seven times the month of the incident. Three to complain about the youth group and
four more complaining about other "concerns," as she
put it, with church leadership. The rumors began fly-

ing that she wanted Micah removed as Youth Pastor. In church communities, gossip can run wild, but Isaiah and Rebecca put a stop to it early and often. Zech's mother, Rebecca, helped diffuse the situation in multiple women's circles, cutting off most of the rumors of Micah's firing before they had traction, while Isaiah declared to the congregation before the next sermon that he was ultimately responsible for all church events. If anyone would like to discuss any particular event, his office door was open every day at 5am. Additionally, he'd be happy to walk through his mentoring methods and development plans. The upset woman soon stopped calling and she never took the 5am invitation. No one came in.

Isaiah had long conversations with the two upcoming leaders. He drilled into their heads the need to plan for events that limited risk, and to be aware of a young male's testosterone. Broomball was replaced with volleyball and kickball.

Additionally, this called out the need to guide troubled males. In Isaiah's opinion, Terrence had social issues stemming from his home life. Micah and Zech would soon be in training for how to deal with difficult and struggling teenagers.

Finally, gender-based groups were formed that encouraged one-on-one discipleship. Zech and Micah were the first participants. Isaiah mentored them each as they grew in the church, and now he positioned them to connect and grow young leaders in the church. Their eyes could not be everywhere, and this not only brought responsible young men closer to the church, but also helped nearly every church ministry as those young men took on more accountability. In the years to come, Rebecca would begin a women's version.

In the end, much good came from this terrible situation.

***

Micah started meeting with Terrence regularly. First one-on-one, and then after six months, asking Terrence to lead a small group of high school freshmen in a Bible study. Micah sat in on those meetings and was impressed.

The high school junior seemed to be finding his stride. He became passionate about the word and studied it deeply. The only issue Micah saw was that the young Terrence still flashed anger from time-to-time, but they were working on it. Micah witnessed Terrence erupt on one of his group mates that showed up without reading the assignment. He told him it was good, he was passionate, but likened screaming at a young follower to leading a horse to water.

"You cannot force them to drink. You must be the example," became that month's recurring phrase between the two.

The following summer, to celebrate the seniors' graduation, the youth group took a trip to the beach. Zech knew of a park in northeast Florida that had a nice beach, wooded trails, and a campground. It was a sort of senior trip for the group and everyone in the high school youth group was allowed to attend.

Isaiah, Zech, and Micah planned it out and had extra chaperons to join. They even created a night-watch schedule with many of the dads. What better chaperons than the God-fearing fathers of the adolescent girls who made the trip. Isaiah had joked that all guns would remain in the pickup trucks, but only a few of the three dozen people on the trip laughed.

Terrence had been in the youth group for nearly a full year now. His freshmen Bible study was still going and he even had hit it off with a few of the girls. It was nothing "official" as the kids would say, but he and a girl named Kristen had been on more than a few group dates together with other young couples. They started hanging around together more and more in the weekly youth groups and events. Micah was happy for the kid; first the Bible study to connect more with God and other boys, now he seemed to finally be connecting with a female.

Kristen and Terrence would never be "official," though. After this weekend, he would no longer be attending the youth group, leading the Bible study, or returning Micah's calls.

***

The trip was a two-day, one-night event. The group arrived Saturday, early afternoon, to set up their camping gear and then head to the beach for a barbeque, volleyball, and relaxing. Later into the day, Zech would congratulate the graduating seniors and hand it over to Micah for a short sermon before dinner. There were two fire pits and six picnic tables with a combination of burgers, hot dogs, corn on the cob, and baked beans (cooked in the can, of course). There were also desserts designed for the fire, such as fire pit pie-making kits and stacks of ingredients for hundreds of s'mores.

As the group cleaned up the beach activities and moved back to the campsite, Zech noticed Terrence talking to Kristen a little too close, and not in a romantic way. His forehead was near hers, but his eyes had rage in them. Her head and shoulders slunk low, half looking in disbelief and half as a dog that had just been scolded.

Zech approached the situation quickly, but Terrence had noticed him and moved quicker. The young male turned and picked up his bag, flashed a look at her, and moved into the trail. He was out of sight behind trees as Zech got within speaking range.

Kristen was still there.

"Hey, is everything okay?" Zech said.

The young girl took a second, coming out of the moment, and then noticed him.

"Oh... Hey, Pastor Light, yeah, of course. I'm fine."

Zech cut right to the chase.

"What was that with Terrence? It did not look all right and it is okay to speak up if something is wrong."

"Oh..." She paused again, seeming to gather her thoughts or coming up with a covering lie, Zech was not sure.

"Oh, oh, yeah... That was nothing. I mean, it was my fault really. I shouldn't have let Trevor carry my bag."

"What do you mean? We were all carrying different bags as we cleaned up and sorted out whose was whose."

"Well, Terrence should have been carrying my bag. It was my fault, really. And no problem. It's cool. Hey, I have to go meet up with Claire and help them build our tent. See ya."

Zech feared he knew where this was going.

He spoke quietly to Micah about it, but surprisingly, Micah seemed to blow it off.

"That kid is doing so much better, and now you're telling me he was getting aggressive with Kristen? Those two seem to finally be hitting it off. You sure you saw it right?"

"I told you what I saw. Something is not right. One of us needs to be close to them tonight."

"There are chaperons all over. We have one for every three kids. I think you might be overreacting. Just think how far that kid has come."

"You know how his father treated his mother. You know how detached his mother is now. His life is coming together and it is a miracle from God, but that doesn't mean he will be perfect. He is still high risk for turning out like his dad."

"Fine. I'll stay close to him. I completely disagree with you, but I'll stay close and watch them through dinner. Then we can switch until they go to bed. Deal?"

"Deal."

Micah sat at the same table as Terrence and Kristen. She was unusually quiet, but Terrence seemed his normal self. He talked with a few other kids at the table, two freshmen that were in his Bible study and another sophomore girl, a sister of one of the other boys. Micah mostly let the kids talk but also chimed in throughout the meal. Kristen gradually said a few words but was not herself. Micah had known her since she was in middle school. She was normally so bright and conversational. He reasoned that it had been a long day, though, and anyone would understand if a few kids were dragging after being in the sun for hours.

As dinner wrapped up, talk of making their own mini-pies and s'mores began.

"Hey, I'll go get the dessert if you all meet me by the fire," Micah said as the young adults began moving their paper plates to the trash.

As Micah filled a plate of graham crackers, chocolate, and marshmallows, Trevor stopped and asked him if he had seen Kristen. He wanted to ask her if she got her bag from earlier. Micah pointed over to their table and commented she had, then he started making another plate. As Trevor left, Micah laughed with a parent-chaperon about each other's memories of camping as a kid. He grabbed a can of pie filling and tried balancing the pie-making kit with all the s'mores ingredients.

He dropped it all in the loose dirt as he heard the commotion.

"I KNEW YOU WERE A SLUT!" Terrence screamed at Kristen.

He pushed her, hard, and she flew towards the fire. Parts of her hair singed on the hot iron fire pit ring as she fell inches from the flames.

Terrence looked down at her with fury then turned to Trevor.

He stepped quickly and cocked back his fist.

As the fist came forward, Micah was there in a flash to catch it. He grabbed the boy by the neck with one hand while the other hand wrapped around the quickly moving fist before he could deliver the blow. Micah's frame engulfed Terrence. His large hands wrapped around the boy, completely covering his neck, lifting the boy off the ground, and holding the clenched fist with his fingers beyond the boy's wrist.

He kept his grip loose enough so the boy could breathe, but strong enough to carry him a full twenty steps past the fire, the shadows of the flames dancing across his stone face. Terrence's eyes widened and his expression changed drastically from the prior aggression. Micah saw a scared boy looking back at him.

Micah held his grip and his composure but was furious with himself. Zech had warned him. He wanted to slap the boy, or shove him the way he shoved the girl, but he simply held the boy and stared, feeling betrayed.

After ten seconds that felt like an eternity, Micah held back his own rage. He stared into the eyes of the young boy.

"I am going to drive you home."

Micah held the back of Terrence's shirt, tightening it without slack, and led him to his truck. Micah drove him home in silence. The two would never see each other alive again.

Chapter Four

Zech and Micah

O ver the next five years, the church grew immensely. The economic boom of the nineties hit the area
and the population increased rapidly. New roads, sub-
divisions, and tall corporate structures quickly shot up,
redesigning the downtown skyline seemingly overnight.
New businesses and people flocked to the North Florida
area for various reasons, including the relatively cheap
real estate, a large east coast shipping port, and nearby
military bases.

The small house and large plot of land that Isaiah
had purchased decades ago were now in a prime location, next to the newly expanded interstate and brand
new Crosstown Expressway. However, the structure was
quickly becoming undersized in the face of the growing
congregation.

Isaiah had planned for expansion in the coming years,
yet there was so much more to be done. He was leading
a rapidly growing church that was now nearing standing
room only on Sundays. They always had two Sunday

services and recently went to a third to handle the extra capacity, which had quickly become filled as well. God was filling the seats faster than Isaiah could handle. It was time for expansion and it was time to promote new leaders.

During those years of expansion, Zech and Micah stepped to the forefront. Zech was tasked with leading day-to-day operations, finances, and the majority of sermons. Micah would now head all the church ministries, including youth groups, prison and economic outreaches, young marrieds, plus give on average one sermon per month. Isaiah took a step back, still giving roughly one sermon per quarter, but now focusing on expansion and long-term strategy, while increasing mentoring time for Zech and Micah.

Isaiah pulled together a small team and developed a formal fifty-year development plan for the property. He would build the church with his grandchildren's generation in mind. Zech and Mary just had their third child, another boy, and named him Matthew. Meanwhile, Micah and his wife, Ruth, had their first only a few months apart from Matthew, and named him Jeremiah.

It was perfect timing for Isaiah, as he could now crystalize his thoughts of leaving this church as a legacy to his children's children. If his plans were to succeed, in his eyes, it would influence the families, the city, and therefore the nation for decades to come. At least that was Isaiah's intention. He communicated it to his new team in their first meeting. "The Temple Team" he called it, and related it to the building of God's original temple from the Old Testament.

What he did not communicate to the church members was his growing concern over security. He knew with a growing church and new leaders that temptation was coming. Additionally, there were family-specific concerns, a long-held family secret that only two other living people knew. Ever since he took the reins from his father Michael, these secrets were now his job to protect. As such, he brought in Paul Stollard to his team. Paul was in thirties, near Zech and Micah's age, and through his twenties had turned his father's failed shipping business into a successful storage and security business.

Paul's father, James Stollard, moved from the Long Island, New York area to Florida in the 1980s. As the stock market climbed, he foresaw increased business and the need for better distribution and logistics across the east coast. He wasn't wrong and secured numerous large corporate contracts. He bought property near the North Florida port and had distribution partnerships throughout the eastern seaboard. He could do it quicker and cheaper than the northeastern companies who were constantly dealing with labor concerns from union strikes and never-ending negotiations.

As great as his market foresight was, his business operations were conversely poor. He decided to increase his leverage in order to expand inland, his sights set on the major shipping companies. He wanted to become national and global, not just a regional player. However, his over-leverage proved deadly, as his cash reserves were not enough to withstand the mounting savings and loans crisis in the late 80s. The oil price shock of 1990 was the final straw. He was forced to sell off costly assets at a fraction of their price to avoid bankruptcy. Additionally, he lost his most profitable contracts and the few of the remaining ones could hardly pay their bills. He lost nearly a year of cash flow and 90 percent of his business seemingly moments after doubling down on expansion.

Paul, however, kept his optimism up through it all. He was a young apprentice in the business during its downfall and learned much from his father's mistakes. He turned the remaining assets profitable in two years, focusing on local contracts and shifting away from shipping but to storage and security. He noticed many high-dollar clients of his father had a problem with timing. As products came in from overseas, they needed an intermediary location before moving on to the retailers or consumers. The rise of malls and big box stores gave more power, and thus higher inventory costs, to smaller companies trying to win shelf space. The timing problem was also a headache for James in the original business plan before Paul, having to shift cargo around the shipping yard to make room for more, then shift it back to be loaded on the trains and trucks. Paul had turned this issue into his competitive advantage. He offered secure storage, for as long as required, giving his clients the flexibility to reroute distribution or change supply levels on shipments as needed. Clients could ship large safety stock quantities from Asian manufacturing plants, hold it in Paul's Storage Yard, and then be fast and flexible in the US.

Paul began targeting technology companies. Personal computers and televisions were expanding rapidly, with larger and costly shipments each month. Paul guaranteed not only security but support in partnering with the national shipping companies. In five years since taking over the struggling business, he doubled business each year and now had a 60 percent profit margin on the majority of contracts.

Paul was also becoming a friend of Zech and Micah through his service to the church, helping out at various events and attending the Men's Night event that Micah had kicked off as a part of his ministry leadership. Paul and his wife also had just welcomed their second child, a young girl named Liz. She was only a year younger than Zech's latest addition, Matthew.

***

Isaiah's Temple Team consisted of five people, three core-team members of Isaiah, Paul, and Jimmy, plus Zech and Micah, so they could learn from the situation and ask questions from an outside perspective.

Jimmy was a land-developer who had attended the church since Isaiah took it over from his father, Michael. Isaiah and Jimmy had grown to be close friends and had worked together when the church moved out of the local high school's gym and into the existing property. The two hardly spoke of it, but the last year of using the high school was a turbulent one to say the least. There was more than one Sunday morning when they arrived to find the doors unlocked, hungover teenagers sleeping under bleachers, and even an inappropriate school principal who was immoral on numerous levels. The dire situation, especially for the young people impacted, ignited Isaiah's passion to grow and help influence change in the community. Now thirty years after the move, it was time to act again if he was going to keep up with the growing city.

After a few shaky months, Zech was soon thriving under the new responsibilities. The growing church brought in more tithes and offerings than they'd ever had, but the expansion project would still stretch them thin. Zech and Isaiah were constantly trying to balance the financial projections to maximize current building expansion without taking on too much risk. Something Paul, in light of his father's errors, would remind them of frequently.

Micah seemed to hit the ground running with the ministry leadership. He demonstrated brilliance in taking successful youth group concepts into men's and women's events. Every month would alternate between a "Men's Night" or for the females, in what came to be called "Ladies with Hats and a Bible." The male events were relatively straightforward, with an activity of some sort that guys could stand around and talk about, such as corn hole, horseshoes, chili cookoffs, and then give them food and a short sermon. It worked like a charm, especially as Micah began encouraging members to bring a friend that would enjoy competing in the activity. Micah wanted newcomers to see the great culture that Isaiah had instilled as well as show outsiders that church goers could have fun too.

It soon became a running gag about how Micah tried to use competition to get someone's guest personally involved and talking to other members of the church. Many of the events were two-person team competitions, and most newcomers thought they would be with their accompanying friend. However, Micah would make a big show out of "accidentally" mixing up the names on the brackets. Behind the scenes, Micah would throw all the names into a hat and randomly pull them out to create two-person teams. This instantly forced conversation and camaraderie with the newcomer and another existing member. Zech reminded him that he could have simply told everyone it was random, but Micah loved the show of it.

In contrast to the simple, yet highly attended male events, the ladies' events were difficult to sustain participation. Ruth, being Micah's wife, was the sacrificial leader with Zech's wife, Mary, and Isaiah's wife, Rebecca, always at her side. A small group of their close friends were regular attenders, but it was not growing. The light bulb finally came when Ruth made a side comment to

Micah. She knew how much it meant to Micah, and she was also frustrated about the lack of growth. In a comment that only a wife would say to her husband in private, she inadvertently gave Micah an epiphany.

"Ugh, I don't want to sit in a stuffy room and make small talk with someone who I'll never see again. Just give me my friends with a fancy hat and a Bible, then we'll laugh and talk about Jesus all night long!"

The comment came right after Ruth and Mary were chatting on the phone and planning the next event. They somehow got on the conversation of those overdressed and obnoxious hats ladies wear to horse races, like the Kentucky Derby. The seed was planted, and the fancy hats soon turned to funny, gag-gift-type hats. Micah and Ruth had figured out that too many ladies felt pressured to be perfect in front of the first ladies of the church. Without regular activities like the men had, the ladies' evenings turned into good conversation but never deep conversation that creates friendship, or the urge to invite a friend.

Once the change was made, the mood lightened and people started returning and bringing friends. The out-fits gave everyone a laugh, and the evening was centered around a Bible study. Many of the guests came back the next time, and they would bring a friend. Females now participated in the monthly event twice as much as males. Ruth and Mary were now brainstorming spinoff activities.

***

As much as Micah flashed brilliance in ministry leadership to drive attendance, he unfortunately became more volatile in other areas. He began to disregard their budgeting process, repeatedly asking Zech to increase his budgets or spending without getting confirmation. Zech gave in to modest concessions, but with every yes, a new and more expensive request came the following month. When Micah made a large purchase of Bibles for the prison ministry, Zech called it out in front Isaiah and the Temple Team. It embarrassed Micah and demonstrated the growing strain on his and Zech's relationship.

Zech wished he hadn't said it as soon as it left his mouth. He was stressed from the numerous financial requests that came in that same day.

One quote for the land excavation, then the bill for blueprints of their latest draft, followed by Micah requesting a fully catered BBQ dinner for a men's event, and finally a second request from Micah for the set of Bibles to give out during an upcoming prison visit. Zech had told Micah it was possible, but to wait a month or two. The cash flow was pinched at the moment.

Micah did not wait and purchased directly after asking Zech. It was only $900 for two hundred Bibles, a good price that Micah did not want to pass up, especially because these were high-quality pocket-size editions. Perfect for prisoners.

When Zech overheard Micah mentioning the purchase to Jimmy, he blurted out, "You bought what?!"

He paused for a moment as Micah looked over, taken
aback by the uncharacteristic outburst, then Zech continued.

"I hope you can pay for it. Because we're not."

His tone drew the attention of the three others. Zech
would rather just talk to Micah individually, but the cat
was out of the bag now. He looked at his friend in disbelief. Would Micah have even told him if Zech hadn't
overheard him?

Micah turned towards Zech and crossed his arms.

"You said yes. What are you talking about *can't pay?*"

"I said to wait a month or two. Since when is the same
day a month or two?"

"It goes on the church card, we get billed next month,
and it was a great deal. What's the problem?"

Zech's tone had lowered, but with the credit card
statement, he hit another level. The two began approaching each other as their voices elevated.

"We don't use credit, genius! Those 'cards' are debit
cards. That cash is leaving our account and now we
cannot pay for something else. You know this. It is called
cash flow. What is the matter with you?"

"Go do math and let me handle the ministries."

The two were almost nose-to-nose now and Isaiah
stepped in. The two friends had not been angry at each
other since they were young teenagers, twenty-some

years ago, and had long forgotten whatever that dust-up was about.

Isaiah helped diffuse the situation and he physically put himself in the thin space between the two men.

"Whoa whoa, hang on. Remember, we're all on the same team here."

He turned towards Zech first.

"You know how passionate Micah is about these ministries. This expansion was my call, and it is putting stress on every other part of the church. Finances taking the brunt of it."

"And you." He turned to Micah. "If you need a reminder, then you can take over finances for a couple months."

He said this with a slight smile, showing Micah he was half-joking, yet half-serious. Micah hated math once it got past simple addition. Even a half-joke of spending a day, let alone two months, in their books filled him with dread.

"Regardless, you know our process and how it works. You can return the Bibles or pay for half the cost out of pocket. The church will only cover $450."

"Dad!?" Zech blurted out.

He called his father "Pastor" when they were in the church and rarely ever Dad. This slip of the tongue showed Isaiah the emotional nature of this disagreement, and the long road each had in front of them to realize their potential.

"No." Isaiah quickly responded, turning back to Zech. He desperately tried to remain an impartial church leader, not favoring his son.

"Micah was wrong, but his heart is in the right place. Prison ministry reaches those at their rock bottom. Think of the company Jesus kept: prostitutes, tax collectors. If Micah is willing to pay out of pocket, then we can find a way."

The situation diffused, Zech and Micah looked at each other with understanding eyes. As Micah left the church that night, Isaiah caught up with him. They packed up their things and walked to the parking lot together.

"Why the sudden push to get into the prison?" Isaiah was not a fan of small talk and went right to the point.

"We have always had that on our list. It's time."

"We have... we have... but why now? Talk to me."

"Come on, Pastor. I'm doing my best to reach this community. You know how hard some kids have it."

"Agreed. If we can help turn men into better fathers, then we can avoid a lot of heartache on the family side, even turn many toward the Lord. But you did not answer my question."

Micah stopped and looked at his mentor.

Isaiah was leading Micah into a discussion that Micah did not want to have. It had been a couple years, and the incident with Terrence still weighed heavy on Micah. In the months after, he called at least once a week and stopped by often. His mother rarely answered the phone or came to the door, and the few times she did, she had no idea where Terrence had been.

"He's not here," was the extent he could get out of her.

Micah later found out that Terrence started living with his father during his senior year. Now it would have been Terrence's first year of college, something Micah and the young man began to talk about. They started discussing how to look for scholarships, practicing for the ACTs and SATs, potential majors, but now, Micah doubted college was still in the plan.

Micah had asked a friend in the police department to keep an eye out for Terrence's dad. When his friend called, Micah held his breath, expecting to hear he was involved in a domestic abuse case. He was relieved to hear it was arguing with a traffic cop.

"He got a ticket for parking in a handicapped spot. The kid allegedly flipped out and tried getting physical with the officer. Thankfully, this was a former marine and not just some meter-maid. He diffused the situation and cuffed him without any injuries. They booked 'em late last night and released him this morning."

"Thanks, Rich. Was there a recent address or number to reach..." Micah stopped mid-sentence.

"Are you still there?"

"Yeah, yeah... sorry. Did you say kid?"

"Yup, nineteen-year-old. You said Terry Shade. This kid came under the name Terrence, figured that was the guy."

Micah hadn't realized it at first. Terrence's father had the same name, but went by Terry. By giving his friend the name Terry Shade, he was actually keeping a lookout for both the father and the son.

Micah got the address that Terrence was booked under and drove out to it that same day. It was a vacant lot on the outskirts of town.

This boy was following in his father's footsteps. He had him in church, and for a whole year! Now he was lost in the world, and it broke Micah's heart.

Chapter Five

The Storage Yard and The Crate

I saiah began mentoring Zech and Micah more often, focusing on how they could grow leaders themselves in order to lighten their load and decentralize command throughout the church. Isaiah hoped it would reduce the day-to-day burdens of the growing church. All three of them were finding themselves working longer hours and getting less sleep.

To help with the church expansion, Isaiah also created a contract with Paul's storage business, simply named the Storage Yard. As certain building material, furniture, televisions, and the like were purchased or moved out, they could use the Storage Yard as a holding place. They got better pricing from the builder, who could now order larger loads and have a place to store it, plus it simply made life easier around the church without so much space used for construction. Namely, keeping the parking lot as open as possible with the growing congregation.

Isaiah also had two ulterior motives for using the Storage Yard. The drives back and forth were perfect times to talk with Zech and Micah. Also, it let him test out the yard's security for a special consideration. His family's responsibility would soon pass to Zech and Micah, and they needed more than the hidden safe in the floor space under Isaiah's bed. He learned the hideaway floor trick from his dad, Michael, and although there were some close calls, it had worked like a charm.

The Temple Team had been meeting regularly for nearly a year now and the fruits of their labors were finally starting to show. Construction had begun. To help the transition during the construction years, they had three temporary facilities in use. These were similar to classroom pods that became so familiar at overcrowded schools. Each had its own purpose: one was church offices, the other for kids' church and ministry meetups, and a third multi-purpose pod. They kept the original house to maintain existing services and were building the new facility behind it after clearing a large portion of the woods. It opened up a large field that overlooked the lake to the east. Isaiah was already dreaming of seeing the sunrise over the trees and reflecting across the pond.

Over the past year, Zech learned the church finances inside and out. He was also leading the day-to-day operations more efficiently and delivering stirring sermons when called upon. The mastery of the finances, along with the completed fifty-year plan, gave him a sense of confidence and comfort, making the prior years' extra hours and effort worth it.

Zech spent many long days and nights at the church while Mary was home with three young boys. Matthew was now approaching six years old, while Luke and Mark were ten and nine. Thankfully, her friend Ruth was also dealing with a husband who was burning the midnight oil. Jeremiah was nearly six as well, and the saving grace to both mothers was getting the kids together to play. They would rotate between houses and nearby parks to keep it fresh for the kids, and a few nights a week, they would plan meals together. The balance helped both mothers keep their sanity during these memorable yet trying years.

As Mary and Ruth became like sisters, Zech and Micah had drifted. They were still great friends, and during this past year, they spent more time together then they did with their respective wives. However, the feud over the budget lingered, an unspoken barrier that gradually wore away their brother-like relationship. Micah still had numerous requests for finances, and the ever increasing requests still nagged at Zech. But Micah stopped bringing them up in their normal conversation. Previously, he would bring it up naturally with Zech and speak to the reasoning to get his friend's opinion and alignment. Now he submitted a handwritten sheet each month with the request for each ministry. Zech would review, make cuts and agreements, then give the sheet back with the final numbers of acceptance. Micah grew hostile to the process every time a request was cut or denied, which happened to be more likely than not. But he never told his friend about his feelings.

The whole process was transactional and their relationship steadily followed suit. They trusted each other but were more of good "work friends" as opposed to best friends who happened to work together.

The small divide did not go unnoticed by Isaiah, and he would use their next trip to the Storage Yard to bridge that gap as well as introduce them to the Light family's historical responsibilities. Outside of lunch with Paul, it would be only the three of them for the entire workday.

***

The three leaders met at the church and carpooled up to the yard together. Isaiah would allow small talk, church conversations, and the like for the first few hours. He wanted to get a sense of their conversation and thus a feel for their relationship. Isaiah felt responsible for their rift.

Did he push them too hard and stress them out?

Should he formally make one of them his second, instead of allowing split responsibilities?

Was today the right day to drop this bomb about their family on them?

He had talked it over with Rebecca and prayed about it daily.

No more questioning himself, he decided. This was the time. Today was the day.

He would gain nothing but added risk by waiting longer. Either this would forge their bonds tighter for a brighter future or...

Well, Isaiah was prepared to act accordingly depending on their responses. Regardless, the secret would be passed on to them both.

As they entered the yard, they met Paul. He showed them the latest shipments from the builders and the three spent a couple hours reviewing the crates, designs, and signage to ensure it matched their orders, and to get a feel for the structures. Then, as they had done weekly back at the church grounds, they walked circles around the supplies and prayed. They prayed for the building to be strong enough to withstand hurricanes as well as any sin that might occur within its walls. They prayed for the past, current, and future families that would pass through their church. Finally, as they started wrapping up their group prayer, Isaiah surprised both young men by praying for their relationship. He prayed for the relationship between the three of them, but specifically between Zech and Micah.

"Lord, these men will carry the torch of our church with this new building. Allow no evil or temptation to come between them, and allow them to serve each other, just as Christ was a servant to your Church. The power you have placed in us, Lord, is their foundation, and with it, they can support a city, a state, a nation, and the entire world.

"Be with them, Lord, in these trying times as you were with our family in spirit and object for all these years.

"Amen."

The two young leaders picked up their heads and looked to Isaiah and then to each other. In spirit and object? They both had a confused look on their face.

But they did not get a chance to ask. Isaiah brought it back to their relationship. He had seen enough. "There is clearly an issue between you two, and if the church is going to succeed, it will require strong leadership. There will be no room for dissension in the ranks, especially at the top."

Zech and Micah were now in their thirties, each with a wife, young kids, and the weight of carrying on their church growing on their shoulders. The weight seemed to lift during Isaiah's prayer, and again when the two looked at each other. They both felt embarrassed and responsible. They could read each other, just as Isaiah could read them, and now they both saw forgiveness. Without a word, they came together and hugged.

"Good. I believe you are both ready for what's next. But first, let's eat."

***

They met in the space outside of Paul's office, where Paul's assistant had lunch waiting, subs from a local spot nearby. A favorite of Paul's and his employees.

Paul had a small office, and that was the way he liked it. In his mind, an office was for paperwork and deep thought. The small office building at the front of the yard was focused more on the community area right outside Paul's office. His assistant had a small desk there, but otherwise, it was set up to encourage gatherings and discussions. Coffee machines, snacks, lots of tables grouped together, and a side area of comfortable chairs and a sofa. All the tables and furniture were secondhand, from friends or fellow church members. Paul was not a big spender, yet even Isaiah gave him a hard time about needing an upgrade.

Paul was an interesting character, not just for his business acumen, but for his seemingly split personality. His friends joked with him about it endlessly. Depending on the present company he was in, Paul would adopt that person's accent. A few people took it as an insult, especially insecure waiters, but most unconsciously loved it. When with a New Yorker, Paul sounded just like his father, a man raised in NYC with decades of life there, but with a southerner or mid-westerner, Paul fell right into the particular dialect without even realizing it. A German or Asian dialect sounded the worst, though, and this was where his friends ribbed him the most, and his wife kicked him under the table. It sounded as if he was mocking them, but Paul's sincerity typically avoided any thoughts of mockery.

Now with three southerners, Paul played to his caricature and exaggerated a Savannah-style drawl as he put the deck of cards on the table.

"Now before y'all go back to work, y'all gonna teach me how you three southerners learned this northerner game of Euchre."

The three men smiled and Isaiah started shuffling the deck.

***

It did not take long to figure out that Paul had secretly known how to play. Isaiah had taught him months earlier and joined him in games often during his trips up to the yard.

Isaiah and Paul won four of six games over Zech and Micah. The younger pair might have split it three to three, but Isaiah caught Micah throwing off trump, the same tricks his son Jeremiah would use, and also be caught by Isaiah and Mary, decades later.

Even in defeat, Zech and Micah enjoyed the game. It helped to ease their prior tensions even further and reminded them of their lifelong friendship. Surprising themselves, they could not remember the last time they were on a Euchre team together. It was a couple of years at least, but their old tricks gradually came back. Isaiah's experience carried the day, along with catching Micah trying to cheat. The cheating was debated heavily in its own right.

"I take risks, but I never cheat," Micah was fond of saying.

The conversations continued, but there was still work to be done.

After cards, Isaiah nodded to Paul and said, "It's time; do you mind?"

"Sure thing, Pastor," Paul replied.

Zech and Micah glanced at each other, confirming neither knew what their mentor was up to next.

Paul went back into his office, then came out a moment later.

"Follow me."

The four men returned to Paul's office, but now, a hidden door was open in the corner of the small office. Paul led them through, with Isaiah close behind. Zech and Micah tentatively followed.

They entered a secret conference room behind Paul's office. The layout of the building hid it completely from sight. Zech and Micah entered onto a smooth marble tile floor and looked around at the thin black leather chairs that surrounded a solid marble table. The white walls had no windows, televisions, and only one other door on the opposite side of the room. Paul took his seat in front of the other door, directly blocking it.

"Welcome to what we call our secure room. Some of our clients have extremely valuable cargo, and we use this room for private conversations. It is soundproof and has no recording devices."

Zech and Micah looked uneasy in these new surroundings, while Isaiah appeared as comfortable there as he was at the standard wood table where they ate lunch.

"Relax. No one gets whacked in here and we don't smuggle people. Most of our secured areas hold family heirlooms that have little value outside of that respective family."

Zech noticed that Paul did not seem to have his southern accent or his New York one. This must be "Business Paul" talking now, he thought, as his friend spoke in a clear, matter-of-fact way.

"So, what are we doing here?" Micah finally allowed himself to ask.

Paul glanced at Isaiah, allowing him to take over the conversation. Isaiah then looked to Zech, "Zech, did you know what our family's name was before we came to America?"

"I... I don't... I guess I've never thought it was anything other than Light."

Isaiah sat forward in his chair, swiftly yet calmly switching eye contact with Zech and Micah to show he was talking to both.

"Well. It wasn't. It was Levit. And before that, it was Levi."

Zech stared at his father. His body was as still as the marble table he leaned on, while his mind raced and eyebrows furrowed.

"As in the tribe of Levi? Jacob and Leah's third son?"

"Yes."

"Yes? In all these years, you have never thought to mention that? I was at bible college for heaven's sake. You couldn't have mentioned it?"

"What would it have changed?"

"I... I don't know... come on, Dad...What are you talking about? I'm confused here. And no, it probably would not have changed anything. I'd want to be a preacher even more knowing we have Moses's brother Aaron in our lineage!"

He looked at Micah, giving his friend a shoulder shrug and half-laugh, showing his unease.

Isaiah spoke again, "Well, Aaron is not exactly the best role model of a priest, but I know what you mean."

Micah sat up in his chair, then spoke.

"Wait a minute. There are people, families out there who have these things traced. People have claimed they were of certain tribes."

Micah stopped a moment to think, then crossed his arms and continued.

"But they are all Jewish. Unless I'm missing something, we go to church, not temple. We're Christians. We're not Jewish."

Zech nodded and swung his attention back to his father.

Isaiah responded, "That's right. Our family became quite private a long time ago. In fact, it was around two thousand years ago."

Silence filled the room until Zech finally broke it. "AND!"

"I remember being in your guys' shoes many years ago." He gave a slight chuckle before going on.

"Let's follow Paul, and if you keep an open mind, it will begin to make sense."

Paul led them through the back door of the secure conference room that his seat was previously blocking. It was a vast hallway with large black doors, none of which had windows, but each held a heavy-duty door handle and pin pad.

Paul stopped at the second door but stopped before punching in his code. He looked back to Isaiah. "Would you like to do the honors? Your number is now active."

"I would. Thank you."

The pastor stepped up. He punched in a long code and then pulled a large lever. The sound of a large deadbolt moving behind the wall echoed in Zech's ears. His curiosity piqued with anticipation.

As they entered the room, Zech was stunned to see how empty it was. He had no guess as to what should have been in there. It could have been Daniel petting three lions for all he knew, but he certainly did not expect an empty room with one crate. His eyes locked on that crate, though. There was something about it that held his attention.

The room was deeper than he expected and the crate was at least fifteen to twenty feet away. Paul held back by the door while Isaiah approached it. Zech and Micah slowly stepped behind.

Isaiah turned before he reached it, saying, "It may hurt a bit if you get too close. That's okay. Just don't grab anything or move too quickly at it, especially if you get that 'hurt'-like feeling through your body."

Zech and Micah both shook their heads yes, both having no idea what Isaiah was talking about.

Isaiah moved forward and opened the old wooden crate. Zech could see a worn green leather box, nearly as large as the wooden crate. In fact, the crate seemed to be built to wrap around the leather box. And if it wasn't for the light coming off the green leather, Zech might have not noticed it in between the wood of the crate. But as he looked closer, the inner box had a sort of glow to it. It was a soft light, but not quite light; more of a warm glow.

Isaiah motioned for Zech and Micah to come in close. Both Zech and Micah stepped forward. They also both felt a twinge of pain, like a push against them, deep in parts of their bodies. Yet, most of them felt totally drawn in, like they were a piece of metal and the magnetic pull was getting stronger the closer they got.

Micah began to feel the pain worse than Zech, but he still approached. He was now sweating, trying not to let the others know how half of his body seemed to be repelled; not only repelled but repulsed. Like a portion of his body's molecules were perfectly happy to jump out of his skin and run off down the hall, and away from this crate, this green box.

The two peered into the box as Isaiah looked down with them.

A large golden wing sat alone in the crate. It glowed and they shielded their eyes, but somehow they knew it was not normal light. The piece appeared to be from something bigger. It was not broken off but somehow removed cleanly and placed neatly here.

As Zech looked at the golden wing, he noticed unbelievable craftsmanship. Each feather of the greater wing was etched out exquisitely. The detail was incredible, like he was staring at a row of feathers from a large bird that was cast directly from life into gold.

His heart stopped a moment.

Not a bird's wing.

This is the wing of an angel.

A Cherub.

Chapter Six

A Ministry Closed

Z ech and Micah decided to have their next finance meeting over lunch. No more transactional budget submissions. They wanted an open and upfront process where each could understand the other's point of view. They also wanted to create a more strategic process, in order to balance the needs of the overall church with the needs of each ministry.

Zech asked Micah to bring an estimate for each ministry's needs for the next three months. The current church's building was nearly paid off, only five years away, based on current payments. Isaiah had wanted to ramp up payments in order to pay it off before the expansion, but with the growing population and after numerous talks with his local mortgage broker, he had worked out a deal he was comfortable with.

Still, the new mortgage was in the seven figures, and as expansion was well underway, the new monthly payments were kicking in. If Zech was going to keep their cash reserves at the appropriate level and pay the new mortgage, they needed to cut back for at least a year, maybe more, in other areas. The new construction filled the congregation and staff with hope, but Zech's heart sank before his meeting with Micah. Asking his friend to dial it back or even temporarily close certain ministries would be a difficult conversation.

Micah dropped Ruth and Jeremiah off at the Lights' house, then he and Zech rode together to a nearby restaurant. It was a local place known for their pastries, cookies, and desserts, but their sandwiches were the best in town. With the popularity of the bakery, the restaurant side of the business was steady but never packed. The owners were members of the church, and upon request, gave Zech and Micah a table in the back in a more private section.

The meeting was supposed to be on finances. They had agreed to hold off all other talk until this was done and each put in hours to get all their numbers and projections and straight. Micah put aside his distaste for getting into the math. He wanted to show his friend he cared about the overall church and its future, not just about asking for every penny he could squeeze for his ministries.

In the short car ride to the restaurant, they made small talk about the kids. Zech's oldest, Luke, was starting to become a handful at home. He was ten years old now and he recently started playing rougher with the younger boys. He was growing a lot lately, and Mary was not surprised if he was more clumsy, but this was different.

Just this week, Mary told Zech on three different days she spanked the boy and sent him to his room. He had a new habit of turning on the TV and ignoring Mary when she asked him to turn it off. As soon as his punishment was over, to her amazement, she'd find him right back on the couch, staring mindlessly at another cartoon and ignoring his mother. Zech told Micah that if the TV trend continued, he might be donating it to the church soon.

Once at the restaurant, they sat down, opened their notes, then proceeded to ignore all the talk about finances in lieu of realizing they never talked about what they had seen at the Storage Yard.

"So what about that crate!?" Micah said excitedly.

***

"...what about that crate..." echoed in Zech's head. He honestly did not know what to think. He had not yet mentioned it to Mary and there was not much discussion between Isaiah, Micah, and himself after that day. Zech had felt a feeling of peace; such over-abundant peace, and joy, and love. It was like getting goosebumps during worship service, when he felt connected to the Lord during an emotional song. Hands raised, along with all those around him. Losing himself to the worship.

But that feeling only lasted a few moments in church. He felt this for hours, and it was stronger. The next day, he woke up confused. Two things picked away at his thoughts.

First, Paul knew how to play Euchre?!

He laughed about this with Micah on the car ride to the restaurant.

The second one was obvious, and both he and Micah gazed at each other trying to piece together their thoughts.

The crate.

That piece inside.

"Yeah, the crate..." Zech's voice trailed off as his response turned more into a thought than a sound.

"You think it really is..." Micah also trailed off as he spoke in hushed tones.

"A piece of the Ark? I do. It sounds crazy, but I do believe it. That feeling when we were there, next to it. At first, it kind of hurt... but once I saw it... Felt it... Stood there in the presence. It just... Just feels right. Ya know?" Zech was trying to put his thoughts into words as he spoke in choppy sentences.

"Yeah. Like nothing I have ever felt." Micah felt the same peace and love, but he did not mention how he also felt the push, the repulsion, like the pain deep in your eyes when staring into a bright light. It kept him awake at night since he first experienced it.

They both had so many questions.

How long had Zech's family had the crate?

Was it really a piece of the ark?

The ARK.

From Exodus?

Did anyone else know?

How old was it?

How long had it been in that crate? At Paul's Storage Yard? In that secure room?

What did this mean for them? For the church?

When they came to the topic of the church, Zech finally steered the conversation back to the original purpose, church finances. It took a moment, but their minds gradually settled on the task at hand, like kids being asked to come in from playing outside and to instantly start their homework.

Zech started by explaining the current situation. The down payment to the builders had dipped into the church's reserves, cutting it in half. Thankfully, Isaiah had over six months of expenses set aside plus a building fund saved specifically for the expansion. However, they were now down to under three months in their emergency fund and their monthly cash flow was strapped to the new mortgage payment. Zech did not even want to mention how the increasing property insurance and utilities were impacting the budget, each more than doubling. Isaiah had not fully budgeted for those increases and they were just another thing that stacked up.

Isaiah and Zech wanted to be at a full year's worth of expenses in the church's emergency fund. They could live with six months for now, at least until the expansion project was completed and the anticipated rise in first-timers gradually became full-time members.

Then the associated tithes and offerings could buoy the church.

Micah listened undisturbed to what Zech thought was a stressful and dire situation for the long-term sustainability of the church. He did not like the risk.

"So what I'm saying is, we don't have a balanced monthly budget. We will need to cut back in multiple places, and immediately," Zech concluded.

The "cut back" comment finally struck home with Micah. He now knew where this was going. Some of his ministries, and maybe part of his staff, or both, would be impacted.

"Hang on. Let's think about this," Micah began. "The city is growing faster than ever. The unemployment rate in the area, and across the country, is dropping. Plus, people with jobs are now being paid more. We need to reach these people, now! This is not the time to cut back; it is the time to expand!"

"Micah, we don't have the funds. Where will the money come from? If your staff can't pay out of pocket, or turn to volunteering for three to six months, then we have to cut back expenses."

"No way. We cannot grow the church and spread the word by cutting back."

"Where?! Tell me where. Would you pull support for missionary families in developing countries or reduce your staff? Would you pay for our staff's medical insurance or go to four prisons next month like you planned? We simply cannot do everything right now."

Micah felt attacked. How come Zech was coming to him and not the maintenance staff or his own? He did not know Zech had already done cuts in every other area. They simply planned their expenses wrong and now was time to readjust their budget in order to build it back up long-term. Regardless, Zech saw anger flash in Micah's eyes, but to Zech's surprise, it left nearly as soon as it arrived. Then it turned into a smile as Micah turned to Zech.

"Why are we arguing over finances when we are sitting on what we now know? On what we now have," Micah said in a calm manner that threw Zech off guard.

Zech felt like he was missing something and he stared blankly at Micah.

"The crate!" Micah exclaimed.

He continued.

"We have an artifact that basically proves the existence of God and is many thousands of years old. The historical value alone is worth multi-millions but think of the people it will bring into the church! How have we not thought of this?!"

Zech looked at Micah uneasily.

"I don't think we should jump into monetizing something we don't fully understand yet. There must be a reason why Isaiah, or my grandfather, or the generations before them, decided against that."

"Isaiah just saddled us with a seven-figure mortgage and in the same year showed us a secret that could have global impact. This lines up!"

"Slow down. Yes. That would be great, but what..."

"Yes! It will be great!"

Micah cut off his friend and started outpouring ideas. "You said how you can feel the presence of God as you approach it. Any place we bring the crate, the piece of the Ark, people will feel it. How could they doubt the word after experiencing that?!"

"But what..."

"Better yet, we hold interviews with some doubting reporters. Every national news program and talk show would want an interview. We could do them all or let them bid on exclusive rights, and that is just in the US. Think about the global rights!"

"Micah, stop."

Micah kept going and gaining momentum like a freight train.

"That solves all our money problems for years. Then we focus on spreading the word. Every school, prison, homeless shelter. Think if we had politicians come see it?! We could convince them about all the policies that..."

"STOP!"

Zech yelled and dropped his fist on the table. Micah looked at him in disbelief.

"I have no idea what to do with the... the... the artifact we saw, if we even do anything. But what I do know, what you are suggesting isn't it. We aren't using it to grow rich and influence politicians. We aren't using it to be the headline on the next *Dateline* or *20/20*. How do you even know we can? You remember what happened when the Philistines stole the Ark? Use it to solve our budget problems and how are we any different from them?"

Micah fired back and stood up from his chair, looking down on Zech in the process.

"Budget? Are you seriously still talking about our budget when we have the Ark? Get a grip, Zech. You would burn the original Bible because you are scared of distributing copies."

"That's not what I'm saying." Zech stood up on Micah's comment. He was inches shorter than Micah but looked his friend squarely in the eye, stepping up to the body language Micah was laying down on him.

Micah continued.

"Stop counting beans and get into this war. Some of us are on the front lines while you hide in the back."

"Micah, knock it off."

"Or maybe your budget can help win over someone on death row."

Micah walked out of the restaurant and kept walking. He walked back to the Lights' house, got Ruth and Jeremiah, then went home without a word to anyone.

***

That night, Zech told Mary about the artifact and what happened with Micah at the restaurant. Mary listened patiently to the unbelievable story her husband laid out for her. Her first response was astonishment, followed soon with wanting to have Isaiah and Rebecca over for dinner the following night. She wanted to know the what and why of this whole situation, and from the source.

Isaiah was expecting the call and was happy to join for dinner, even on short notice. He actually wished he had done something similar with Rebecca when he first found out the secret from his father. He had waited months to bring it up with her.

No babysitters were available on short notice, and they were hesitant to ask Ruth, so Mary held the kids without TV all day. When Isaiah and Rebecca showed up, she popped in a kids tape into the VCR and brought out dinner. She was not proud of using the TV as a short-notice sitter, but she knew they had at least one hour, maybe ninety minutes for discussion. She also knew her in-laws would understand given the circumstances.

As the four sat down to eat, Zech started off by asking about their family history.

Isaiah started, "We have been protecting the Ark for generations."

"So it is *The Ark*?!" Mary interrupted. "Sorry, go on."

"No problem. I was excited when I learned too. And it is not quite *The Ark* but pieces of it. I don't fully understand aspects of this myself. But, as I was saying. It has been under protection for at least a few thousands of years, with no written documents, passed down solely as an oral-tradition. That is why it is hard to say for sure, but keeping it oral also helps protect it.

"My father, Michael, told me that at some point in ancient Israel, before the Babylon invasion and Jewish captivity, our family became responsible for the Ark. As you now know, our family were priests in the tribe of Levi, and quite likely, we were responsible for the inner portions of the Temple, the Holy of Holies, and that is how we became caretakers of the Ark."

"That is the real *Ark*? I mean, the piece we saw was actually from it?!" Zech said quietly with shock and awe written on his face.

"That is a good question, and we will come back to that." Isaiah continued, "Your grandfather did a lot of research on this, and best he could gather was that in the years in between the prophet Isaiah and the fall of the first Temple, a special group was formed to protect the inner sanctuary, more specifically, to protect the Ark.

"Our family must have been in that group, and more than likely, it was made up of only priests; they were the ones most familiar with the cleansing rituals that allowed someone to get within close range of the Ark and not be, well, for lack of better term, disintegrated by the holy power of God held in the Ark."

"You mean how the Lord struck down people that touched it?"

"Yes. And after my time with it, standing near the crate, I believe it's not necessarily God reaching out to strike down people. I think it is our internal sin that the Ark is burning up. I am sure you felt that pain as you approached it?"

Zech nodded.

Isaiah continued.

"I have felt varying degrees of that. One time in particular when I was less of a Christian than I would like to remember." He paused for a moment, thinking of the time he moved from the high school into the small church house they were now reconstructing.

Isaiah continued, "I believe that pain is from your inner sin. I'm not sure if it is from the Ark pushing against us or because the sinful portion of ourselves is trying to run away, but either way, everyone feels it to some extent. No one is without."

"Dad, I have to ask, why all the secrecy? Shouldn't we make this public? Share that holiness with the world?"

Isaiah looked thoughtfully at his son.

"We already do."

"How? This is the first I've heard of it and I've been in the church my whole life."

"Zech, we share it every Sunday when we preach. We share it every time we help someone in need. We share it every time we pray. Or when we put someone else's needs in front of our own."

"You know what I mean, Dad."

"I know exactly what you mean. But do you know what I mean?"

Isaiah and Zech locked eyes for a moment upon this last comment.

Mary was about to speak up, but Rebecca beat her to it as the boys began stirring.

"Come on over, children. Who is ready for a bedtime story?"

The three kids were all peering around the corner, interested in the conversation far more than the movie playing behind them. Rebecca opened her arms wide and welcomed the kids over to the table.

"Dad, can we step out back?" Zech said to his father.

"No, it is time for this grandpa to enjoy his grandkids. We can continue this another time. Meet me at church on Saturday evening as the worship team is ending their practice session."

***

The next day, as Zech was walking up the rickety metal stairs to the temporary building that was now the church offices, he caught sight of Micah pulling into the parking lot. He thought of keeping his head down like he had not seen, but he forced himself to stop and wave to his friend before going into the office. If he was going to figure out this crate stuff, he would need to work with Micah. They were a team, and best friends after all. They would do this together.

The door stuck as Zech unlocked it and gave a hard pull to open it. This door always seemed to stick in the mornings. As he confirmed the deadbolt was unlocked and broke the door free, he noticed the temporary platform shift under his feet. Two of the bolts attaching the hard steps were coming loose from the main structure's siding. Most likely from pulls on the door, just like this every morning. Zech thought to himself that he was like those stairs, gradually coming loose with every extra effort. He made a mental note to get it fixed, then went into the office to start the day.

Micah did not enter the office for another hour. He had a few things to take care of in the main church area first, but really, he was avoiding talking to his friend. How could Zech be so short-sighted? he thought to himself. But just as Zech realized, Micah knew the two would need to work together if they were to be successful. They were on the same team.

He swung open the door to find Zech was the only one inside. Perfect.

"Sorry to interrupt, but let's settle this."

"Finances or the crate?" Zech replied.

"Both." Micah paused a moment, then added, "Separately."

"Crate first?"

"Okay."

They stared at each other a moment, then blurted out like teenagers talking about the latest gossip.

"*The Ark* was in that crate!" Zech began.

"A piece of *The Ark*!" Micah responded.

"How cool is this?"

"Oh, I know, this is... big... I mean REALLY... BIG."

After a moment, the giddy friends lowered their voices.

"So did you feel it? The joy but also the hurt?" Zech asked in a serious tone, leaning forward in his chair.

"Yeah... I didn't want to say anything, but pal, it really hurt. I'm not sure how long I could have stood there with it."

"You know what bugs me?"

"You mean outside of the fact that your family has been hiding an artifact that God lived in and still has his power in? And outside of how it will likely change the world? And how we have never heard of it for the last thirty years? Yeah. Outside that, what's bugging you.?"

Zech dismissed most of Micah's sarcasm with a half-smile, then built on the comments.

"Well, yeah. All that. I mean, if it's real, which after seeing it, we both think it is real, then why hasn't anyone in my family brought it out in the open? Used it for the church? Or to dispute those who are against the church or causing violence around the world in what they claim is God's name? I just don't get it."

"Let's talk to your dad. Pastor Isaiah has to have his reasons or know more. He didn't tell us much when we saw it. Honestly, I'm not sure I would have listened. I was in a daze that entire day."

"I tried talking to him already. We were cut off by the kids, but he was saying something about already sharing it. He didn't really make sense."

"Well, I know a few ways we could use it." Micah looked at Zech, raising his eyebrows in suggestion.

"Come on," Zech said dismissively.

"No no no, hear me out." Micah walked closer, pressing his hands in a playful pleading motion as he continued.

"What if you did not have to worry about this budget, or mortgage, or ministries?"

"We are not using this to drive church profits," Zech said with a sigh.

Micah kept going.

"I've put thought into this. We could get lawyers and license it. That is completely reasonable. Get it into the world, make it free for any personal use, but charge for corporate usage."

Zech turned his head, trying to think through what his friend just said, pausing before instantly dismissing it as he had planned.

"You know. That's not a bad idea." Zech started thinking of how great it would be to have the new mortgage paid, looking into developing other land on the property, and even flashed more churches in his mind's eye.

Micah saw the agreement in Zech's eyes.

"But still." Zech backtracked and caught himself in greed.

"We would be the financial benefactor of God?! God can bless you with it, give you more or take away, but we're talking about turning God's former home in the Temple into our passive income stream."

"Well it sounds awful when you phrase it that way! Think of ALL THE GOOD WE COULD DO! You are underestimating this. Walk that crate into any building, a school, sporting event, prison, a church for crying out loud, and watch as they are in awe. Watch as they worship and dedicate their lives to God."

Zech felt himself pulled into Micah's train of thought more and more. It would be an incredible tool for gaining believers. *God is behind us, but now he'd literally be behind us!*

The fact that he had to stop his thoughts from running away for a second time gave him even greater pause.

"Look, I'm not saying we hide it forever. But let's talk with my dad more, learn about why he did what he did, and then we can create a plan. Agreed?"

Micah took longer to respond than Zech would have liked.

"Fine. I don't agree. But fine."

Zech moved to the other topic they needed to clear the air with, back to finances.

"All right now, let's settle this budget. We are over and still need to cut back."

Micah rolled his eyes but then sat near Zech in an agreeing fashion.

"You can't fire all my staff, end contributions to good causes, and stop our visitation trips. You can't."

"I don't want to end all of that. I want to figure out a way we can do it for a year on a tighter budget. If we do that, we grow our reserves back to comfortable levels in about a year. Then we can gradually increase back up as tithes increase. Likely cutting back to half of what you have now."

"Half?! No."

"Isaiah did most of these things with a tenth of the budget." Zech began to voice his frustration. "I don't see why this is a big deal. We cannot afford to have multiple full-time staff members in multiple ministries. We can have one admin, not two, and ideally none. Most of these positions were volunteer positions, areas for people to serve and meet new people. It was that way for decades. Only since *WE* have taken over have we increased headcount so much. It's my fault as well. I will be asking people to cut hours or laying them off."

"Headcount? Headcount..." Micah stared at his friend with a blank expression. "When did this become a corporation? Next thing you'll tell me is we need to optimize expenses to help our share price."

"Oh, knock it off." Zech's frustration rose again, and this time, Micah responded in kind.

"NO. You knock it off! You might not see a lot of tithes and offerings from it, but we reach people." Micah stood and stepped toward Zech. Zech stood to meet the implied physical challenge as Micah continued. "We support worthy causes, like orphanages, trafficking victims, prisons, women's shelters. Some of those could NOT stay afloat without us. You are not asking me to cut a couple thousand; you are asking me to cut spreading the word and helping those in need. Those like..."

Micah stopped and trailed off.

"Like you mean like Terrence?" Zech said as quiet filled the air. "You tried. And who knows, maybe he will come back, but you can't save everyone."

There was a long pause. Zech broke the silence and reached for a piece of paper from his desk, the one he was finishing as Micah entered the room earlier.

"This is your budget," he said, holding up the paper. "We can do more later if we cut back now. We can do it together."

Micah took the sheet. He was still breathing heavily, and Zech noticed that his friend was sweating from their argument.

"Come on, let's take a walk," Zech suggested. "I could use the fresh air."

Micah nodded and they went for the door.

Micah stepped out first but before stepping down, he turned to his friend.

Zech thought his friend was calming down and getting rid of the sweat that now showed through his collar. He was wrong, though. Micah was now sweating more after holding in his frustration.

As Zech walked out on the stairs, he was caught off guard by the look in his friend's eye. It was pure rage that flashed through a waterfall of sweat.

"If you think this is enough, you're wrong. You're no better than the guy who turns his back on abuse or trafficking."

At this comment, Zech could feel his frustration mounting again and he tried to suppress it as Micah continued his onslaught.

"You're no better than the guy who put the girl in..." As Micah spoke this last insult, he shoved the sheet of paper in Zech's face.

Zech responded with force to combat the arm raising towards his face, pushing Micah's hand and body backwards.

The rickety steps could not hold the two men as their weight quickly shifted. The stair panel shifted and came off the wall.

Micah stepped back to regain his footing, but his foot found empty space where the stairs were descending.

He plunged, falling backward down the short metal stairs, smashing his back on the third step. Then his neck turned, unable to compensate as his body hit the ground below. The noise from Micah's body against the loose steps echoed in Zech's head.

He was rushed to the hospital.

Three days later, Micah Grey was pronounced dead.

Chapter Seven

Watching Jeremiah Grey

The empty feeling left by Micah's death was heavy in Ruth's heart. She came to realize it would always be there. Her sadness, her longing for her husband, her longing for a father to her son. It became a part of her now. No longer something she prayed to remove. Every night, with tears in her eyes, after putting Jeremiah to bed and dreading the thought of him mentioning his dad, she would pray for God to help her feel better, to remove the scar. But no more; she accepted the hurt. The empty.

It was not so much that she embraced it, but more of realizing that it would never go away. It was there and it would stay the rest of her life. The best thing she could do was to be the best mother she could be. To continue loving Jeremiah like she always had, continue getting him exposure to the right friends, exposure to the church.

The Lights were the closest thing to a family they had within a thousand miles. Ruth's family was now based in West Texas and Micah's only family, a sister and brother, were in Northern California and rarely heard from. Ruth's parents, Gary and Barbara Freed, flew in for the funeral, and Micah's siblings sent flowers. Her parents knew Isaiah from their younger days when they grew up in the North Florida area and even went to Isaiah's youth group during a trying time in the church. They stayed with Ruth a few weeks and visited with the Lights, but once her parents returned home, Ruth had only her church friends and the Lights.

Ruth and Mary started having lunch, just the two of them, more often. In the weeks after the funeral, Mary reached out but mostly gave Ruth space. However, after a series of unreturned calls, Mary started dropping by throughout the week. She would find Jeremiah playing quietly or watching TV while a distracted Ruth was halfway through a mundane task, staring into the distance, usually with tears in her eyes. One time she found her friend halfway through washing dishes. She was staring out the window, crying, while the original hot water had long turned cold. Ruth hadn't noticed the water temperature.

Mary was cautiously optimistic as her friend started to turn the corner, and not long after, their meal planning and playdates with the kids were back, now happening three to four times per week, and an effort to have one meet up together without the kids. Just Mary and Ruth.

On those days, Zech would come home for a long lunch or take the afternoon off to watch the boys while Ruth and Mary went to lunch or had a long walk.

There was more than ever to do at the church in Micah's absence. Isaiah stepped back in to help with the day-to-day operations and give more of the sermons, while Zech kept finances and took over the ministries. Zech enjoyed getting away to be with the four young boys. Work was busy enough and helped him focus, but every time he pulled into the parking lot, he expected to see Micah's car. The void left by his friend stuck with him.

And he blamed himself for his friend's death.

***

Micah's official cause of death was a pulmonary embolism. He was rushed to the hospital after his fall down the shaky steps. His back and neck were significantly damaged but thankfully no breaks, only three small fractures that doctors expected to heal in due time. However, during treatment, the doctor noticed one of Micah's legs was swollen. Initially, she attributed the swelling to the fall, but the swelling stuck in her mind and she ordered diagnostic tests on the second day to resolve it. The tests would show what the doctor had feared, blood clots, but the clump of blood had already broken free. The following day, it made its way through Micah's veins and eventually to his lungs, where it lodged itself and ended the young church leader's life.

Zech had no idea of the clot, and he seriously doubted if Micah even knew. Zech thought of the situation in two ways. The first way, Micah's fall and trip to the hospital could have saved his life. Or the second way, the fall proved to be the catalyst to shake the clot loose and find its deadly resting place in Micah's lungs. Zech's mind drifted toward the latter.

At first, Zech buried himself in his work, but being at church only reminded Zech of Micah. Watching the boys did too, but at least he could see the boys smile. Jeremiah's smile reminded him of Micah's smile. It reminded Zech of the incident on the stairs, but in time, the young boy's smile gave him solace in the tough times.

Zech decided he would always be there for his boys and for J. He etched in his mind that he had four sons. Micah had joked with Zech years ago that he and Mary needed to have one more boy and name him John, so they'd have all four of the New Testament evangelists: Matthew, Mark, Luke, and John. Now with Jeremiah around, and most people calling him J, many folks who met the Lights thought that was exactly what had happened.

With Micah gone, Zech thought he must be the father figure for the young boy. Micah would have done it for his boys. Both men had seen the struggles children face without a father. Zech's mind often went to Terrence, shoving the girl near the fire, and Zech's resolve to be there for Jeremiah would harden.

Zech would never stop blaming himself for Micah's death, and decades later, once Jeremiah learned about what happened on those stairs, he would blame Zech too. For now, the boy could remain innocent of the situation and enjoy his friends.

***

Jeremiah missed his father dearly. He was only six when Micah passed, but he was old enough to know something was wrong. His mom cried when she saw Micah in the hospital and then even more often after the funeral. When his mother started regularly meeting with the Lights again, Jeremiah, like most young kids, became a creature of habit. Playing with his friends took over his mind. He also saw his mom cry less and less. Ruth had not noticed, but Jeremiah was having trouble understanding the situation. All he knew was his dad was gone and his mom cried a lot. Jeremiah started pulling apart his toys on the days he would see Ruth cry. He did it quietly, and his mom never noticed. He would stay awake after his prayers, find a stuffed animal, and poke his finger in the seams. Eventually, he could get a grip and rip the seam, pulling it apart. The head and all the limbs would eventually come off. Cotton stuffing would pile up in his closet, where he did this quietly, but

Ruth would never see it. Jeremiah destroyed, and then cleaned it up quietly each time.

Jeremiah liked Zech and spending more time with the Lights. Matthew was his best friend, while Luke and Mark were already like his brothers. Now the added time only reinforced the bonds.

Zech took them fishing, backyard camping, and filled their time together with tag, football, Bible readings, and even how to play card games and board games. Zech found that Jeremiah was somehow brilliant at Monopoly. Mark fancied himself the house Monopoly expert, mostly because he would never stop playing and declare himself the winner. But Mark typically did not get the chance to outlast the other kids when Jeremiah played, though. Jeremiah had inadvertently stumbled into the house trick. It took Zech weeks to finally figure out the young boy was actually gaming the system in his favor. At first, he thought it was luck, simply that the boy had done well in a few games, the luck of a small sample size, but it kept happening.

Jeremiah did not like the hotels; he thought they were too big for a property and did not like the red color. "Why would anyone put a barn on their property," he would say. So in response, he put up four houses. He would put up four houses everywhere he could, and as fast as he could. As the game went on, he began using up all the houses, limiting others from using them. Others would get a hotel or a house or two, but on the whole, Jeremiah was the first and fastest to build. The money saved on not buying hotels left him with only more houses and the strategy rolled on, limiting others because all the houses would be used up.

Zech laughed and thought to himself how bright the young boy was. He was already street smart, just like his late father.

As the weather cooled, Zech kept the kids outside as much as possible when he watched them. Backyard football, where Zech was "all-time QB," was their current favorite.

It was a Friday afternoon, when the five played on the side of Zech's house.

Then Terrence pulled up.

***

Terrence sat in a tan four-door Toyota Corolla. It was his father's car and he parked it one house down and across the street, within view of Zech's house but not too close. As he looked out of the windshield, across the rusted hood, he was not sure of what he would say. But whatever it was, he knew he had to say it.

His original affection for Micah had gradually turned to anger, and then to hate after leaving the church. It was Micah's fault that Terrence did not last in the youth group. Micah's fault that he had to now live with his father. Terrence's father took his anger out on his son, but now that Terrence was older, he could fight back.

The two had given each other numerous black eyes and had evolved a symbiotic-type of relationship. As long as one of them had a job, then that would fuel both of them being able to eat and go out to bars. They developed into more of a partnership instead of father and son, and Terry began bringing his son with him to happy hours after work. They would typically stay long into the night. Terrence would observe the drunken behavior and sometimes even listen through thin walls if his father brought home a woman, sometimes solicited or sometimes under the influence.

Their alcohol-sparked behavior changed after one of Terry's prison stints. He came home claiming he found someone who knew Jesus. How the savior was preparing to fight back against the sin in the world, against the sinners' unwillingness to listen to righteousness. Terrence couldn't hear it, thinking too much of Micah, but something about the fighting back held his attention. His attention gradually turned to passion. The two began going to weekly meetings to hear from the local leader, the same man who met Terry in prison.

"I am a Christian, and the strongest Christian you will ever meet" was how the man started every meeting. It became a tagline for the group and they would all repeat it to start and end each session.

Terrence never knew the man's real name; in fact, he only went by "Christian," and that was just fine with the small yet growing number of followers. They began calling themselves "New Christians," claiming to usher in

"Heaven on Earth." Their meetings frequently cited Revelation and the reckoning that both the misguided believers and non-believers would both face. The message was not about saving lost souls but showing the world the punishment they had in store if they did not change their ways. If they knew the sorrow, the heartache, the pain they would inevitably face, then surely they would follow the New Christians. If Revelation preceded Heaven on Earth, then they would help make the prophecies of Revelation a reality.

Terry and Terrence soon stopped drinking, except for during group celebrations when the entire meeting would be extended. The whole group would stay up long through the night, enjoying many spirits.

Only men were allowed in the "New Christians," as they were the "strong ones" in their eyes. They were tasked with protecting, or "enlightening," as they called it, the weaker men, women, and children.

Terrence had all the New Christian talking points in mind when he started walking towards Zech. He wanted to tell Zech what he had learned, and he wanted the kids to hear it.

As he walked up, his mental focus was shattered when someone stepped in front of him.

"Hello, Terrence," Isaiah said calmly.

***

Terrence was awestruck. The old man came out of nowhere.

"How can I help you, young man?" Isaiah said, with eyes locked on Terrence. The young man could not look away.

Terrence had taken a step back, nearly a fear-induced twitch, when he heard Isaiah. He was so focused on Zech, he had not even noticed the head pastor's car pull up in the driveway ahead of him.

"I'm here to talk to Zech," Terrence finally said, desperately trying to muster back his resolve.

"Well, he looks busy," Isaiah glanced over to see two of the children celebrating a touchdown. "How can I help you today?"

Terrence stood another moment, looking at Zech and kids, then back to Isaiah. This old man was stopping his plan, stopping his satisfaction. But no matter, if he had to go through Isaiah first, fine. He would tell Zech and the children soon enough.

Terrence remembered an opening line that Christian had used in a mock debate. Terrence ran with it. "Is your flock ready, Pastor?"

As he spoke, Terrence began to gradually find his courage for the first time in the conversation.

"My flock?"

"YES." Terrence came in with a more direct and confident voice. He centered his eyes and lowered his brows on Isaiah. "Yes. Your flock. Are they ready? Are YOU ready?"

Isaiah remained calm and solid in his stance, not flinching.

"I see behind these accusations, Terrence. And I see behind you, back to the accuser backing you," Isaiah said in the same tone as his first greeting.

"Accusations?! The time will come for accusations against your watered-down message. But..." Terrence slowed his talk and forced a smile. "You can help prepare for Heaven on Earth. Ready your flock. Be a shepherd. A *real* shepherd."

The final comment, "a real shepherd," was said with insult in his voice. If the young man was trying to negotiate Isaiah to his side, he had a lot to learn about emotional intelligence and understanding his audience.

Isaiah looked deep into the man's eyes. A mere boy, he thought. So misguided, caught up with the wrong kind of hope. The wrong kind of power.

"Son," he said slowly and directly, "there will always be a place for you here. You do not need to chase power and dreams of control. Control yourself and you have all the *power*, as you put it, you will ever need, through Christ. Do not go down with the accuser. Leave it behind and find peace."

Terrence's eyes lost their resolve. He broke eye contact with the older man and looked to the kids. The good times of youth group, making new friends, and long talks with Micah flashed in his mind. Then his anger sprouted back up to the surface.

"Peace?! You can have your false peace. You and your foolish flock will be worthless in the end. Adrift in the ocean of lost souls. You had your chance, old ma..." Isaiah interrupted the last insult.

"And you will always have another chance. Now it is time for you to leave."

Terrence fumed at being cut off, but he decided this was not worth his time any longer. Plus, he would never admit it, but he was afraid to continue looking into Isaiah's gaze. The older man kept eye contact the entire time. Terrence was uncomfortable, even at his peak of confidence. As if Isaiah was looking deep within him, almost through him.

Terrence walked briskly back to his car. He opened the door, but before getting in, he looked back. Isaiah was in the same spot, with the same piercing stare as if Terrence had not moved.

Terrence then looked at the children. To Jeremiah. He looked intently at the young boy and smiled wide. He flashed the smile to Isaiah as he drove past.

Chapter Eight

Weeks Ago

M atthew sat in the early morning darkness. Liz and the girls still slept. It was only him and their cat, Porkchop, in the cool morning hours. Porkchop had devoured the food Matthew laid out for him and now he hopped up on the couch armrest, close to Matthew. Such a loud eater for being such a quiet cat, Matthew thought as he closed his Bible. He smiled and petted the cat. As Matthew began to reflect on the past month, the fluffy companion purred at the chin and ear scratches from his master.

One month ago, his father Zech had told Matthew and Jeremiah about Terrence and the "New Christians." He and J had only vaguely heard of the group. Maybe a mention on a news report or headline, Matthew was not sure. Zech explained how he and Isaiah had been keeping an eye on the group since the boys were kids. Their local presence ebbed and flowed, but most of the group's work was in the Middle East. They were loosely linked to various attacks on churches, temples, and mosques.

At a high level, it was hard to decipher this group with all the other fighting and terrorist threats in that region, especially for local or national news in the states. The New Christians rarely, if ever, made the news, so Zech and Isaiah had been relying on missionaries in the area to keep them updated.

Zech explained the group's circle of violence and how they believed it related to recruiting. Every two to three years, the group would hit a series of religious build-ings or events. The first few sets of attacks were more demonstrations than violence, but their latest round dis-turbed Zech and Isaiah. All of their actions centered on the Seven Bowls from Revelation. Early demonstrations were around dying water red, to show the blood refer-enced in the second and third bowl the Angels poured out. Lately, rumors were they tried infecting drinking water in small towns in order to mimic the first bowl, and even burning down religious buildings to show the fire of the fourth bowl. It appeared they targeted Judeo-Chris-tian buildings just as much as mosques, whoever was not onboard with their "Heaven on Earth" plot.

Now with Terrence returning at the Christmas Eve ser-vice, Zech and Isaiah were concerned the group might be branching out. Their contacts overseas had reason to believe the group might go after a broader audience this time for recognition, potentially making a global effort.

The best Isaiah and Zech could gather was that the cycle of attacks came every two to three years, and increased in violence because of leadership changes and recruiting. The group would grow with new recruits, excite themselves with the thought of action, and then die back down after their actions concluded. Then a new leader would emerge in the group, rallying another batch of new members, eager to make their mark, and the cycle would repeat. Each time a more extreme leader, more members, and more resources would carry out the next round.

Zech estimated that if Terrence was in town, he was planning something domestic. Likely, he needed people, going for recruits that were easily convinced with the thought of power and control. Just as his father was recruited, and then himself through his father, Terrence likely had been going to the prisons and low-income areas, growing a leader on the inside who would be released in the coming months and could convince a group of followers.

After hearing of what happened thirty years ago, and the threats Terrence had made, Matthew was bothered by this revelation. As Zech had told them the origin of Terrence in the church, Matthew saw Jeremiah step back as he heard the story.

Jeremiah had led prison ministry, even been a guiding figure in their outreach to the lower-income and crime-ridden parts of town. He'd never seen anyone like Terrence or others claiming to be "New Christian." Had he simply missed it? Had he overlooked the insidious threat right under his nose? He was so focused on combating Islamic talking points in the prison, he may have been priming new recruits for this blended message all along. The New Christians seemingly evolved to utilize specifics of both Christianity and Islamic brand messaging. They gain recruits with a message of love and welcoming. That Jesus is your savior, you are loved. That He died for you, but then the message quickly pivoted from "being saved" into "how are you showing your gratitude," and into "how are you proving your worth to the creator." Any peace or tolerance-based aspects of Islam quickly dissolved into paralleling the radical Islamic view that many terrorists found solace in, centering on violent action to prove oneself in this life to earn favor in the next.

In Zech's view, the entire movement was hypocrisy, but they all realized the power in the messaging, especially to young men in a world growing more and more politically correct. Males without proper guidance were like a speeding car without a driver.

Matthew's mind drifted back to his current moment. He was still petting the soft cat.

"Seven bowls," he said quietly to his companion. "I know, I know. You only care about one bowl being filled. Don't worry."

***

Matthew also reflected on the changes in his and Jeremiah's careers in the last month. Starting in January, he was promoted from senior manager to director. Director of Industrial Engineering was his new official title. With it came a raise and an annual bonus related to business performance. He now had a total of four project teams underneath him.

In the past, Matthew had been on the verge of promotion due to his flashes in strategic thinking and leadership, but it never came to fruition. However, his recent shift in mindset was timed just right, as everyone in the regional firm gathered for annual planning in January, it took only two days of observing Matthew in the large group setting for the firm's owner to take notice. Matthew's manager told Matthew of his promotion the following week.

Ever since Christmas Eve service and the talk with his father and J on Christmas night, Matthew had proactively tried to be more intentional with his days. He bought a yearly planner and started making a slash for every morning he read the Bible. He had a streak going now that he did not want to break. Plus, he was sick of his dad, Zech, always reminding him how he should be in the Lord's word daily. Now he knew exactly how many days in a row it had been. Porkchop was also loving the new morning routine, as he was fed right when Matthew made the coffee and cracked open his Bible early each morning.

Matthew's shift to proactively planning his morning bled into his day. He now limited his drifting through email, viewing various websites, or hallway talk with his colleagues to start his day. He knew his first priority, and thus focused on it, more readily delaying the various requests and distractions that inevitably popped up. His afternoons became lighter, not scrambling to finish his most important task, and thus he was more free to explore the rest of his to-do list and head home for dinner with a clear head. Previously, the stress of work had him feeling brain-fried during dinner and playing with the girls afterwards felt like a chore. His morning routine and change in demeanor were subtle, but his bosses noticed his new focus, and so did his family. Not only was he getting more done, but his already quality work was now top-notch. As Matthew got better, he found himself caring more about the work and more present with his family. His own development was now leading towards a passion for mastery in his field.

The new work and daily plans took up the majority of his headspace, but the reason for his shift to being more proactive still loomed top of mind: Jeremiah.

He kept replaying Christmas Eve service in his mind. The point he stopped the replay was when he avoided walking over to his friend before service, and thus felt he gave Terrence the opportunity to talk with his friend. It was not that Matthew felt he had to protect J, but he felt he left his friend on his own at the wrong time. J was a grown-up, he rose through the church, and was involved in numerous ministries and outreach events. He spoke with people in dire situations and varying levels of intention, from mentally ill to scared, from feelings of helplessness to those with a drive for power and violence. Matthew knew J could handle himself, but still, he did not feel right.

This last thought nagged at Matthew. Terrence had not seemed like such a bad person based on appearance, but the background that Zech gave told an entirely different story. That was thirty years ago, though. Things change day-to-day, let alone decades later.

Still. He thought of his friend, J.

And now, he felt responsible to help.

***

Pastor J, as most of the church called him, also received a promotion that January. Not as formal as the one Matthew received, but pivotable nonetheless. Zech had given him more responsibilities with the church, essentially splitting all of Zech's responsibilities with Jeremiah.

Zech had learned from the stress he and Micah had experienced when they started leading more of the church. He hired staff deliberately for those who took accountability for their respective areas. *Competency*, *accountability*, and *communication* were his three hiring pillars, his three legs of the stool, as he liked to say. He also joked if he could make that stool into a chair, *curiosity* would be the fourth leg. This was his way of trying to get his team to ask questions and seek improvement. Zech's strict criteria netted quality church members into staff roles, but those skills were hard to come by, especially in someone who would take a church's salary full-time. The staff was small but capable.

Zech's first official hire after Isaiah retired was a former CPA. She was to take ownership of the finances. The same topic that cracked the foundation of Micah and Zech's relationship would now have professional support, so the same crack did not happen within the next generation. The new hire, Millie, was now in her seventies but still sharp as a tack. Decades ago, she originally worked two nights a week with the church, and at a reduced hourly rate, partly because Zech could not afford her normal rate, but also because her services were so in demand within the growing city that she could not spare much time. As she aged, Millie retired from her private practice and came to work for the church full-time. Her salary was still based on working part-time, but she was happy to be around, and she stayed over forty hours most weeks. If Zech's wife, Mary, was the informal church mom, Millie had sort of become the church grandmother, not only leading the financials but also taking a large role in the women's ministry with Mary, especially after Rebecca's passing. Millie especially loved continuing the "Ladies with Hats and a Bible" tradition as her way of honoring the late Rebecca. Millie had grown close to Liz through the ladies' ministry, a mentor and friend type relationship similar to that of a close aunt. Matthew and Liz's girls had started calling her "Aunt Millie."

***

J was now leading three sermons per month, leading all the ministries, and had Millie reporting to him on the finances and budget decisions. Zech still held one sermon per month and was the church's connection to their national and global church network, but gradually, J was learning all the day-to-day and taking it over from Zech naturally. The aging pastor was impressed with the young leader's capability, drive, and natural leadership abilities.

The increase in responsibility was also partially a test. Just as Isaiah had watched Zech and Micah closely when extending more responsibility, Zech was now doing the same with his young heir apparent.

Could he handle the added workload?

Would he delegate to his staff or work more and more hours to do it himself?

How would he handle Millie's strict financial process?

Would his discussions with Zech stay focused on short-term tasks or would he start to step back to understand the big picture?

However, the biggest question was obvious in Zech's mind.

How would Jeremiah respond to learning about the crate, the artifact, *The Ark?*

Would he seek its power for financial gain, to solve his worldly problems, or would he see it as an example for what God can do inside each and every one of us?

Zech watched J closely, and Isaiah watched both of them intently.

***

J started the new year giving the sermon on the first two Sundays. Zech would take the third Sunday with J back to finish the month. In between services on the second Sunday, J noticed he had a missed call from an unknown number. His first thought was *thank goodness,* as he kept his phone on silent and off the altar while preaching. Then he remembered he had two missed calls, also from an unknown number, the prior week, both during his time on stage, matching this recent call right in the middle of his sermon.

Were some friends trying to see if he turned his ringer off while on stage? He had friends in the church who would easily try to embarrass him in that way. But why call back the next Sunday? He didn't even keep the phone on him while preaching; anyone who knew him knew that. J dismissed it as a poorly timed and failed prank call. He prepared himself for the second service.

While on stage, he unconsciously noted the time he started and stopped preaching, so it was obvious when he picked up his things after the second service and saw a fourth call. The missed call came again and was exactly five minutes into his message. He scrolled through and looked at the older missed calls. Each missed call was five minutes into his message. He thought curiously for a moment before walking out of the office area and through the rotunda toward the coffee shop within the church. Halfway across the rotunda, he paused when he felt his phone vibrate.

He looked down.

A voicemail had come through from the fourth call.

He pulled the phone to his ear and listened.

"I have heard you out for five minutes each day, but have to say, when will you stop going through the motions of this watered-down message and really get into saving people?"

The familiar voice paused and then carried on in a lower, more direct tone.

"You have such potential. Your father did too. Don't let it go to waste."

J was confused as his mind thought of who the caller could be. His mind raced as he walked to the coffee area. He bought his cup, a large black, and said hi to the volunteers running the shop today. He liked to sit for a while and think in this area after sermons. Plus it was a great open spot if anyone wanted to come join him and chat. Zech was a fan of hanging out by the door, greeting and chatting and saying goodbye. However, J wanted to show he was open without directly infringing on Zech's method, hence the first table in the coffee area.

As he sat, his mind raced back to the unknown caller. It came to him in a flash. It was not a prank from a friend or youth group leader, it was Terrence. They first met a month ago close to this very spot. He referenced J's dad then just as he did on the message.

J sat quietly as the church cleared out, greeting and chatting with folks as he finished his drink. His mind pulled back to Terrence often. He was trying to reconcile the image of their first meeting with the one he had from Zech's description, when Terrence was thirty years younger and just getting out of high school.

He checked his watch; it was time to head to Matthew's house for lunch. Every month or two, he'd drive out and spend the afternoon with them. His favorite part was heckling his friend about watching online instead of joining in person, but that would not happen today. Matthew, Liz, and the girls were there each week since Christmas. J and his friend did not talk this morning but had noticed each other before first service. A quick wave and thumbs-up from each told the other their lunch was still on as planned.

J sat up in the chair and pulled out his phone to text his friend that he was soon on his way. But his eyes were drawn to an unread text. The number was not "unknown" this time. He could text or call back.

The text read, "Lunch? Let's talk about your message, and your potential!"

It was no doubt the same person.

Terrence.

J responded, trying to confirm the person's identity. "Who is this?"

"1:30. Larry's, off Southside."

J did not respond a second time. It was obvious who the caller was and J knew the sandwich shop well. What was not obvious was if he would accept the invitation, which also meant canceling with Matthew. He could be there ten minutes early if he left now.

J pulled up his text string with Matthew. The last messages were about what food they'd be having that afternoon and what games the girls were eagerly awaiting to play with their "Uncle J," as they called him. Monopoly Junior was the latest choice.

J smiled, skimming through the series of quick messages. Then his smile broke to a solemn expression as he texted his friend, "Rain check?"

He then waved goodbye to the few people still in the church area and headed for his car, and the strange invitation.

***

Matthew was surprised. It was not like his friend to cancel plans, especially on short notice and especially after confirming that same morning. Did Matthew read the head nod and thumbs-up wrong?

No.

That was plain as day. What was going on?

The message J gave that morning was good. He seemed full of focus as he preached on defending yourselves and loved ones from the perils of the world. The consistent attacks of the flesh that were popping up in the workplace, through media, and even the insidious versions within children's shows. Zech would be giving next week's sermon, following up on the same message but from the point of view of a parent to three grown boys and as a father of this church.

Matthew asked about rescheduling for the following week, but J was noncommittal.

"Let's talk later in the week," J had responded.

Matthew did not see him later in the week or the following Sunday.

Chapter Nine

Where's J?

Zech gave the following week's sermon about the pressures of the world, how it can tear down Christians and nonbelievers alike, and ways Christians could prepare themselves. Zech phrased the overview as "Building a wall of defense, and storehouse of weapons, during a time of peace. So you are ready when the war comes. Because it will."

He focused a large portion of the message on children and young adults. How their innocence is so easily lost when they are exposed to sinful things, or even righteous ways, before they are ready. Giving a fifteen-year-old young man open internet access without talking to him about the dangers of the internet and pornography may be just as bad as sending your twelve-year-old daughter off to evangelize to her teachers. In both cases, the child must be ready. The accuser, the enemy, will be there. Have we helped prepare that young man so he does not click on that ad of the scantily clad woman? Have we helped that young girl be an example of the Lord's Word

and how to navigate the social pressures of nonbelievers?

As Zech completed his message, he saw Matthew, Liz,
and the girls. He smiled as he caught Matthew's eye before his final prayer to the congregation. The smile faded
as Zech looked up and stepped forward after the final
announcements and dismissal. He noticed the empty
seat next to his.

Jeremiah was not there.

He was sometimes late to service. Caught up speaking
in the rotunda with guests or long-time members. But he
never missed the service.

Had Zech missed him leaving?

Had Zech been so oblivious to not realizing he was
gone the entire message?

His thoughts were interrupted as Matthew walked
over. He smiled and gave his dad a hug.

"Hey, Dad. Good message. Although I am surprised
you did not turn that message into a 'read your Bible
daily' or 'join the Bible Project.'"

"Whoa whoa, did you not hear me exclaim 'Don't go
into battle without your sword' as I held this old book
up?"

Zech extended his old green Bible and smiled, poking
it towards Matthew like the corner was the end of a
longsword.

His father's Bible was still a few feet away, but Matthew
seemed to notice the Bible more in that moment. He was
slightly embarrassed; a small part of him slightly flinched

at the motion his dad made towards him. But it was not the motion, it was something else. The Bible held his gaze and he lost his train of thought.

Zech took up the gap in the conversation.

"Hey, have you seen Jeremiah today?"

Zech was likely the only person who still called him Jeremiah instead of J.

"No. And that reminds me, that's what I was going to ask you. He canceled lunch last week and didn't respond last night. We were going to grab food today, just him and me, after service. Liz and the girls are heading to a playdate, so no afternoon lunch at our place."

"Hmmm." Zech looked off in thought. His eyebrows furrowed and eyes squinted, showing his concern as his mind raced. Now he was sure that he hadn't seen J that morning.

He put his arm around Matthew as they stepped through the sanctuary, toward the exit.

"Well, I don't have lunch plans either. And if Liz and the girls are not joining us, let's make it a father-son date. Just wait for me to say goodbyes and then I'm ready. What do you say?"

"You had to call it a date, huh, Dad?"

Zech laughed and his arm shook Matthew and pulled him close as they walked, bringing them tightly shoulder-to-shoulder.

"But sounds good, Dad. Any place in mind?"

"How about Larry's?"

***

Lunch between the two went by fast. Too fast, Matthew thought. They laughed and enjoyed each other's company from the moment they met up in the parking lot and went inside to order.

Zech ordered the Italian sub, his favorite at this place. It came warm and loaded with slices of meat that dwarfed the large bread that held it together. He subsequently joked with Matthew about his order, a meatball sub with added mayonnaise.

"You really need mayo on that thing?"

The meatball sub was a good choice, but not if you want your hands and face kept clean. The overflowing red sauce was bound to spill out, as well as a meatball or two trying to roll away.

"You know, J actually got me into this when we were kids. Ever since he had me try it this way, I can't ever remember eating one without mayo."

"Well, it's disgusting. Enjoy."

The woman taking their order asked if they were father and son. As they ordered and waited near the counter for their food, she ended up on the topic of family heritage, saying her dad was seventy-five. For his and her mother's fiftieth wedding anniversary, he surprised her with a trip to Europe, traveling through the parts of Italy, near places they could trace old family members.

She asked Zech and Matthew where they hailed from. Matthew deferred to let his father give the answer.

"Mostly Central Europe before crossing the ocean, just like you, ma'am, and best I know, it goes back through the Middle East a few thousand years ago."

Matthew never heard his father mention a Middle East aspect of their heritage.

Once they were sitting alone with their food, he asked about it.

"Middle East? I never heard you or Mom talk about that. It was always primarily a mix of German, Italian, and Belgian."

"Well. You never asked."

Matthew stared blankly at his father, motioning him to move along from his joke.

"Okay, okay. We have our roots in central, and even parts of Eastern Europe. Those DNA tests place us there too. However, those tests only picked up a few percentage points on where our family was before Europe. The Middle East and Egyptian areas."

"Wow. I never knew. That's cool," Matthew said innocently.

Zech studied his son for a moment.

He was proud of him, all the boy had accomplished and the family he was raising. Zech noticed the slight changes Matthew had made since Christmas. He previously would prod his youngest son about coming to service in person or reading his Bible more often, but now that Matthew was doing exactly those things, Zech did not have to ask. He knew it instantly. Matthew had a certain presence about him, and it was growing. Not an arrogance or pride, but Zech felt like his son was coming into his own, finally feeling comfortable in his own skin.

Zech also did not mean to put the Bible so close to his son's face earlier in the day. He had noticed Matthew flinch, but Matthew had not mentioned it. In fact, it was much less than Zech would have thought, given what he'd experienced in the crate for himself.

As he contemplated where to take the conversation, he did not want to force things. Having three sons was amazing for a young pastor. Surely one of them would follow in his footsteps, but it seemed not meant to be. He was proud of his sons, and Mark was a missionary, the tip of the spear for preaching God's message in harsh social and political environments. However, Zech was secretly disappointed, even though he hid it well. He did not want to guilt-trip his boys but wanted them to make their own life choices. Regardless, he was saddened how none of his three were taking over the church.

Thank the Lord for Jeremiah, he thought. He struggled in his prayer time after he lost his friend, Micah, and still felt guilty about what happened. But he knew he was too small in this universe to understand God's plan, so he was thankful that Jeremiah, essentially his fourth son, was now in line to take over the church.

Zech had plans to talk with Jeremiah soon, within the next couple weeks, of what his father had told him and Micah. Where their family name came from. And show him the crate, the artifact hidden inside, and the piece in

Zech's Bible. Plus, Zech was eager to show J what Isaiah and he had learned in recent years.

Zech decided he would tell Matthew about the family name, not the Ark, but just the history of their family name. Keeping it at that. For now...

***

Matthew felt like a kid in school as his father told him their family name was originally Levi. He recently finished Exodus in his daily readings and thought the personal connection was unbelievable. However, he did pause a moment thinking of the contrast between Moses coming down from the mountain to see Aaron at the forefront of idol worship. The difference between the two was stark, with Moses having glowed like a presence of God was within him and Aaron leading the creation and worship of a golden calf. Matthew wondered which side he would have been on.

Zech and Matthew got up from their table and began their goodbyes while talking about what the rest of the day had in store for each of them.

Matthew pulled out his phone and texted Liz he was on his way home. She should be close to home with the girls by now too.

As he texted his wife, his dad became silent. He looked up to see a confused yet angry look on Zech. An unfamiliar one for his father's face.

Following his dad's eyes, he saw J.

Great! There he is, Matthew thought. The concern from the unreturned texts and calls faded away. There was his friend.

But as Matthew looked on, he saw J was with someone. It was Terrence.

And the two were walking into the restaurant.

Together.

Chapter Ten

What Happened to Micah

Matthew was confused. Why was J with Terrence? Zech had warned them! The New Christians were radicals, and J was not!

Was he?

What was he doing?

J and Terrence walked toward the small sandwich shop, smiling and chatting, looking as if they were long-time friends meeting for a meal. He had not even known of this guy a couple months ago.

Matthew looked toward Zech. The flash of rage in Zech's face had subsided. He clearly was not happy, but he controlled his urge to kick the door open, right in their faces, and speak right down to both of them. Strongly. Directly.

But the head pastor breathed in deep through his nose, closed his eyes, and gripped his Bible tight. Matthew could see the white in his father's knuckles around the green, radiant spine of the great book. Zech had brought the Bible into the restaurant, mostly out of habit from carrying it every morning and nearly all day Sunday, but Matthew had noticed his dad had it with him more often than not recently.

J walked through the door first and paused when he saw Zech and Matthew. The look on J's face was like a teenager trying to sneak in past curfew, only to find his parents waiting just beyond the front door. Caught red-handed.

The awkwardness stunned Matthew. This was his best friend, and for all intents and purposes, this was his brother. Outside of a two-week period when they were in eighth grade and had a crush on the same girl, their relationship had never been awkward. Being offbeat with his best friend was bad enough, but what surprised him more than the fact that he was with this new person in their lives. This *Terrence* character that seemed to pop out of nowhere and who held an extremely troubling past.

Zech broke the tension by stepping forward and smiling at J. Then he said hello to Terrence as he walked in behind J.

"Hello, Terrence. Been a long time. How have you been?"

Terrence was much smoother in his conversation than he was thirty years ago. His confidence oozed as he saw Zech. He knew that J was not in service this morning, and Zech surely noticed, because J had been with Ter-

rence. Terrence's tan skin gave off a feel of Mediterranean and his short yet full beard was trimmed with
precision. He had aged well and clearly kept his body
in shape, almost unnaturally fit and muscular for being
nearly fifty years old. Matthew thought to himself how
Terrence seemed the type of guy to go on a cruise
ship vacation alone, with the goal of seeking out single
women solely for one-night stands.

As Terrence looked to Zech, he held his head up
higher than normal. The overexertion of pride was not
lost on Zech. Here was his heir apparent, now missing
service to spend time with someone suspected of having
far from the same values.

"Ah, hello, old friend. A long time indeed. You have
come a long way since last we saw each other. And so
has the church, I might add, under your leadership of
course."

"So what brings you into town after nearly thirty
years?"

"I may have left from time to time, but I was always
here, close to home."

"How was it overseas? The Middle East? Were you
spending time in Israel, or was it Iran?"

The mention of Iran and inherent extremist connota-
tions were not lost on Terrence. He half-smiled at the
barb and avoided the geographic portion of the question.

"It has been well. I have learned to live for God, and not for people. I have learned how to teach, and how to sacrifice. True leadership."

Zech knew he was referencing the New Christian propaganda. He and Isaiah had studied it after hearing of one of the group's smaller-scale attempts to mimic one of the seven bowls from Revelation.

He did not take the bait for a theological debate in the middle of a sandwich shop, but he did fire back.

"All leaders have a cross to bear, agreed. Especially when they are the ones carrying its weight instead of thrusting it on others."

Terrence squinted his dark green eyes toward Zech for a split second. It was enough for J to enter the conversation.

"Good message today, Pastor. We watched together, online. Terrence and I have been connecting on the Word lately and decided to watch together so we could discuss it live."

"Interesting," Zech responded calmly. "If only we had a coffee area built specifically for discussing the message while staying close to the church."

J knew Zech's form of sarcasm well, and typically enjoyed it, but that one hurt.

J's stomach dropped with guilt, because he knew Zech was right. Why did he agree to watch outside of church with Terrence?

No matter, J thought. Zech does not realize what he was trying to do. Terrence knew his dad and hearing about Micah was a whole new world to J. He would not readily admit it, and he appreciated being brought into the Lights' family, but always yearned to know his real father more. His mother told him about Micah, but it wasn't the same. This was someone who said Micah helped him see the light. To follow the Lord and change his life. J was always drawn to ministry, especially when there were hard-to-reach people, like lower-income parts of town, prison, and even difficult youth that made their way close to the youth group. Now J was hearing about his dad from Terrence, and how his late father was drawn to the same types of ministry, and how it led to Terrence's salvation!

Matthew stepped into the next short break in the conversation, looking to J.

"Hey, missed you last week and this morning, pal. We good for next Sunday afternoon? My place?"

J was pleased to be distracted from Zech and Terrence, who had been locked in eye contact during their quick verbal exchange.

"I think so. Thanks. Text you later?"

"Sure." Matthew looked around at everyone quickly. The slight weirdness when no one wants to end the conversation.

"Well..." Matthew said as he patted J on the back and moved past him toward the door. "Enjoy the food. And be careful with the meatballs. They're extra sloppy today."

J laughed.

"Has it ever *not* been a mess?!" J said as he nodded goodbye to Matthew.

Zech broke the gaze with Terrence and looked directly into J's eyes.

"Talk tonight, young man?"

"Of course. See you at six."

***

Zech and J had been meeting at the church every Sunday night at six to review the prior week, plan the next week, and discuss various other topics, urgent or otherwise.

Zech noticed J seemed a little distant in their Sunday evening meeting the prior week. That was after J heard from Terrence, canceled his lunch with Matthew, and went to see Terrence. J's mind was loaded that night from the conversation with Terrence, and Zech could not put his finger on what was wrong. He now wished he had been more direct and asked his young mentee.

Zech pulled up to the church before 5 pm. He wanted to get his thoughts together and write out notes before the 6 pm meeting. He was surprised to look across the empty parking lot to see Matthew stepping out of his car to meet his father. They began talking as they walked into the offices of the church.

"Hey, Dad, mind if we talk before J gets here?"

"Sure, but why so urgent?"

"Well, the girls are gone for another couple of hours, and I couldn't get this afternoon out of my mind. And... I mean... Why do you think J is hanging out with Terrence? It does not make sense. J is not an idiot. He knows enough about Terrence from what you told us, and I'd be willing to bet he has been studying the New Christians heavily since you brought them up."

"Agreed. And well, there are a few things I can think of." Zech paused as they both thought for a moment in the silence. Then Zech started again with a question.

"First, why do *you* think he'd be with him?"

"It does fit J. He wants the challenge, he wants to talk to the lost souls. Like the prison ministry or outside a bar during happy hour. If you ask me, no chance I'm going there. Sounds awful, but to J, it's... it's like when we were kids again playing against the older boys. It was tough, but at the same time, a fun challenge to play against Mark, Luke, and the other kids their age.

"For J, if he loses, so what, it was doubtful to begin with. But if he wins! Then wow, what an accomplishment.

"Does that make sense?"

"It does. And it reminds me of his father," Zech said.

"Micah?"

"Yeah. What do you remember about him?"

"Hardly anything. I remember him being a giant." Matthew laughed slightly. "I remember being a kid and thinking my dad was so huge, so strong, and then I remember when Micah would come over. He was so big, it was like he wasn't human to me. If he was bigger than you, then he couldn't be real."

"Ha. He was a big guy. And his heart was his biggest part. He cared for people, especially strangers, more than most. And I see it in Jeremiah."

"Yeah?"

"Micah ran the church ministries before he... before I..." Zech paused, and Matthew sat down, giving him a moment. They were in Zech's office now.

Zech's eyes began to water.

"You all right, Dad? What is it?"

Zech shifted his gaze and sniffed, as if trying to pull back the moisture from his eyes. Then he continued.

"Micah ran all the church ministries before we had to do various cutbacks to pay for the building expansion. I started to cut back on his outreach work to help cash flow and bump up our reserves... And we were never the same after that. Financially, it was the right decision, and I would do it again. But, what came next, I would not..."

Zech held his composure as he turned away from his youngest son. Matthew got up and walked around the desk to see tears silently streaming down his father's face.

Zech continued, struggling to talk without allowing the tears to take him over.

"It was petty money. Budgeting. Sacrificing the short-term so we could have a stable long-term. Micah did not get that. He thought losing the short-term was allowing lost souls to stay lost. That we were abandoning them.

"His size betrayed how gentle of a man he really was, but his strength was certainly there. In times of necessity, his quickness and strength showed, like when he stopped Terrence from hurting others all those years ago. He had arrived and picked the boy off the ground before most of us could react. But there were other times, when his emotions bested him, and his strength frightened others. Including myself."

"Dad?... What do you mean?" Matthew said softly as Zech took a deep breath, overcoming the weight of moving his guilt from his mind into his words.

"We argued about finance a lot in his last days. It was really so silly, looking back on it. But maybe tragic is a better word. It was not much money and we had done more with less. I think losing Terrence weighed so heavily on Micah's mind, and heart, that he felt like his heels were at the cliff's edge. He couldn't give an inch.

"The day he went into the hospital, we were at the church together. I thought we had come to an agreement, but as we left the office, he disagreed...

"His anger flashed and I... Well... I pushed him before... before he could strike me...

"At least, I thought he was going to... I don't know what I thought anymore."

"Dad. Micah fell down the stairs. They were not attached right, they were shaky, the two of you on it at the same time."

"Yes. All that is true."

"So what are you saying?"

"Micah did not just trip or lose his balance. He got in my face, and in that small space, with the door behind me, I had nowhere to go... I struck back.

"I pushed him...

"I pushed with every ounce of strength I had. I was reacting... but... I gave it everything. All the frustration over the budget, our arguments, all of it went into that push.

"He may have died of a blot clot in the hospital. But I killed him."

Matthew sat in silence. Stunned, yet sympathetic.

Zech grabbed his Bible with one hand, held it tight to his chest, and covered his eyes with the other. He made no sound as tears streamed down his cheeks.

"No, Dad. You can't say that. You were reacting, unconsciously, and it would have been nothing if you were on solid ground. The stairs. And the clot! Who knows if that would have been caught with technology back then. You can't know."

"I know, I know. I have prayed about it, and talked to your mother about it, more times than I'd like to admit. I have made my peace..."

He took another deep breath.

"But that doesn't mean it doesn't still hurt. How I was the catalyst to ending my best friend's life. How I widowed Ruth. How I left Jeremiah without a father."

Matthew walked to his father and hugged him. Even as an adult, Matthew still saw his father as a wiser, stronger man. Not quite invincible, but revered in a sense a young child sees an admired adult. But now, more than ever, he saw his father as a person. A human.

He still saw him as wise and strong, but now he respected him more than ever. Somehow the admission to his son brought Matthew to think of their relationship as more than father and son, where he was always looking up, but now as equal love and respect, on the same plane. Matthew knew of his own faults and sin, but now seeing his father's sin made him realize that his dad was not perfect. Just like Matthew.

And that was okay.

He did not have to be perfect.

And at this moment, all he had to do was hug his father.

That was enough.

As the embrace began to loosen, Matthew's eyes caught his father's Bible. Zech had released it, but it was still pinned between the two men. As Matthew stepped back, Zech pulled his hand in to grab the book before it slid off his hip. The top of the book moved past Matthew's line of sight, and a glowing light flashed through the spine, near the binding of the pages. It could have lit the entire room. It was warm and welcoming. Matthew felt good to be close to it.

He opened his mouth to ask but was cut off.

The hallway door outside Zech's office slammed shut with a bang.

It was five minutes until six o'clock.

They both knew it was J.

Chapter Eleven

History Rhymes

J pulled into the Church parking lot well before the six o'clock meeting. He saw Zech's car, as well as Matthew's and another car he did not recognize.

Matthew's car was unexpected, but "Good," he thought.

If Matthew was there, he could explain it to them both at once.

J needed to tell Zech there was more to the Terrence lunch than it appeared. He felt sorry for not explaining to Zech or Matthew beforehand, but it all happened so quick. J knew Terrence was likely a bad guy. The story from Zech about Terrence and Micah said enough, but that was thirty years ago. Shouldn't Terrence get another chance? And if he was beyond coming to Jesus, then J could at least learn more about the New Christians and why Terrence was back in the area. However, J knew deep in his heart, the biggest reason he wanted to hear from Terrence was because it was a chance to hear about his dad, Micah.

J loved hearing the random stories about his father. Some he had heard from the sages in the church over a dozen times. The time when Micah did this or that. The time he had this person or that person laugh, or made them think, or even those people that said they gave themselves to Jesus because of Micah. Those were the best. J could see the family tree still attending the church and look right at the grandfather or grandmother, or sometimes both, and know that it was his father who helped them come to Jesus. A whole family tree was changed because of God working through his father, Micah.

J wanted that for himself. It drove him. Not only to introduce Jesus to non-believers or to strengthen the faith of current believers, but for the generations to come. Every person had the chance to have an impact on future generations "as countless as the stars in the sky," he would think to himself.

Now here was a man claiming to know J's father right before he passed away. Based on Zech's recollection, this man was someone Micah desperately fought for, prayed for, but ultimately lost. Terrence was obviously bright and charismatic, and had the traits and confidence of a natural leader. Micah must have seen that! Now it was J's turn to learn more about his father and also get a glimpse into Terrence's life and the "New Christians."

He thought of it as low risk, high reward. Any conversation point would be fruitful.

Zech would understand. He had to.

The only thing that surprised J, as he walked through the rotunda and to the hallway, was how come Zech was not as interested in Terrence as J was.

He went through the whole story of their past, and warned Matthew and J of Terrence, but why not take advantage of the situation? Why not try to learn from him about the New Christians? Was it that risky?

As J opened the hallway door leading to the offices, he figured Zech and Matthew must be in Zech's office. He leaned into the door, which was notorious for being a hard door to open. Going into the office area meant going against the oncoming pressure from the large AC unit. The office portion of the building had an oversized air handler unit. It was designed to help the cool air be constantly funneled into the rotunda, however, the higher pressure made the door open quietly as it pushed against the steady flow, but it slammed hard if not held tight.

The habit of all the staff was to close it quietly, to respect anyone who might be in deep thought or prayer, and J held it firmly as he guided back with minimal noise.

As he turned toward Zech's office, he was frozen by the discussion.

It was Matthew speaking about Micah.

"Dad. Micah fell down the stairs. They were not attached right, they were shaky, the two of you on it at the same time."

"Yes. All that is true," Zech replied.

Why were they talking about Micah's death?

J lost all thought of moving his feet and walking into the room. His mind raced as his body locked up like a statue.

Matthew responded to Zech.

"So what are you saying?"

"Micah did not just trip or lose his balance. He got in my face, and in that small space, with the door behind me. I had nowhere to go... I struck back.

"I pushed him...

"I pushed with every ounce of strength I had. I was reacting... but... I gave it everything. All the frustration over the budget, our arguments, all of it went into that push."

J could not believe what he was hearing.

His fists clenched. White-knuckled, he stood, his hands trembling.

"He may have died of a blot clot in the hospital. But I killed him."

J's jaw dropped, his fists loosened, and his eyes watered.

He knew the story of his dad's death. He always thought the fall on the stairs was nearly his dad's saving grace. The fall put Micah in the hospital, and where else could his father have been to give him a chance against the fatal clot flowing through his veins? J would not understand God's reason to take his father, but he saw it as inevitable.

But now, J's view was challenged and he saw the situation differently.

Zech was not there to call the ambulance, as if placed by God. J had always thought that Zech was in the right place at the right time to get Micah to the hospital.

But now... No.

Zech caused the fall.

And the fall may have been just what the clot needed to dislodge!

J caught himself going down into dark thoughts. He pulled back to his prior alertness and continued to listen as Matthew sought to justify Zech's actions, to make it remain an unfortunate accident.

J took a deep breath. His mind had forgotten all about Terrence and the reasoning he would lay out for Zech and Matthew. That was long gone.

He heard Zech sniff, pulling up his tears. J's eyes had been watering and now a small stream of an escaping tear ran down his cheek as he overheard his mentor. The tear curved to follow his jaw and waited under his chin.

Zech began again. "But that doesn't mean it doesn't still hurt. How I was the catalyst to ending my best friend's life. How I widowed Ruth. How I left Jeremiah without a father."

How I widowed Ruth.

How I left Jeremiah without a father.

The two lines echoed in J's head.

They grew louder.

How I widowed Ruth.

How I left Jeremiah without a father.

They were deafening.

All the thoughts of walking into the room faded from J's mind.

He could feel his feet again and his face wore a stern resolve.

He turned swiftly, pulled open the door, and walked quickly out.

The door slammed behind him.

***

Matthew and Zech jogged out to catch J, but all they saw were his taillights leaving the parking lot. Matthew called J's phone.

After numerous rings, the generic voicemail message picked up.

Maybe he had it on vibrate or "do not disturb" came automatically while driving?

He called again.

Ring. Then voicemail.

Matthew waited a moment and tried one more time.

Straight to voicemail.

J had turned his phone off.

Zech patted Matthew on the back.

"I'm not sure how much he heard of that, but let's find him."

"Agreed."

They each walked to their cars and yelled out a few ideas of where each could start.

As they turned to swing into their respective cars, they saw the other car in the parking lot. Zech did not think much of it as his mind focused on J.

Then he saw two men just off his sightline around the building, near the car, and recognized them immediately.

It was his dad, Isaiah, and his friend Jimmy. They often came to walk the property together. Being a part of building the property, Isaiah's "Temple Team," these two took special pride in walking the land they helped to form.

It had been Jimmy's car all along, and the two elder sages of the church waved to Zech and Matthew as the younger two backed out and left the parking lot.

***

The search was fruitless. Matthew and Zech drove around for hours, mainly doing larger loops from J's house to the church, trying to take different routes, and driving slowly by favorite restaurants to look for J's car. They both left a voicemail and decided to head home.

Liz had put the girls to bed by the time Matthew was home. He told her about it, still frustrated he could not find his friend.

"I'm missing something. I should know where he is."

"Maybe he just needs time. Think if you were him."

"I know, but... it's just... I should find him."

"It was your dad involved with Micah. Maybe he should be the one to talk to him?"

"You are probably right. They see each other at church way more than I see either of them anyway."

They had a glass of wine and talked as they picked at leftovers from the girls' playdate lunch. They stopped by a nearby Mexican restaurant for cheese quesadillas, the girls' favorite. Now Matthew and Liz ate the last few slices, dipping them straight into the large plastic sour cream container from the fridge.

Matthew thought the wine would calm him down and put him to bed. He was not much of a drinker, and two to three drinks was his limit. Any more and he typically had a nagging headache the next morning.

Matthew stared into the deep purple drink in his glass. Thinking of J and now gazing into the wine brought Matthew back to his early twenties, when Matthew and J were more accustomed to having a few drinks. The church, and J included, had an unwritten rule that no staff member would drink in public to respect those with alcohol problems. But before J was full-time, he'd meet Matthew at a local sports bar to watch sports and split a couple pitchers. There was a place not far away that had the best chicken wings.

As Matthew started feeling hungry, realizing he skipped dinner, he tried to remember the name of that place. He wondered if it was still there.

Then his mind snapped back. A place he did not think to check. The sports bar.

He stood up quickly and reached for his nearby keys. Before he could tell Liz, she walked around the corner from the bathroom, toothbrush in one hand, her phone in the other.

"Hey, did you hear from my dad?"

"No..."

His hand went to his pocket. It was empty. Where was his phone?

He'd set it in the kitchen drawer when talking to Liz earlier, an old habit he had to avoid checking it while around the girls.

He felt so stupid. What if J had called?

As Matthew stepped quickly toward his phone, Liz spoke up.

"He said he was watching football over at Mulberry. And he said J was there, acting a little weird. You going?"

He was right. Mulberry! That was it.

"Yup. I love you, babe."

He kissed her quickly and snatched up his phone. She called out "I love you too. Be careful," as he opened the garage door and quickly backed out.

He had a text and voicemail from Paul Stollard, Liz's father.

Football playoffs were on that Sunday, the conference championships, and Paul met friends for wings and to watch some of the games.

"Hey, Matt, this is Paul," the voicemail began.

Matthew always thought, Why does he leave his name? We have known each other's voices for years.

"J is up here, and he seems a little off. Nothing too crazy, he's mostly keeping to himself, but he's not talking to anyone. You know J, he can be the center of attention at a moment's notice. Oh, and he's drinking in public. Isn't that a rule he has now? I know your dad has that one. Well, actually..."

Matthew wished he could fast forward the message. Why couldn't his father-in-law get to the point?

"Well actually, I'm not sure he is drinking. He has a full pitcher sitting in front of him, but he hasn't touched it. Anyway, you probably already know, but I was with your grandpa and Jimmy. They called and wanted to meet here today instead of that new place we had been going to this season. Isaiah talked with J a bit, but Isaiah did not say what about. I said hi, and J was friendly, but obviously not himself. Well. I love you. God bless."

***

Matthew entered the sports bar and found J in a back corner of the bar section, sitting at a booth by himself.

As he walked up, the bartender hollered his way. She was keeping her eye on J, and Matthew could not tell if she was angry with him for not ordering or if she was sympathetic to him somehow. The place was busy that day with football going on, but most of the crowds had filtered out, leaving the place just under half full.

"Whatcha drinkin', hun?"

He almost ordered the same wine that Liz had poured him but stopped himself.

"Soda water, please, club soda?"

"Yup," she said softly as she quickly looked away, clearly not interested in the non-alcoholic choice of someone in her bar area. She was a younger woman, early twenties and attractive with long dark hair. It was pulled back in a ponytail through a ball cap of a team playing that day. Two things Matthew had noticed was the bright shine of her nose ring and the blue design of a tattoo creeping from her shoulder and reaching up her neck.

Matthew sat down and J looked up. It appeared to be the first time he looked up in a long time. A pitcher of beer, a full basket of fries, and a cup of water sat in front of him. They all looked to be there a long time, and none of them appeared to have been touched.

The top foam of the beer was long gone as thin trickles of bubbles still persisted. Full beads of sweat were built up on the pitcher and on the generic hard plastic water cup. The fries, which had come out steaming hot from the fryer, were now cold with hardened cheese topping them.

"That's a big glass for one guy," Matthew said, nodding to the pitcher. "You with someone else?"

"You know? I'm not quite sure anymore," J said passively.

"What does that mean?"

"I heard you today. Your dad, talking about my dad…"

Matthew snapped back quicker than he meant to, "Did you also hear him crying at the loss of his friend? The impact of the loss?"

"Yeah. Must be tough to hear your dad cry. I don't have that problem," J spoke in a bitter tone. "Never had to hear him, for my childhood or entire adult life. That must be tough for *you*."

As J spoke, he began to lean forward in his seat, pointing at Matthew's chest, dropping his eyebrows and face growing red.

Matthew was taken aback by his friend's aggressive tone and sarcasm.

"Come on, J. This isn't you."

J sat silently, thinking of the conversation he'd had earlier with Isaiah, trying to limit his frustration and focus on the positive. Thinking of the love he had experienced regardless of the hurt he endured as a child. His mother, Ruth. His relationship with Ashley before she moved to New England. He wondered if she was still in that area. Isaiah reminded him of what could still be. But now, the discouragement came back in as Matthew responded to J's sarcasm and distance.

Matthew continued, "You can't change the last thirty years. And Zech was as much your father as he was mine."

J sat there, pulling himself back into the present moment from the abyss of remorse and regret that filled him before he spoke with Isaiah. He wanted to be alone, and he would not admit it now, but he was thankful Matthew was there.

J exhaled a deep breath that took part of his anger with it.

"It's... It's just hard to take...I know Zech loves me and loved my dad, but this feels like... like I have been lied to somehow. Like I have been betrayed."

The mood lightened yet became solemn.

"Yeah. I can understand that."

"Look. I'll be all right. Thanks for coming. How did you even know I was here? Isaiah call you?"

"No, Paul."

"Paul! Ha. The only man who could somehow be confused for a native New Yorker and a redneck in the same conversation."

They both laughed and then silence fell. The drinks and food still sat, growing closer to room temperature every second.

***

Eventually, J spoke up and nodded to the TVs elevated above the bar area.

"So, math man, you have the right side in today's games?"

"Nope. Good thing I didn't bet it. They won't have to take my thumbs this time."

Matthew had created numerous models for football predictions years ago. He even tried his hand at becoming a full-time sports gambler, having two successful low stake years before suffering large losses the year he went high stakes. He had saved up and worked on his bankroll. He and Liz could absorb the financial impact of failure, but it hurt his pride, confidence, and motivation for gambling. He now looked at it as closer to the lottery and day trading rather than long-term investing, but at the time he thought he could beat the market.

He came out of his funk over the following offseason, motivated more than ever to improve his math models, and even convinced himself he should ramp up his stakes, going higher than the prior failed year. Only this time, his bankroll couldn't support it. He would have had to dip heavily into their savings.

Matthew had all the statistics to back up his model, and swore last year's losses were only poor variance. He was simply unlucky that particular season. If he had gone bigger the prior two years, when he profited at lower stakes, he would have already been considering quitting his full-time job to become a professional sports better. If he could do it in football, one of the hardest sports to crack, then he could do it in other sports. The earning power was unlimited! Or so he let himself think.

It wasn't until he let his plan slip to his brother, Mark. As Mark was preparing to leave for another missionary trip, he and Matthew went for a long run together.

Matthew had mentioned his plan, and Mark saw the greed overtake his younger brother.

It was the same look Mark had seen in all those young one-in-a-million entrepreneurs, so successful so early, and unable to handle the pitfalls. Mark had seen the life it led them down, and it was a big reason he left finance and followed the missionary path. Wealth, in Mark's opinion, was a slow build. "401ks make more millionaires than the lotto ever will," he liked to say.

Mark had calmly asked Matthew leading questions, encouraging his brother to consider the risk.

"So what do you think your odds of succeeding this year are?

"What happens if you lose?

"What would Liz do if she knew you put your family's emergency fund on the line?

"And what are the odds she leaves you if you can't stop yourself?"

The final two questions turned the tide and hit Matthew like a ton of bricks. He pulled back from that moment on and began using a cost of capital model on all his financial decisions. If the market returned between six and eight percent annually, then sports betting fell too far outside the bounds. Too much variance, too much risk for the given reward.

A couple years later, enough time had passed, and all the brothers, including J, now joked about the "math man" openly.

Bringing up the old "math man" jokes and talking football steadied the conversation.

As the conversation wore down, and they realized the warm beer and cold fries were still staring at them, an off comment by J got Matthew thinking.

"Well, we're not touching these. Maybe we can bet them against some cold chicken fingers. You see any suckers out there, or any bookies taking old fries as a deposit?"

Bookies... *Book.*

As Matthew heard "bookies," his mind went to "book" and instantly to Zech's Bible. The interrupted question he never asked his father, what was that glow? That light?

It must have been a trick of the lights, or the water in Matthew's eyes after hugging his dad tightly. But it seemed to be more than a light. Like he could feel the light.

He spoke up to J, who spent more time with Zech than anyone. He might have seen it too, known what it was.

"Hey, have you ever noticed Dad's Bi—"

He was cut off by the bartender. The nose ring caught the light as she turned to face J, showing the blue tattoo to Matthew. It was some sort of creature's claw, likely a dragon, drawn to be grasping for her throat.

"Sooooooo you've been here for like hours. All I can imagine is you are waiting for me."

J smiled as he sat back in the seat and glanced at Matthew. The smile was half in surprise and half due to embarrassment. The young woman continued, not missing a beat.

"I'm off an hour. Meet me by my car out back?"

She waited for a response and Matthew nearly laughed out loud in astonishment. All those years they were teenage boys and dreamed of women. Now, seeing this display and having two young girls at home, Matthew felt more pity for the girl than excitement.

But J was single.

No kids.

He almost drank a full pitcher by himself a few short hours ago. Would he go along with this?

Matthew remained silent, watching his friend. He thought no way his *PASTOR* friend would even consider this.

But why hadn't he not already said no? Or preached to her?

J reached down and pulled out his wallet.

The bartender had the tip of her tongue out, held tightly in her teeth as she waited and eyed J with her eyebrows raised.

"Tell you what," J began as he opened his wallet.

"Close our check? And then how about my place?"

The girl shifted her balance to take the two cards from J's hands.

Matthew could see one of them was his debit card; the other he was not sure. Was it his number?

J then spoke up in a more direct tone, which Matthew recognized from his sermons. He saw the second card was a business card, with the church's address.

"We have service at 9 am and 10:30 every Sunday morning. Plus, a great young singles group. Ma'am, there is a lot more joy to this life, in a life for Jesus. You don't need to focus on the physical to be fulfilled."

The young woman rolled her eyes and walked away.

Matthew laughed.

J put his hands up and exclaimed, "Hey, she took both cards!"

Chapter Twelve

Power of the Ark

P astor J's sermon the following week was titled "God Making a Way." It was a stand-alone message that J or Zech had delivered in late January in each of the past few years. Right around the time people were losing their New Year's resolutions, they wanted to encourage the church members to stick with it or to pivot accordingly.

J was at the top of his preaching game on this particular Sunday, delivering a witty and thoughtful message that kept the crowd captivated.

He came out directly addressing the crowd.

"Stand up if you made a New Year's resolution."

Nearly half of the large crowd stood.

"Now sit if you've already broken it. And be honest!"

Only about ten percent of the crowd remained standing. J gave them a round of applause and the whole church followed.

Matthew usually did not stand for this type of active participation during service, but he stood with pride this time. He had become more engaged in the recent messages and had kept his morning routine. He had not considered it to be a New Year's resolution, but why not? He started it the week of New Year's Day and kept it every day since.

Matthew smiled as he stood, holding back a laugh as J smirked and nodded his way after seeing he was in the remaining standers.

J continued into his message.

"For those who now feel guilty about giving up so soon, feel free to lean over to that other guy or gal who sat down as well. Ask them 'Why are you a quitter!?'"

The church gave a soft laugh, recognizing the joke.

"But seriously, first, recognize you are human. And it is hard to change yourself. There is a multi-billion-dollar self-help industry that prints money as people constantly strive to improve themselves."

J's tone dropped as he slowed his pace, speaking loud for all to hear him clearly.

"How often do we think we can do it?

"How often do we think, if only I work harder, I can do it?

"Or after failing, saying that wasn't for me, I need something else?

"If only I can find the right thing, then I'll have it made. I'll make my way."

The church was quiet as Pastor J paused.

"How often do we ask God for his help with our goals? Better yet," J quickened his pace and increased his volume, "better yet, how often do we give him credit for accomplishing our goals?"

J looked around the room. He saw Zech in his typical front row seat. Matthew and Liz were near the back on an aisle, just back from dropping the girls off at kids' church. Then he caught a glimpse of Terrence in the far back opposite corner of Matthew.

"And not only giving God credit for our successes. Thanking him for the path he laid to put us in that position. Well before the success, God was there. Well before that new job, or landing the big contract, or your girlfriend saying 'YES, I will marry you.'"

He gave a poor impression of a female voice and received further laughter from the women in the crowd.

"Before all that, there was the job you hated, the contract lost, the ex that didn't work out. The things that hurt. That *hurt bad*, but those things taught us, and prepared us. The things we learned from that laid a path. A path for the better things to come.

"I want to make sure you remember this today, the things that *hurt*. And if you had already given yourself to Jesus at that point, you probably prayed for God to take it away. To not let it happen. To save you from the hurt, the pain, the agony.

"But, if those troubles prepare us, if they make the *good* things better, then we need the hurt. We need those troubles to prepare us.

"So how often do we give God credit for our troubles? For preparing us.

"How often do we thank him for the thorn in our side, as Paul did? Paul prayed for the Lord to remove his thorn, multiple times! But eventually, he thanked God for it."

J went on to discuss the varying levels of success and variations of hurt. From a young child learning to walk, to a CEO accomplishing a major business deal. A skinned knee after falling off a bike, to cancer taking a lifelong love, or a parent, or a child.

"I don't pretend to know God's plan, or make light of a loved one's death. But I have learned that if you keep trying, if you keep moving forward, and MOST IMPORTANTLY... keep praying. Work, pray, work, pray. God will make a way."

He closed his message, emphasizing the work-pray-work relationship we can have with God.

"Moses had to put his staff in the Red Sea before God parted it. God could have parted it at any time. His staff, a piece of wood, surely did not part that sea. But a piece of wood showed the faith, the commitment, to let God make a way for him as Moses demonstrated his faith.

"The priests who carried the Ark across the river had to bring their feet to the edge, to touch the water, before God stopped the flow of water. Again, it wasn't dusty sandals and dirty feet that stopped the river. Those feet showed they could step out for God. Those feet demonstrated faith.

"And finally, Paul's thorn. We can only guess what that thorn actually was based on historical studies of

Paul, but it honestly doesn't matter, because we all have thorns. And I think it was left out of the Bible for a reason. We all have thorns. Some are big, some are smaller, but we all have something we have tried to pray away. Something we absolutely hated. *HATED*. And begged God to remove it.

"I suggest it is time we pray on our thorns. We work to get past them. And most importantly, WE THANK GOD FOR THEM. Because without those thorns, we might not have the path to success that God has planned for us."

***

Matthew caught J in the rotunda after service as he and Liz brought the girls out of kids' church.

"Great message, Pastor!" Matthew said as he patted his friend's shoulder.

"Thanks. Are we still on for lunch next week after service?"

Matthew glanced at Liz before answering.

"Excuse me, I should have asked the decision-maker of the house," J interjected and motioned toward Liz.

"Yes. Excuse you. My partner handles my social arrangements. I'm much too busy to schedule my own luncheons with various local pastors, thank you kindly," Matthew joked.

Liz rolled her eyes at both of them before responding.

"Babe, we have 'Hats' next week, and our Life Group is going shopping and to dinner beforehand. I'll be leaving straight from church to meet up with your mom and Millie. You'll need to take the girls."

"All day for dinner and a women's night," Matthew said.

"You can take the girls on your lunch, you'll be fine. Better yet, J why don't you come to our place? He can make you lunch."

"So he'll order us a pizza? Sounds good."

Matthew smiled, knowing pizza was precisely what he would do to supply lunch.

J said goodbye to the Lights as he headed for his customary after-service coffee and a small table on the edge of the rotunda. Terrence was in a booth, waiting for J, and popped out a moment after J sat.

"So what is your thorn?" Terrence said as he sat down next to J.

J nearly blurted out "you" in jest but stopped himself. He wanted to help Terrence, help guide him into the church and give himself to Jesus, or at least learn more about Micah and the New Christians. He couldn't be rude. The older man rubbed him the wrong way, but J had to admit Terrence was growing on him.

Something about the man gave a sense of action, of doing. A default aggressive attitude that J recognized in successful ministries and missionaries. Zech was geared toward action too, but was often too conservative for J's liking. Terrence's attitude reminded J of his old sports teams as a kid, the "1-2-3 Team!" style chants that all opponents' teams had a version of before hitting the ice or field. He could imagine Terrence doing the cheer and then running into battle. A King Leonidas giving the rallying cry to the three hundred before battle.

"Glad you made it in person. So was I right? Way better in person than online."

"You certainly had a command of the room. Your dad would have been proud."

"Thanks. So what stayed with you, what did you take away from the sermon?"

Terrence thought a moment and J realized this was one of the first times he ignored a question from Terrence and then asked his own. He had rarely been leading the conversation.

The two were far from friends but were growing more comfortable with each other. Somehow it did not seem like a friendship but more of a business relationship. J felt like he was constantly being interviewed.

"You were too passive. That will stick with me."

"How so?"

"Why do you talk so sympathetically about God giving us thorns as a blessing. If you want to help people get to God, and you are using their troubles, Paul's 'thorn,' as you put it, as a way to show God's love, then how come you are NOT helping people find that thorn?"

J thought about the question for a moment.

Zech approached before J could respond.

"Speaking of thorns," Terrence said, looking up to Zech.

"Hello, Terrence. J, you mind a word in private?"

Zech and J stepped out of earshot. Zech warned him about staying too close to Terrence.

"I know you want to help him and learn about his group, but don't let him fool you. He is not an honest man. He will lie and he will show his rage."

"If I don't take on challenges like this, how will I become a better leader for the church? And yes, of course, I'll be careful."

Zech looked at the younger man for a moment. He decided not to keep pressing on Terrence and changed the subject.

"You mind if I invite Matthew to our meeting tonight? There is something I want both of you to know, to see. You should find out together."

"Of course not. Everything okay?"

"Yup. See you tonight. Oh, and come early if you can. Let's talk about your father as well."

J was silent as Zech hugged him and left.

***

Matthew arrived at the church at 5:30 pm and saw that Zech and J were already there. Jimmy's car was also there, which made Matthew smile. Jimmy and Matthew's grandfather, Isaiah, must be walking around the lake again. Matthew made a note to look for them after this meeting. He wanted to ask Isaiah if he could join them sometime. The North Florida winter was a great temperature, fitting for a light jacket and a long walk.

As Matthew walked into the hallway offices, he over-heard Zech and J talking. He thought of stopping to hear more before entering but decided it was best to show himself. He could always say hi then wait outside. When he turned the corner into the room, he saw Zech and J hugging. Both of them were red-eyed and sniffing, like they had just been crying.

"Hey. Sorry to interrupt. I can wait outside," Matthew said after being spotted.

"No, no. Come on in. We were just remembering a great man," Zech said, patting J on the back.

"Yeah, come on in," J said after clearing his throat.

Matthew walked up and hugged J, knowing the emo-tion he must be feeling after talking about his father's death. Zech was a great man, not only Micah's best friend and the father figure in J's life, but now a side of him contrasted what J and Matthew always knew. Zech was now also the primary person involved in Micah's death, seriously injuring Micah and maybe even causing his death.

Matthew was surprised J had not reacted harsher, but seeing the full pitcher in the sports bar last week told him that J was close to the edge. He still respected and loved Zech, and by the looks of it, the prior conversation demonstrated the mutual affection.

"Well, Matthew you are a bit early, thank you. Let's get started. There is something I want to show you boys. Isaiah showed Micah and me not long before Micah passed, and I have thought about telling each one of you boys since the day you were born.

"Luke and Mark do not know about this, but one day, they may. For now, I have decided to follow tradition and only let two people know. One main caretaker and a backup in case anything happens to that caretaker. Micah and I were the two after Isaiah. After Micah passed, your mother, Mary, was my backup. Since Isaiah was still alive and all you boys were growing up, Isaiah and I decided to wait until you were ready and able.

"That time is now."

J and Matthew looked at each other with a curious expression.

"You have a trust fund or something you want to give us, Dad?" Matthew said jokingly.

"No, no. It is not money. Although, I want to warn you, money will be one of the first things that come to mind once it sets in. We have worked hard over the years to create a strong cash reserve for the church and belong to a financially sound global network of churches. That is not only for emergency funds, but has a dual purpose, so that the caretaker and backup do NOT need to consider using this for money.

"Isaiah showed me at the Storage Yard, where we have part of it under lock and key, but I want to show you right here, with the part I carry with me at nearly all times."

Zech pulled out his worn green Bible. Matthew was reminded of the light he saw coming out the spine.

J spoke up, "Zech... we know the Bible is important. Is all this secrecy your way of getting us to think of it as treasure? We do think that... Just not literally."

"No, I don't mean that, but wait a minute, you should treat every Bible in print like it's a treasure!" Zech stood up holding the Bible in both hands like a small treasure box, teasing J and Matthew. He then returned to his low serious tone.

"But no, I am not trying to be cute about an upcoming message. Tell me what you feel when I do this, and if it hurts too bad, then back away quickly."

Zech held up the Bible, holding the spine in his hand and touching J's and then Matthew's chest. He held it for a few seconds each with the open edge of the Bible pressed against their chest.

"Feels fine. I mean, I feel good, but I also cried with you about my dad for the last half hour," J responded.

Zech smiled in agreement.

"Feels fine here too, I guess... I do have goosebumps and a warm feeling. But it's not like I was struck by lightning," Matthew replied.

Zech nodded, once again in agreement.

"Okay, what about now, and I'll go slow. Do your best not to step away, but you may if you need to. You'll feel it, quickly and painfully, if you need to step back."

Zech turned the Bible around, now with the spine pointed out.

He motioned toward J first.

J closed his eyes as Zech softly pressed the old Bible against his chest. J felt a warm, welcoming sensation that embraced him. He did not want to lose it. But at nearly the same time, he felt a piece of himself pull back, hurting, like a sliver or needle being pushed out of closed skin. But this wasn't just one sliver; it was somehow throughout his entire body. The painful feeling was mixing back and forth with the warm, loving sensation. J could not describe it, but part of him wanted to hug and hold that Bible forever while the other part of him wanted to run like the wind away from it.

J was speechless as Zech pulled it back and he opened his eyes. It had only been five seconds, but to J, it felt like hours. Matthew noticed J's eyes twitch and slight spasms go across his body.

Zech turned and motioned to Matthew. Matthew looked at J, confused by the slow shake of J's body and facial expressions. He did not know what to make of it.

As the Bible approached, Matthew felt the pain first and flinched back, but he forced himself to stay close, obeying Zech's instructions to hold close if possible.

The pain was intense, but as the full spine of the old book pressed against his chest, Matthew started feeling the loving, welcoming warmth. The pain remained but was overtaken and minimized. It was like dipping a toe into a hot spa, flinching at first but then embracing it, loving it, craving it as you begin to submerge yourself.

Matthew was also speechless as Zech backed away and leaned against his desk. No one said anything as the two men looked at their elder, mouths open but unable to comprehend.

"There is something that our family has protected for centuries."

Zech motioned his finger into the tiny space in between the outer spine and the page bindings. His finger moved in the space and there was a click, and a soft, warm glow started to poke through the shadows of his hand. Zech carefully pulled his hand back slowly and softly, like he was holding a hot bowl fresh out of the microwave. Matthew noticed a slight flinch in Zech's expression. He knew that his father was not immune to feeling the pain he and J had just experienced.

"This is a piece of the original Ark of the Covenant."

***

All three men stared at the artifact silently. Matthew felt the urge to get down on one knee, bowing to the piece, but he could not take his eyes off the soft glow. He remained motionless.

The piece was the width of two fingers and a few inches long with curved ends running from one edge down the long side, like feathers, and a smooth break on the other edge.

J and Matthew squinted and looked closer, but their silence was shattered.

The door slammed in the hallway outside the office.

Only someone not familiar with the office doors would let them slam. Instinctively, Matthew and J stepped in front of Zech, as Zech skillfully replaced the unique piece back into the tiny compartment within his Bible. He snapped the lock closed.

They looked to find Terrence walking into the office. He had heard more than they would have liked, and his broad smile showed it. Terrence was followed in by a younger man. He was slightly shorter than Terrence but far more muscular. His arms nearly popped out through the short sleeve t-shirt. He wore a short yet full cleancut beard in the same style as Terrence's. He carried marks and scars on his face, implying a long-time boxer or mixed martial arts fighter.

Matthew was closest to the door, and he remained silent, unsure of what they had overheard, but Terrence tipped his hand with confidence.

"Well, I came to talk to you about your church, and how we can improve your watered-down message. And to introduce you to my friend and fellow follower here, Ignace." He motioned towards the young man. "But I can see you have more pressing matters to attend to."

Zech placed the Bible on the desk behind him and stepped forward through J and Matthew.

"Yes. Let's talk about our *message* as a church and let's talk about the *path* you are following." Zech emphasized message and path, dividing what his church was doing with what Terrence was attempting.

Terrence was not pleased with the statement and his facial expression changed from smiling like a winning politician, which was the only way J and Matthew had seen him, into a straight-face stare directly at Zech.

Terrence began, "I always held out hope for you, Zechariah. All those years ago, I enjoyed my time in this church, or at least what it once was. Micah knew he had to reach people, but even he was foolish, going along with your love message."

J stepped forward, but Zech side-stepped to stay in front.

Terrence continued, "You are patting a child on the back instead of putting them back on the bike. You understand there might be a few skinned knees in the process? *Don't you*?!"

His eyes flashed anger as he nearly yelled "don't you" and Zech was reminded of the young boy. The boy who was lost and gave in to the anger that only pushed him away further.

"It's not my message, Terrence. It is from Jesus Christ. Love your neighbor as you love yourself."

"While you hug and cuddle, I will help our savior. We will show this city, this state, this nation, the error of their ways. I thought your church would help to push that message, but why wait months or years influencing you and your church members, when you have such a precious piece of history that will speed it all up?"

Terrence raised his hands, palms up, in a "can you blame me" manner as he looked around the room. He had not realized the Bible's hiding place and was now scanning the room.

"So, where is it?"

"I would not focus on the physical aspects if I were you," Zech replied. "I can help you focus on the inner you. That is the only place you'll find it. The only place it will truly take hold and grow."

"You don't understand how the world is changing. You don't understand that God gives us gifts. He puts us in charge to help people. And why would he do that? Why? If not for us to help them reach God. To help them realize their errors."

"Terrence, we agree in many ways, but the ends don't justify the means."

"Oh please, continue to water it down, continue to forget about what will happen during the second coming. You'll be left here with the rest of them and then you can tell God that *HIS* ends don't justify the means."

Zech looked patiently at Terrence, who was still glancing around the room for a clue to where the Ark was located. He had come in confident, assuming he'd find what he was looking for with a single look.

"Terrence," Zech said patiently.

"What?!"

"You cannot pour out the bowls of Revelation. You are not God."

Terrence's eyes stopped jumping around the room and fell plainly on Zech. His facial expression was of pity as he looked at his elder as a parent may look at a child, then in an instant, his eyes showed rage. He stepped up to Zech and reached for his shirt, but as he came forward, J and Matthew were synchronous in their defense and beat Terrence to Zech, blocking his way.

Terrence stopped his advance and dropped his hand. He turned back to his young follower.

"Search around the desk, where Zech was as we came in."

"No. It is time for you to leave," Matthew said strongly, looking straight into Terrence's eyes.

"Oh, the young one speaks. Welcome to the conversation. Speak to me that way again and I'll break your arm. Then you can tell your daughters how you broke it. It will teach them a valuable lesson."

J responded quickly, "Terrence, this is not for you. It is time for you to go."

Ignace now stepped forward, looking inches taller than he was, with his hands clenched into fists. His presence gave Terrence confidence.

"No, I think we will only leave on our terms, when we have what we want."

Matthew and J stepped up to the seasoned fighter. Both were far from trained fighters, and in a one-on-one, they did not stand a chance against Ignace, but they now had each other. They could at least neutralize him in defense of their father and the artifact they just learned of.

Ignace appeared to welcome the disadvantage, and took a quick step forward as J and Matthew turned their eyes to him.

"Stop," Zech said, holding his arms out and glancing at J and Matthew. "If they want to search, let them search."

J and Matthew reluctantly agreed and stepped back.

"Yes, always avoiding the conflict, just like your message. We shall search. Thank you."

Zech edged in front of his two sons and motioned them to the side.

Ignace stared into Matthew's eyes as he walked past, and Matthew returned the strong gaze.

Terrence came opposite Zech and watched Ignace as the younger of the two men began to search the desk area. He looked around and under the desk before opening any drawers. He began scattering papers and books from drawers as his eye caught the Bible on the far corner of the desk. It was opposite the side he walked around, and now he motioned over to it.

J spoke up, "Leave the Bible," but that only increased Ignace's speed to come around the desk and reach for it.

They would never forget what followed.

Ignace quickly reached for the old green book. His arm darted forward like a quick jab from a seasoned fighter.

But as his hand approached, it was as if an invisible force field was around the book. Ignace's left hand was like dough being smashed. With equal quickness to his jab, the Bible seemed to push back. His hand coiled back, bending and snapping bones, the skin shifting alongside muscles as water runs down a mountain.

Ignace let out a deep and painful scream as his hand was deformed into a mangled ball up to his wrist. As he pulled it back, he held what was left of his misshapen hand, watery-eyed and in awe. He gasped for words, but only silence left his mouth.

He stepped back and away from the desk, toward Terrence. Terrence stood in disbelief and only when Ignace reached him did Terrence help guide him out of the room. As they quickly retreated from the room, Matthew caught Ignace's expression. He saw in the fleeing man's eyes a pain-filled emotion. Horror and awe.

Chapter Thirteen

Life or Death

"What is more contagious, life or death?"

Zech looked out over his congregation, pausing to give them a moment to think. Many remained silent, pondering the question.

"We can think of life as purity, as holiness, such as the presence of God. And we can think of death as sin, something that harms your soul. Think of the Old Testament, how there were things you had to be cleansed of, such as certain animal carcasses, diseases, or certain bodily fluids. These things that represent death, that you must be cleansed of.

"Life or death... What is more contagious?

"Two things we are going to talk about today. First, we will talk about the dark and the light, the sin and the good, within each of us. Second, we will discuss individual accountability.

"Now I want to ask another question: why do you think God told the Israelites that a King was not a great idea?"

Various people in the crowd spoke up as Zech nodded and pointed at some of the responders.

"Yes, yup, because he wanted the people to worship him, not a person... To keep focus on how *He* was in charge, okay, okay.

"Now I understand that we need structures and government to help society function, but God certainly knew that putting such power and control in one person was a problem waiting to happen. He has seen what people have done, and are capable of doing. Take a peek at the book of Judges if you don't believe me.

"All the leaders in the Bible have some sort of checkered past or fall from grace. Moses kills an Egyptian, David commits adultery, and fast forward to the New Testament. Saul of Tarsus is snatching up men and women, throwing them in jail or stoning them if they worship Jesus. He literally watches Christ-followers get executed and then BOOM! Jesus comes in, knocks Saul off his horse, and then he's Paul the Apostle building churches all over the region.

"What I'm saying is that Man is fallible. God can still use us, and he usually picks someone you'd least expect, and thank God for that. But putting a single person in charge?

"Man is fallible, that is the point, and we can all agree on that, amen?"

Zech raised his hand encouraging the audience to participate, getting a soft amen back from the majority of the congregation.

"Once Saul became Paul, he certainly was not following a worldly king or the Pharisees anymore. And we know he ticked off plenty of local authorities by how many times he was thrown in jail. I'm certainly NOT saying disregard all government and be an anarchist; we have laws and structures in the world to help society. And we must honor who is in charge. But if you put those humans above the true King of Kings, Jesus Christ, then you put your spiritual life at the mercy of those people and their man-made laws."

Zech paused and looked at his Bible. The same worn green backing that held the spiritual secret his family protected.

Then he continued.

"God put his temple here on earth. He gave specific dimensions for the Israelites to build it. He gave specific commands to the people many times in the Bible. Not only the Ten Commandments, but also all the laws of cleanliness in order for someone to enter the holiest parts of the temple. Laws and instructions directly handed down from God. Oh Lord knows we have a hard enough time following just ten things, let alone anything more.

"But God pivots his style as we go into the New Testament. And you know what... I think he was setting us up. Preparing to show us something. To show us that we are so flawed that the only way for us to truly be with God is to let him lead. For us to let him inside us, to embrace him, and to let him guide us.

"He took a major part of our relationship with God, all those ritual cleansings and the human representatives of God's church. He took them out of our hands and put them into his son's hands. He improved the process so he could be closer to us. So his light could shine away the darkness.

"If you have ever followed the Bible Project—that's an app we use here to read the entire Bible in a year—you may have seen a wonderful video on holiness. If you have not heard of it, check it out, bibleproject.com, great stuff. In that video on holiness, one view they show is a person, filled with dark black to represent our sin. It shows how we must be cleansed through ritual to be filled with light, to be cleansed. We get filled with the blackness, the sin, the death, by external happenings, such as a dead animal, by our own sinful habits, et cetera. The darkness spreads into you, like it is a contagion, and we periodically must cleanse ourselves before it takes over. This darkness, this representation of death within us, keeps us from getting close to God. You would die in his presence if you were not cleansed; he's too holy and we have too much sin in us. Think of it this way, if we had a backroom temple in our church here, where God made home to his presence on Earth, just like the Holy of Holies, it would be so holy that it would blast you away as you approached. If you were not ritually cleansed, don't even think about approaching it. God's light illuminates the darkness, and if that darkness is us... well, we might be blasted away too."

Matthew and J were in sight of each other, listening to Zech's message. They caught each other's eye as they both mentally recounted the piece of the Ark Zech showed them. How they experienced its push on the sin within them. They remembered what it did to Ignace's hand. But they also felt the urge to embrace it, to be within its welcoming warmth and love.

That welcoming feeling, it must be the parts of them with less sin, parts where God had a spiritual foothold within their bodies.

"Now continuing with the video, there is a part I absolutely love. As they transition from showing death, that sin, that blackness that infects and spreads within us to the point where we need to be cleansed to get closer to God, they then use a prophecy of Isaiah. In the prophecy from the book of Isaiah, Isaiah is dreaming, and in his dream, a weird six-winged creature, sent by God, flies up to him and presses a burning, white-hot piece of coal to his lips. It is searing hot and all white.

"I know what some of you are thinking, 'That sounds wonderful, Zech, his mouth is burned shut. You want us to keep quiet and have more "The Fear of God" type stuff.' Great." Zech said sarcastically.

A soft laugh went through the captive audience. Then Zech continued, "No, that's not it. Stay with me, Church. Think of the white-hot coal emanating light that is striking the black death inside of us. The death that always spreads through us is now being pushed away. Now the light of the coal is a more powerful force in us. Previously, death spread within us like a virus, but now, the light wipes it out like the antivirus. The death has no chance, retreating and running away, leaving us filled with the light. Filled with life."

Zech motioned his hands, pushing and pulling, showing the internal back and forth as he spoke.

"Now if you had to go perform rituals to be cleansed, would you ever miss an appointment? That's a nice way to phrase the question, isn't it? It's easy for you to think, 'NO WAY! I'd be there, get that death away.' Well, let me phrase it this way...

"How often have you missed reading your Bible?

"How often have you skipped going to church?

"The dozens of simple habits that bring Jesus into your life every day. We don't even need to bring our best-looking goats and rams into town! We just have to show up. Or to open the book! But we drop the ball.

"Now that everyone feels bad about themselves," Zech gave a guilty smile, "let's flip this around, let's go back to how so many Israelites and so many leaders in the Bible have fallen away from God. This is comparable to modern times as well. But going back to the Old Testament ways, instead of you participating in the rituals, which we know is hard enough for us, what if you were the head priest in charge of them?

"Have you ever let some power, even a tiny little bit, go to your head? Ever think that you know better than someone else? Or how about, ever think you know better than your boss? If that little bit of power can begin to corrupt us each day, what if hundreds or thousands of people are coming to you for their religious purity. AND you have the authority to say if they are cleansed or not. If it is hard enough for us to cleanse ourselves, it may be even harder to do it for others. It may be even harder to not let it go to our heads, like we are the ones responsible for it. Just like God was warning us about when we put a single person in charge instead of always putting him first. We give into our own nature, and then we tend to think it is us that did it. That we were the greatness, instead of God using us to do his will.

"We have a hard enough time fighting back against sin in our life, let alone the corruption of letting a single person run the show.

"One of the many things I love about the Bible is that it recognizes our weakness and then God comes to help us. We are a mess, aren't we?" Zech raised a hand to show he included himself. "God gives us exact instructions on what to do, even has someone write it down so we can go back and check the notes, but even with an open note test, we screw it up. But that's okay. God isn't surprised. You won't shock God by praying about your weakness, like he'd say 'whoa whoa! Are you kidding me?! I just told you! You can't even follow ten simple rules?! Be gone, FLOOD!'"

Zech laughed at himself after this last comment.

"Just kidding. He said he wouldn't do that one again. Thank God for rainbows, amen."

Zech waited a moment, returning to the center of the stage, and leaned onto the small podium. He had been pacing back and forth, speaking to each part of the congregation as he emphasized parts of his message.

"As we get into our weaknesses, and realize that we must put God first, we move into the second part of today's message, individual accountability. If we put a person in charge, what do we have a tendency to do?

"If you ever trained an entry-level person at a job you probably have seen this more than you would like to remember. We have a tendency to simply *do what we're told*. And this is NOT just in early career, people, I see it all over. And I highlight it because it is a destructive habit if you are looking to grow. When we simply do what we are told, not adding our own thoughts, not adding in our own accountability, then we are safe."

Zech paused a moment and began an impression as his voice dropped to a low baritone and he bounced his shoulders in jest, mocking an overly masculine-looking guy.

"Hey, hold on, that's not my fault. I did what *YOU* said. Hey. Hey. Come on. Not my fault. Not my fault."

He smiled as he returned to himself and let the laughter settle.

"Nope, it's not your fault, friend. And now I know that none of the successes are your fault either. Thanks, I can outsource your position.

"Former Navy SEAL Jocko Willink has a book called *Discipline Equals Freedom*. Great book. And the premise is: if you control yourself, then you have the freedom to do anything. Such as taking care of your body. If you have the discipline to work out, then your body has the freedom to do more, to live longer. If you have the discipline to budget, spend less than you make, then you have freedom to buy what you couldn't otherwise.

"Mr. Willink also has a book, *Extreme Ownership*, that directly discusses taking ownership of your situation, whatever it is. Because once you take ownership of a situation, a job position, a problem, whatever, then you begin to work towards improving it. If you are constantly 'not responsible,' then you are passing the buck. You end up blaming your boss, or your employees, or your spouse, or whoever around you. And you know what, who do all those people, all the people you say have something wrong with them, who do they have in common. *You*. It sounds like the common denominator in all that blame is *YOU*." Zech pointed to the crowd to emphasize his point.

"To me, as a Pastor, both of those books and premises sound like following Jesus. Like picking up your cross. God will make the weak become strong. Sacrificing for the sake of others. Stepping up to solve a problem, if even you did not CAUSE IT, for the sake of others. For example, taking accountability for your faith and having the discipline to read your Bible daily, then you will have the freedom to live more like Christ. You are picking up your cross, taking accountability.

"Working out and finances, 'yeah, yeah,' you might say. 'We are in church, Pastor, come on now.' Well how about this, have the discipline to attend church *every week* and go to life groups *every week*, and you will have the freedom and connection that comes with a support network of Christ-followers.

"In Tony Evans' book *Kingdom Man*, there is a sequence of chapters based on Psalms 128. The chapters step through the Psalm to discuss first being obedient to God and how your life will be blessed. But not only will you enjoy your fruits, not only will you be blessed, but your marriage then becomes blessed, your children become blessed, then your church, then your city, then your state, then your country. One person, following God, can have an impact on an entire country.

"There are so many grey areas in life, that the enemy, the accuser, can take advantage of. If we are not taking charge of our lives, then we sit back, we look to others, and we lose. If we are not accountable for our own lives and those of our families, then we will lose because we will be following culture. We will be following the crowd, letting the world dictate to us our days. We will be letting in the darkness and not allowing Jesus to speak through us. We will be no different than the Israelites that drifted from God and ended up in captivity in Babylon. Ask yourself, what did we learn from all the falls of Israel?"

Zech paused for the last time as he then went into his conclusion.

"We need God to fight off that darkness within us. It is in us all, and if you let Jesus in, you can have a bright light in a dark room. A bright light that blasts through the sin. Jesus is that light, and we put him first, knowing he is within us. We can be more like Jesus. We can take accountability of our lives, to do our best to act, pray, love, help, all of it, but only through Him. He is our example, and if our bodies are our temples, and God is within us, then the old temple of Jerusalem is no longer on a mountain, it is right here." Zech pointed to his chest. "It is right here, within each of us. THE POWER TO MOVE MOUNTAINS IS WITHIN US ALL! And each of us can decide what fills our temple."

Zech looked out over the quiet, listening people as his keyboardist started playing a soft tone.

"What fills your temple? Is it Jesus? I hope so. And if it isn't, then let me recommend a good book."

He smiled and held up his Bible.

Matthew noticed that it seemed to glow.

***

As the service ended, Matthew thought about Zech's message. He realized that his morning routine and improvements at work were him taking more accountability in his life. He was now reading his Bible daily, praying more, attending church more, playing with kids more, and talking with his wife more. He was not feeling the sense of overwhelm he previously did when he tried to do everything. He knew he had a long, LONG way to go, but he was becoming the person he wanted to be. And it started with a small morning change to put God first.

Matthew looked over to J, smiling as he sought to say hi to his friend and chat before picking up the girls. J was uncharacteristically up the aisle and heading out of the sanctuary. Matthew thought he saw a disheveled look on J's face as he opened the door and walked out into the rotunda.

Chapter Fourteen

From Within

M atthew was surprised to see J show up for lunch. After seeing his friend walk out of service so quickly, he wasn't sure what to expect. He did not think his friend would retreat to the bar again, but it did cross Matthew's mind. A lot happened in the past month for J. He was the perfect heir apparent to Zech, but then Terrence showed up talking about his father Micah, then he discovered Zech's role in Micah's death, and now the discovery of the Ark and what it did to Ignace. Based on how he left the church that day, Zech's latest message on individual accountability seemed to top it all off for J. Matthew had never heard that sermon from his father before and thought he must have been saving it, or recently inspired to create it.

Matthew and the girls were there as J arrived. Liz was enjoying time out of the house with her friends. They were meeting for lunch, some shopping, and preparing for their Ladies with Hats and a Bible night that evening. Matthew ordered two pizzas, just as Liz had joked, and had splurged on stuffed crust and wings. His daughters loved the stretchy cheese at the end of each slice.

J arrived right as Matthew and the girls returned from picking up the pizza. Matthew was eager to ask his friend why he had left service in such a rush, but first, lunch with the girls. They would talk about more serious matters as the girls played and the youngest took her nap.

It was over an hour before Matthew and J got on the subject. After lunch, Matthew's oldest daughter broke out the puzzles and insisted on doing a large one with her Uncle J. The time was enjoyable and Matthew wondered if J ever longed for kids. The times they spoke about family, usually Ashley came up and J would tend to grow quiet or change the subject. Matthew did not want to push it but still wanted to show he was there for his friend. He caught J looking off in the distance a couple of times, and wondered what was on his mind. Was it something at church? The Ark? Ashley? Terrence?

As the girls began playing on their own, Matthew began the conversation and J started with the Ark.

"So what's on your mind? You left pretty quick earlier," Matthew said.

"A few things..." J paused "But hang on, we haven't had the chance to talk about the Ark yet! I mean, come on. First, how cool is this, second, what in the world?!"

Matthew laughed; he was so caught up in trying to read his friend's mind, he moved right past talking about the supernatural event they both witnessed.

"Yes! And honestly, 'what in the world' is a good way to phrase it, because it really is not part of this world."

"Agreed," said J.

"Have you seen Terrence since? I thought we might get a call from the cops or hear about a hospital trip. That guy's hand was really messed up."

"I have not. We had been texting regularly, but I haven't heard from him since. I texted him this morning to see if he was coming to church today, but no answer."

"So what do you think about the Ark? That piece Dad had in his Bible," Matthew said.

"If we weren't religious, I'd say it was magic," J said with a slight laugh.

"It was like a force field. It melted and pushed that guys' hand like soft butter," Matthew responded as he motioned his hands, crumpling one hand into the other.

"If that thing is really from the Ark, and it did that to someone's hand, it basically proves God's existence and the entire Old Testament, right?"

"I think so. We may be biased, though, since we are already believers," Matthew said as he grabbed two cans of soda water out of the refrigerator. "You know if it were ever made public, some scientists would claim it is a new form of electromagnetism or radiation that interacts with tissue or something like that."

J nodded. "Probably. Well regardless, I'm convinced. And who knows, electricity was once considered witch-craft. Maybe this is a physical sign of God on Earth."

"Hard to prove that, though, when it was held up against our chests just a moment prior, and it didn't melt us like the Wicked Witch."

J smiled. "I don't think I would have let Zech hold it up to me if I saw that melted hand first. It makes me feel for Uzzah."

"Uzzah?"

"He was struck dead when he touched the Ark. In short, King David wanted to move the Ark to the City of David, Jerusalem. While moving it, the Ox pulling the cart stumbled, the Ark faltered. Uzzah tried to keep it steady and he touched it, which disobeyed God's law to not touch it, and God struck him dead."

"That seems a bit harsh," Matthew said, not remembering the Bible story.

"Yeah, but there are a lot of different ways to interpret it. It is easy to think of the harsh Old Testament God that smites people who disobey Him. But, if you study that part of scripture it is not so simple. That could be God enforcing his law, showing us that He is steady and constant, or it could be an example that we can't save God, but that only God can save us."

"Or it could be Uzzah was sinful and he crumpled like Ignace's hand."

"Could be." J nodded.

"Did Dad talk to you about his sermon this week?" Matthew asked. "I feel like he brought that up just for us."

"Nope. Usually, we plan the details of sermons a couple of months at a time, or at least a few weeks out, but not this one. It was not on the list." J paused for a moment, and Matthew let the silence do the work instead of asking his question. He knew J had left for a reason and now it was at the forefront of conservation.

J soon continued.

"That one hit home..." J said as he furrowed his brow and looked down at the table.

"How so?"

"Being an individual, taking charge of your life. It's hard to explain... But it was screaming in my head the whole time."

"What do you mean? You have done great in your life."

"Have I? I basically followed in your dad's footsteps without even questioning it. I went to seminary, moved right back, without a second thought. Now when I look back, I'm not sure who's life I'm living."

Matthew did not know how to respond. He had never heard his friend talk this way. He stood there with his jaw hanging open, eventually making scattered comments.

"What do you mean... You are so steady, so good at being a Pastor."

"Yeah, I guess, but all this... I mean, it's great... but is this really what God put me here for? I feel like my life is passing me by. Like I'm in the passenger seat, and don't get me wrong, I'm enjoying the ride, but if I see the other cars or look to the driver's seat, I feel alone. I feel like I'm not accomplishing anything."

"Soon you are going to be head of one the fastest growing churches in the area. Thousands of people already hear your message. You impact so many people's lives for the better."

"Yeah...This is more than 'grass is greener,' though. Something doesn't feel right. Like I'm not in my right place. And another thing, and hear me out, I know the guy is misguided, but Terrence wanting to be more direct with the church audience does make sense," J said, looking away from Matthew.

The conversation held in the air as silence took over.

Matthew looked at his best friend in disbelief. He felt he could have been saying the same thing, as if he were the one that drifted through life. Going to school, then working at various companies. Even now, he was enjoying his new responsibilities but occasionally wondered why he put so much mental energy into improving factories and manufacturing plants. Was he really making an impact? He should be doing more. But Zech's message that morning inspired him; he felt he was doing his best. Putting in his full effort for Jesus. To make his small part of the world a better place.

Even with his newfound appreciation for his daily grind, if he compared his contribution to the world against J... It was no contest. J was a pastor; he literally showed people their first glimpse of God. He taught and brought people to God. How could anyone in that role not feel like they were fulfilling God's purpose?!

But Matthew's disbelief was proven right before his eyes. His friend was not lying, he felt that way, and Matthew noticed J's posture slump over in a defeated manner as they sat quietly.

Matthew hated the mention of Terrence, but he could understand the pull J was experiencing. Looking for a way to blaze his own trail, J was open to the New Christian's message of aggressive pursuit for the Lord. Matthew could see the powerful recruiting message Terrence was employing.

As the silence lingered, J snapped out of it before Matthew spoke, bringing his posture back up and looking at Matthew as he changed the subject.

"Let's go back to the Ark. Zech mentioned there are always two people, one in charge and a backup. Does this mean we are the next two? And part of me still burns to figure out how to use it. It seems crazy it has been a secret for thousands of years."

J continued, "So we both obviously believe it is real. That Ignace guy clearly wasn't ready for it and was hurt, but it did not hurt us. So it cannot be too close to just anyone, or at least until they're ready; otherwise, the person's character is going to get them hurt. What if it is something we could study, or make available on some sort of basis? The example of electricity's discovery is a good one. What if this is a spiritual version of it? That sounds crazy, but we saw its effect. And think of what it could do for the church and bringing people to God; the evidence case alone would persuade so many new followers. So many lives would be changed for the better if they were following God."

J had obviously thought about this already. Matthew had as well, but not as far as J.

Matthew spoke up. "Yeah, but let's back up. What gets me is that this has been private and protected for thousands of years. Why?"

"I have no idea," J responded. "I told you, Zech never talked to me about that message, but he just preached to us on individual accountability, the law, and rituals from the Old Testament. It feels like a cryptic message to us."

"Are you two meeting again tonight, the usual Sunday night meeting?"

"Yup, we can talk to him there," J said.

"Perfect, now let's think in the meantime." Matthew's business training now kicked in. "There are two ends of this spectrum, keeping it on lockdown or going public, and everything in between. If we "use" this in any way or talk about it to others, then it'll become public knowledge. You know how gossip spreads, and what would someone love spreading more? It'd be on the news in days, or hours, especially if someone posts online about it."

J responded, "But is that a bad thing? Let's say it does get announced and it's a media storm. It'd be a podium to talk about God and how he left this proof for us to share with the world."

The introvert in Matthew blurted out a quick response.

"You really want to be the one to have all those reporters and whoever else ask you about it for years to come? Ugh."

J disagreed with Matthew's line of thought. "Yes. Why not?"

As J responded, Matthew knew his friend had all the right intentions, but he still feared for his friend in this "going public" situation. If J was the face of the church for the Ark, then some would see him as a hero, as almost God-like or saint-like, yet others would see him as a false prophet, a hoax, a snake oil salesman. He knew J could handle it for a while, and even steer plenty of non-believers to the Lord through these conversations. But what about in years to come, when the media died down and yet potentially hundreds or thousands of pilgrimages would come to see the Ark, would come to see J. He wouldn't have a personal life, and the Ark would be in control, not J. If this thing turned global, J would be consumed by it. That could be a GREAT thing, and maybe this was J's purpose. His life's calling to shepherd this artifact into the world for God. But what if J lost his footing, what if he was influenced by someone like Terrence? And J was just talking like he wanted more autonomy in his life. This could be a shining beacon to help rid the world of so much sin, or it could be the first step into greed and despair. Misusing God's gift just as the Israelites did so many times.

Then it dawned on Matthew what Zech had been trying to get at in his earlier sermon.

The law and rituals.

The Old Testament.

The Ark.

It was so obvious now.

The laws were meant to clean people of sin, so they could get closer to God. There are numerous examples in the Old Testament of people getting too close without being cleansed or leaders, kings, or priests, falling from grace.

That did not work because man is flawed. We have too much sin that even when God gives us the way to get close to him, we still screw it up.

God sent his son, Jesus, to be with us so that he could be in us. You cannot wash away sin with a man-made process, if even inspired by God, because the man-made process leads to following man. But if you follow Christ, you can have the light inside you grow, you engage in the never fight against our sinful nature from the inside out. As Zech had said, "The power to move mountains is in us all."

You take individual accountability.

You look to the Bible instead of a human figure.

You center yourself to Christ.

Matthew's mind was spinning with thoughts. How could the Ark supplement Christ? It felt like two warring ideologies. The Old Testament versus the New Testament.

As he thought, the process improvement engineer in his head was now taking over and applying itself to his new revelation.

If God had a process for reaching us, and a point in that process was constantly failing, it only made sense to design out the failure mode. Just like a machine that requires three parts to work for the whole structure to operate, God is part, and He is one hundred percent reliable, but we are the centerpieces of the other two parts, our lives and coming to God. And we are not reliable! So if God doesn't bring us to him, we won't get there! With Christ, God was eliminating a piece that depends on us. He was improving the entire system by showing us we are not in total control. He was helping us get closer to him.

A piece of our flawed humanity was replaced by a piece of God himself.

***

As Matthew started explaining his epiphany to J, he could not seem to form the words right. His mind was racing, and he lost J with his scattered communication. He backed himself up to start from the beginning, trying to connect the dots to Zech's message. Then the girls came over wanting to play, climbing onto their dad.

As Matthew tried to ignore the interruption, J looked at his watch and realized it was time for him to go as well.

They agreed to discuss it later. Matthew would join J at the church for the normal weekly discussion with Zech, and they would ask their questions about the Ark.

Chapter Fifteen

Raided

After J left, Matthew saw he had a couple hours before needing to leave. He and the girls played one more game and had an early dinner before calling Liz. The ladies were all having a good time and now most were arriving at Millie's house. Millie was this month's host for dinner and fellowship. Normally, they met at the church, but this time, Millie had insisted. She said she was inspired to make her favorite enchilada recipe and wanted to do it in her own kitchen.

Matthew and Liz joked that Millie secretly wanted to make a few pitchers of frozen margaritas for the ladies. Millie was as steady and hard-working as they come, but she certainly knew how to let loose as well. She was a classic example of work hard, play hard. She and Liz had hit it off, and they got together at least twice a month for lunch or for Millie to stop by to see the girls. Millie was such a spitfire yet had all the grandmother-like qualities, and the young girls took to her as well. Grandma Mary was the steady and sweet grandmother figure the girls needed, while Millie the wildcard great Aunt. The girls often asked for "Aunt Millie" to babysit them.

Liz and Mary had left the shops early to help Millie set up for the night. She was there when Matthew called to say hi and let her know he was stopping by the church, with the girls, to talk with his dad and J.

As they briefly chatted about the church, Matthew heard Millie shout out, "Be careful or you might start working there!" Matthew smiled and was surprised to realize the church had become a sort of part-time job for him. All the talk about the Ark, regularly attending the Sunday night planning meeting; it was all adding up. Thankfully, it had not been too much of a strain on home life or his career. He made a mental note to talk about it with Liz, to make sure she was okay with the recent shift in his time.

As they wrapped up their call, Liz added one more comment that gave Matthew pause.

"Hey, babe, you still there?"

"Yeah, what's up?"

"So I don't forget to tell you, something weird happened earlier. A van pulled up outside of Millie's place."

"A van? Like a moving van or a family car van," Matthew asked.

"No. It was like a work van, a huge work van. No letters or anything on it. I figured it was a delivery, and thought I even heard a door open and close, but after a few minutes, it drove off."

"So nothing happened?"

"No, nothing happened, but it gave me the creeps. Seemed sketchy. I had just gotten here and was unloading the car, but after it pulled up... Well, just sketchy. I stopped carrying in bags and we watched it through the window. It ended up leaving."

"Hmmm, well, okay, babe. Glad you have a lot of people showing up. Maybe it was a delivery truck, but they pulled over to rearrange, or maybe a real estate person scoping out the neighborhood."

"Scoping out the neighborhood is right. Seemed weird. But anyway, other ladies are arriving, I have to go. Love you, babe."

"Love you."

***

In the moments before leaving, Matthew began using his phone to search for "God within You", "Prophets of Jesus from Old Testament", and "The Ark of the Covenant in modern times." He saw a church in Ethiopia claimed to have the full Ark of the Covenant.

"Interesting, well, I'd bet they don't have all of it," Matthew said as he looked over to his cat, Porkchop, who was now rubbing on Matthew's leg in search of dinner.

After feeding the cat and getting food for the girls, he continued his search. It led him to a site titled "The Bible Project." He recognized it as the program his church used for daily readings and the one his dad mentioned. Zech had used it often and had groups within the church join in order to finish reading the Bible in one year and watch the associated videos.

One particular video drew Matthew's attention. It was on "Holiness" and the uniqueness of God. The description of the Old Testament prophet Isaiah and the dream of the burning coal hit him so hard, he nearly stumbled. Zech had mentioned this in his recent message. It stuck with Matthew, but he was unfamiliar with the story. The burning coal that seemed to push away the sin was just like Zech's piece of the Ark.

However, in the dream, the contagious light of the coal stayed within the person. The piece of the Ark seemed to have a proximity. And if it was thousands of years old, it seemed to have a never-ending life force. It did not need to be recharged like Matthew's phone, which he realized was getting low.

As Matthew began the video for a second time, the girls now took notice and joined him on the couch, peering over the screen to watch with him. He was recalling Zech's sermon and the feeling he received when the Ark was close.

A popup for low battery came across his phone and it shook Matthew's trance. He was now running late. They loaded into the car and started off for the church.

***

The forty-five minute drive to church was a fun one. The girls led a sing-a-long and Matthew happily joined in, the three of them belting the latest princess songs. They missed nearly every high note, but their timing was spot on, built up with all the repetition of the familiar songs.

The sun drifted lower and the soft light was pleasant as Matthew smiled, pulling into the church parking lot.

But flashing red and blue lights erased his smile.

The parking lot held three police cars, lights flashing, at the front of the lot near the main rotunda doors.

The only other cars were Zech's and J's. Matthew wondered where Jimmy's car was, as this was their usual time. He and Isaiah must have already left or decided against their walk today. Matthew voiced a quick prayer for God to protect everyone in the situation and thanked God for the police. The prayer helped steady Matthew's nerves. He spoke it out loud for the girls to hear and it helped calm them as they approached the unfamiliar lights.

As he parked, he looked at his phone. It was on vibrate, and with all the singing he and the girls were doing, he had not noticed the buzzing. He had a missed call from both Zech and J, followed by two texts from J.

"Church has been broken into."

"Cops on the way."

Matthew gathered the girls and found Zech and J talking with two of the officers. The lights of the police cars now seemed brighter as the sun sank lower.

"What's going on? Everyone okay?" Matthew asked.

"Yes. Thankfully, no one was here," Zech replied. Matthew was immediately grateful the ladies were meeting at Millie's house tonight.

"Someone broke in and ripped up all the offices," J added.

"Really?" Matthew said.

"We didn't find anything missing, but they sure made a mess," J said.

"Any damage?"

"All the windows on the backside and around the offices," Zech said coldly.

"We were just talking to the cops about that," J said. "They were saying they will write the report as a breaking and entering, but since we could not verify what was stolen, it may have been more an act of vandalism. And that it can be common for churches to experience vandalism like this."

"It's not common for us. We have never had vandalism as long as I can remember, and it's not like we are walking distance from heavy crime areas. We are mostly in the woods," Matthew stated while looking around at the tall trees bordering the property.

"Yup," Zech said, still with a cold tone in his voice. He only broke his solemn expression as he turned to smile at his granddaughters.

Matthew's oldest girl spoke up. "Maybe they were camping. And they just came out of the woods!" She started walking toward the woods to go look for herself as Matthew pulled her in close, keeping her near as he held their toddler.

"Beth does have a point," J said, smiling at the young girl as she smiled proudly back. "This had to be deliberate. No one would just walk by and break over a dozen windows and toss all our offices."

"Maybe they were looking for s'mores," Beth said in an innocent yet detecting way that made Matthew proud. He patted her back and steered the conversation back to the break-in.

"Don't we have floodlights and cameras?" Matthew asked.

J responded, "And a costly security system. Zech got a call from them before either of us arrived. They thought we might have caused a false alarm."

"So maybe they caught something on tape?"

"Hopefully. They said they need to check the recording and they will get back to us soon. Apparently, since they record to the cloud, any recording takes up to four hours to recall."

"Well, that's good, but it doesn't help us now," Matthew said as he looked at the large building. He stopped to think how dark the building looked. Normally, there were multiple emergency lights on, even at night. "Wait, why is it so dark in there?"

Zech responded, "The main power was cut. And not just turned off, I mean cut. The cops found it when they arrived. Said it looked like someone took an axe straight to the live wires. And they took chunks out of the building around the wires as well."

"Geez. Will that impact the security cameras?"

"Hope not," J responded as he grimaced. "Didn't even think of that until now."

Matthew's oldest daughter, Beth, noticed J shake his head. She walked over to him and patted his back, "It's okay. We can still play tag later." The girl's innocence broke the tension. J thanked and hugged her.

None of this made sense to Matthew. It was a church. And sure there had been a few random protests over the years, but they were harmless and seemed to be more about posting online comments than actually doing anything extreme like this.

The way J explained their earlier conversation with the cops, it seemed like whoever did this was looking for something. And when they did not find it, they got mad and started breaking everything in sight. J said there was even a desk split with what looked like axe marks on it.

Matthew turned to look at his father, who seemed to be in deep thought.

"Dad, you've been quiet. What's on your mind?" Matthew asked. But before Zech could respond, Matthew blurted out another question.

"Do you have your Bible?!"

Now it all started to make sense to Matthew. Of course. It was Terrence and Ignace. They wanted that Bible. Matthew had thought they would stay away after what happened to Ignace's hand, but of course not. The power of it, whatever Terrence thought it was, clearly still drew him in.

Matthew's heart stopped in the split second he waited for his dad to respond.

"Yes. It's safe. And excuse me. Speaking of security systems. I have a few calls to make."

J and Matthew watched Zech step away as he began to search his phone and make a call. A moment later, J pulled out his phone as he received a notification.

***

The notification was from his doorbell.

He installed a smart doorbell last year, complete with motion sensor alerts, night vision, and a speaker. He got the biggest kick out of talking to the delivery people as they left packages. He would proudly belt "thank you" and "bless you" through the intercom, even if he was home. He felt like the Wizard of Oz behind the curtain, speaking to Dorothy and her friends.

J lived alone and he bought the doorbell more for novelty than for security. He did not pay extra for the cloud storage and monitoring like the church's system. However, there was one feature he never cared about, but now loved. If the power was cut, the device would obviously stop transmitting, but with the last bits of power from a small internal battery, it would send a notification on why it stopped.

"My power is off..." J said as he looked at Matthew.

J and Matthew quickly told Zech and the police, who were preparing to leave. Zech had abruptly ended his phone call and agreed to wrap up with the cops as they finalized their work. They quickly planned their next steps for checking out J's house and covering the windows of the church to shield the offices from the weather.

J would go to his house and make sure everything was all right while Matthew would bring the girls to Millie's house. They both would return and help tape up the windows.

As they left, Matthew hesitated and stopped mid-step as a thought crossed his mind.

Zech noticed the pause, "Matthew, what is it?"

"Something Liz said earlier. She said there was a large van that pulled up to Millie's house right after she arrived."

All three of them looked at each other and stepped in closer to hear each other better in the evening air.

Matthew noticed Zech look at his phone and then back to Matthew, as if Zech had expected a van to pop up in the story.

Matthew continued.

"She thought it was weird. Like it was watching them. But as they unloaded her car and kept an eye on it, eventually it left."

"You know the color? Or make?" Zech asked.

"No. I'll ask."

Matthew called Liz as he took the girls back to the car. J left to investigate his house.

Zech walked over to the police and let them know about the suspicious van and other potential break-ins.

***

Liz did not remember much about the van, except that it was big and all blacked out.

"It was really tall, with heavy tinted windows, and all black," she told him.

He asked again, about make and model or any other identifying marks, such as stickers or numbers and letters on any windows. She couldn't recall. Matthew texted Zech what Liz had told him so he could relay it to the police.

He had no idea if the police could even do much with a "suspicious-looking, unmarked van," especially since the suspicions were from recent victims of an apparent vandalism.

Liz was concerned, and a little agitated, when Matthew called to ask about the van and say he was dropping the girls off. It was their ladies' night and many of the moms in the group were looking forward to a few hours with their friends and no children hounding them for more snacks. However, she knew Matthew must have had a good reason and when he explained there was a break-in at the church and the "creepy van," as Liz called it, might be involved, then Liz and all the other women were primed to do what they could to help.

Matthew had told them not to worry, that Zech was with the police and it was probably just some high school kids screwing around. He was not sure if he was trying to calm Liz or himself more with his downplay of the situation.

Millie overheard the conversation as she welcomed the two young girls to her "fabulous, exclusive ladies only PAAARRR- TAY!!!" Matthew smiled, Millie could be cold and direct when evaluating balance sheets, but she sure was great with kids. The girls moved through the crowd of women and found their grandmother, Mary. She had beat Millie to hugging the girls first and now walked over and hugged her son tightly. Zech had called her right after calling the police, but she did not see the call. She checked her voice mail when Liz told her what had happened.

Liz kissed Matthew and told him to stay in touch and be careful. She could see something in his eye that he was not telling her. She did not like it but figured he had a good reason. They had a very open and honest rela- tionship. Matthew had learned early in their marriage that anything he withheld, even if he had all the best intentions, would eventually be sniffed out. Liz had a knack for reading his moods, and she had the bluntness to blurt out her opinion. That caught him off guard while his mind was in whatever other world or situation she was pulling him back from.

She did not ask this time because she feared his response. He had previously told her about Terrence and his concerns of the New Christians. Thankfully, he had not yet told her about the Ark and Ignace's hand. He planned on it but was glad she had not known that part yet.

He gave her a tight hug and they locked eyes as he stepped back. Millie leaned in over Liz's shoulder as Mary went back to the girls and said the ladies would all be on the lookout. She added that Matthew should say a prayer. Matthew thanked her and began to step backward away from the door.

Before he turned away, Liz called out, "You know you don't have to be the hero... Right?"

Matthew froze in his step. She continued, "You can stay here, and hang out with us, and it will all be okay. You know that, right, babe?"

***

Years ago, they had an in-depth conversation about the military. Matthew had a few friends that went into the Marines right after high school, which was not long after 9/11. He told her that he felt guilty not going in to serve his country. He had an academic scholarship and played hockey through college. Matthew saw a recruiter multiple times but was still on the fence. When the scholarship came through, he took it, thinking he might go in at a higher rank once he completed his undergrad. But it never happened.

He started dating Liz in college and never wanted to leave her, getting married soon after graduation. Liz had darkly joked once that Matthew would have been "one of those heroes who is remembered but doesn't come home."

Matthew didn't think it was funny and it led to a few deep conversations about if a terrorist, shooter, or whatever sort of life-and-death situation, occurred. Liz knew that Matthew was the type of person who thought it was his duty to rush the shooter. He was bigger than average size, played contact sports his whole life, and had done a couple years of Jiu Jitsu. By no means was he a trained fighter, but he thought he could hold his own, or at least slow them down enough for professionals to arrive, before they could hurt more people. Liz admitted she was being selfish of her husband, but said let the professionals handle it. If something like that happened, then call 911 and get away, run, go.

The old conversations flashed in Matthew's mind as Liz said, "Right?" one more time. Matthew stopped before he turned to his truck. It had been over five years since the conversation about being a hero had taken place, but now it resurfaced quickly. While the chances were slim he would be in a life-or-death situation, somehow they both knew the odds were much higher tonight.

Matthew looked at his wife and said in a clear and strong voice, "I love you, Elizabeth Light," and then turned away.

***

J arrived at his house to see his smart doorbell cracked and pressed in on itself, as if someone had kicked it in. He examined the doorbell but was confused to see the front door was still shut and locked. If someone had broken in, they had gone in another way. Or maybe someone simply came up to vandalize the doorbell. J did not buy that theory; it was too much like the church scene, and simple vandalism did not explain the power outage.

J walked around the side of his house and everything appeared normal. A friend from three doors down had waved to him in the glow of the streetlights as he took out the garbage. The normalcy broke as J went through the fenced gate and peered across the back of his house. It mirrored the situation at the church, where nothing was touched on the front, but the back had all the windows broken out. The mayhem of broken glass and debris from the internal damage filled his view. The incoming power line to his meter looked like an axe had cut right through. It ate deep into the stucco beyond the wires.

As a young pastor without a family, he did not own much, especially high-dollar items that could make him a target for robbery. Just like the church, nothing seemed to be gone, but nearly everything was ripped from its place or damaged in some way. His TV had a fresh crack running from corner to corner, the refrigerator had multiple dents from a bat or large hammer, and the door of his microwave was ripped off and thrown across the room.

The scene was like a shotgun spray of anger bursting out under pressure.

J spent a few moments walking around the house quietly, confirming no one was still in any of the bedrooms. After investigating the damage, he cleared a spot on the couch. He leaped up nearly as soon as he sat. He sprinted down the street to the neighbor's.

His neighbor, the one who had just waved to him while taking out the garbage, was usually out front with his kids playing before sunset. If their theory of the van was true, then maybe it went to his house after the church. His neighbor and his kids were usually outside playing at that time. Maybe he saw something.

J had talked with him plenty of times over the years and they had become friends.

"Hey, Tim, sorry to bother you after dark."

"No problem, the kids are still up and we're just heading for bath time. What's up?"

"Well, someone busted out the back windows of my house."

"What? Really?" Tim interrupted, surprised.

"Yeah, really. But it must have happened recently. Earlier tonight. Did you happen to see anything?"

"No, I don't think so," Tim said as he walked out front and looked down toward J's house.

"Nobody walking around or near my place? No vehicles, maybe ones you didn't recognize?"

"No, sorry, man. Is your place okay? Did they take anything?"

"A lot of damage, frustrating, but that seems to be it. If you think of anything, could you let me know? I'll call the cops and let them know, it'd be good to give them any info."

"Yeah, okay. Man, sorry. You know, on the community page they were saying a lot of folks were complaining about packages going missing. I bet it's some kids in the neighborhood, getting into trouble," Tim said as J was turning away.

J thanked his neighbor and stepped backed toward the street.

As J reached the street, Tim hollered out a last piece of conversation, "There's so many packages nowadays anyway. Wish you could ask some of those vans that are always coming through."

J stopped and leaned back toward his friend.

"Vans? You said there were not any weird vehicles around here today."

"Well, you know those delivery vans are out constantly. There was one closer to your place. One of them was a jerk too. He didn't get over far enough and then he yelled at the kids. Saying they were too close with their bikes."

"What'd this van look like? Company logo?"

"No. It was black, one of those newer ones, that are really tall and have a long back."

***

Before learning of J's power outage, Zech had stepped away to call Paul. They had a close relationship going decades back to before Micah's death and the first time Isaiah had shown him the Ark. With Paul being in security, Zech knew to call and ask his opinion on the church break-in. Plus, Zech wanted to warn him.

Zech had mentioned Terrence to Paul, but not with specific guidance for adding any extra security. Zech preferred Paul to keep it business as usual. Terrence was never supposed to find out about the piece of the Ark, and for all Zech knew, Terrence still didn't know. But he knew the look of rage, the desire for power on the young boy's face. As much as Zech wanted to be the picture of forgiveness, he could still see the rage ready to break out every time he saw Terrence. The stories of the New Christians looking to grow domestically, and by the looks of it in North Florida right near Zech's church, had kept Zech on high alert.

Paul was not puzzled by the vandalism masking a breaking and entering scene. He said it quickly and plainly.

"They were looking for something and didn't find it."

The conversation was brief as Zech responded.

"These same people may come your way. And they could be dangerous."

"Agreed. Isaiah gave me a heads-up on a van just a bit ago. A weird call, but you know your dad, and I sure know to listen when he talks."

"Van?"

"Yup. I'll keep an eye out and you do the same. A newer model Ford, one of their large work vans, all black with raised roof and extended back. The biggest you can get within that line. Everything is good here, but I'm going to head to the yard and double check just to be sure. Call me if you hear of anything."

"Thanks, Paul."

Zech just realized that Jimmy's car was not in the parking lot today. With Paul mentioning Isaiah, Zech wondered if they saw something and called it in. The cops did seem to get here quickly and they said "Mr. Light," not Zech. Did that mean anything? Regardless, it gave Zech a sense of security knowing someone out there was helping, especially his father. The sense of security did not last long, though, as Zech then flipped the track in his mind, now thinking his elderly father was somehow involved.

He started saying a quick prayer as he overheard J saying his power was out.

Zech knew that Isaiah had seen something and was ahead of them when Matthew mentioned that Liz was creeped out by a van outside of Millie's house. How he wished his father had a cell phone.

After Matthew and J left, Zech spoke to the police and warned them of the large, all black work van that seemed to be making its rounds at key church officials' houses. The police were engaged and listened to Zech, but they could not do much outside of keeping an eye out.

"Call 911 or us directly if you see anyone from the van doing anything illegal. Or if something comes up on the break-in," one of the higher-ranking officers said to Zech as he handed him one of his cards.

As the cops left, Zech asked to say a prayer over them, and to his surprise, all of the officers agreed. One of them even said he used to attend the church. That cued Zech's response, "Next time we talk, I'm going to have to find out why you said 'used to' in front of that 'attend.'"

As Zech began the prayer, they overheard a call coming from their radio inside the cars. Zech did not make out the communication, but the officers moved quickly and ran to their cruisers. Whatever it was, it sounded urgent.

Zech stood and watched the officers speed away with their lights on. After they were out of sight, he looked at his phone and saw texts from J. His house was in similar shape as the church and a neighbor saw a black van parked outside. Zech knew his house was likely in similar shape and he thanked God that Mary was at Millie's.

Zech returned to his car and exhaled a deep breath.

This was going to be a long night.

In one hand, he phone-called Matthew and then J, while his other pulled the worn green Bible from under his driver's seat. He told them to meet at Paul's Storage Yard as soon as possible. He held the Bible tightly as it glowed softly in the evening light.

Chapter Sixteen

Emboldened Evil

T errence looked at the piece of mail and smiled. It was a regular-sized envelope with a company logo in the corner, "Paul's Storage Yard," with the tagline "Advanced Security and Storage" under the company name.

He called off the trashing of Zech's house and shouted to Ignace. They had a new destination that night. There was no need to visit Matthew's house. Terrence knew the prize was locked somewhere at Paul's.

Terrence had thought it would take at least a year, maybe eighteen months, to infiltrate the church. He would recruit multiple key members to join his efforts, whether they realized it or not. First and foremost, he would make friends with the young up-and-coming pastor, Jeremiah Grey, and gradually convert him into an asset for the New Christians. He would do to J what Micah had failed to do with Terrence. With Jeremiah on his side, many other young men would follow the cause, starting with the young males in the youth group. They were not as physically gifted as the recruits Terrence would select from the halfway houses, but they would serve their purpose.

Eventually, J would have to give up any youth group stragglers who disagreed or had no value to the cause. Leaving anyone behind would be tough for J, but Terrence thought it was possible. Next, Terrence would "help" J shift his messages from the "feel good" and watered down messages into ones outlined by Terrence. Messages that reflected the New Christian point of view. Again, it would not be easy, but over time, Terrence knew he could get J on his side. He was driving action while Zech was too passive.

Terrence had to admit, Micah did have a good strategy for outreach. Lower income areas and prisons were fertile ground for Terrence. A message of salvation through Jesus gave all his recruits a strong moral code and foundation, something that deep inside they knew would make their grandma or parents proud. But talking about Revelation, opening the eyes of the world through power, always sealed the deal. Through "God-Inspired Power!" as Terrence put it. He even began and ended each of his meetings with three firm bangs on the table from a clenched fist and accompanied "G-I-P" shout. These lost men needed guidance, and Terrence was going to give it to them. Terrence firmly believed he was doing right by Christ, that he was empowered to bring what Revelation spoke of, and therefore prepare the Earth for Christ's second coming.

The eighteen-month plan seemed daunting to Terrence. He was not sure if he was going to make it more than a year listening to J's or Zech's messages as he worked on the younger pastor. He could not stand the weak message, but he bit down and continued to put up the charade. He had a crucial role to play in the New Christian's strategy for the United States. He was the first one officially deployed to the US and the starting point of a five-year plan laid out by the New Christian's president. Terrence liked this new leader and was flourishing under him. He felt the group had accomplished more in the past three years under this man than in Terrence's previous twenty-seven with the organization.

After spending nearly all of his adult life away from the region, he could hardly recognize the North Florida area when he came back. He spent years drifting within the New Christians organization, doing petty jobs with his father as they sought to prove themselves the first few years after moving to the Middle East. A few more years of petty assignments left him with multiple stints in Israeli or neighboring jails. Over the years, he learned how to build explosives, train on multiple firearms, and practice numerous martial arts. However, in the past few years, he found his calling in recruiting and it left him with a crucial leadership role in the organization. His role was also relatively safe amid the volatile leadership positions and risky terrorism-related missions that others were required to partake.

Through Terrence's lead in recruiting, the group's enrollment grew every year, frequently doubling from the prior year. Frustrated young males, once convinced, often brought one or two of their closest friends. The numbers alone were impressive, but the family wealth was what made Terrence's recruiting so valuable to leadership. The funding that flowed in with particular recruits made Terrence a rising star in the organization, and ultimately led to him being chosen for the inaugural US mission. However, Terrence was no fool and realized the money was why he was so valued. He ensured the new recruits kept loyalty to himself, and he ensured that leadership was aware of all financial contributions he helped secure.

Any rumor of a wealthy family's young son getting into trouble or hanging out at the wrong places was Terrence's cue. He would swoop in and speak to the boy about how he could become a man, and make not only his Earthly father proud, but more importantly, his Heavenly father. The strategy worked and soon some of the wealthiest families in the area were linked up with the New Christians. This emboldened leadership, and in recent years as the wealth kept increasing, their goals left the regional turmoil of the area and began to develop into global plans. The organization had thought if they could make an impact in the area where Christ had walked thousands of years ago, then it would proliferate to the entire world, and Jesus would strengthen them until his ultimate return. However, that strategy now shifted. As media grew and even desolate areas of the Middle East watched the news and had internet connections, they realized how the right plan could magnify their impact around the globe.

The group made the decision that they would lead no more foreseeable events in the Middle East. They would also minimize efforts in Europe.

They would go directly to the US.

The largest media market, with the largest economy. It was filled with sin, a prime target for many religious groups, and the world media would pick up all the news. If they made an impact in the US, the whole world would see it.

The goal was to bring multiple plagues to major cities in the US. It hinged on a key strategy, which was a lesson Terrence had learned from studying 9/11, another reason he was chosen to lead the first deployment team.

With border patrols and law enforcement always a threat, Terrence realized that many of the 9/11 terrorists had been in the States for months, maybe longer, before the attack. But instead of sending in international operatives, like the ones in 9/11, Terrence's recruiting could grow them right in the USA's backyard.

Why risk sending over high-ranking men or unproven recruits when they could grow it all organically from the States? Plus, these domestic recruits were expendable; if the mission went downhill, Terrence simply had to cut ties and escape.

Christ was patient and therefore the New Christians must be patient. Embedding themselves, recruiting, and then executing the plans would take at least two years, maybe more, but in their eyes, the payoff would last an eternity.

***

All was going according to plan. Terrence was working on J and he also began speaking multiple times per week at area halfway houses. As Terrence figured, every person at a halfway house that he convinced to follow him was one of two potential uses. Either they screwed up legally and had to go back into prison, where they would help plant the seed for more recruits, or they stayed out and Terrence would help to mold their new habits now that they were on the outside.

The only real issue was sorting through all the mental health issues. Some mental health issues in his recruits were fine, it could even be used to his advantage, but sorting out the "Non-Called," as he mercilessly called them, did take some time. Regardless, he was making progress.

Ignace was proving to be a loyal second-in-command. He was not the brightest young man, but he was strong and passionate about the cause. His physical presence alone helped convince people there was power in Terrence's message. Ignace often stood behind him, arms crossed with his large forearms dominating the view. Terrence used this to his advantage, like a business leader might use a large desk and high-back chair to symbolize his authority.

The plan was in motion and making progress, but it was now derailed and for the better. Terrence was ecstatic and thought that he could soon escalate the entire timeline.

Whatever it was in Zech's office that mangled Ignace's hand, Terrence knew that was the key. If he could get his hands on that, whatever that was, then he wouldn't need the support from the base organization. He could lead it all himself. He believed that with himself in charge, he'd be many more times successful than someone leading from thousands miles away. Less delays to wait for approval. All decisions through him.

It was now his for the taking.

Whatever this thing was, if Zech had it, then it certainly had religious significance. Just seeing what it did to Ignace made Terrence envision ways he could use whatever it was. He convinced Ignace that the incident was not an injury but a transformation. It was now his badge of honor. That he should have immense pride that he was chosen by God for such a demonstration.

Ignace was smarter than a box of rocks, but not by much. He deeply bought into Terrence's ideas and the New Christians, so much so that he never thought twice about his hand once Terrence explained it as being a demonstration from God. He had thought it was electricity of some sort, a live wire that he did not see or something. He did not know. But now, he knew it was God using him.

Terrence ramped up his efforts, energized by his new-found goal. He used every day to the fullest. He spoke at each of the three halfway houses where he had begun building relationships. Soon, his small group grew rapidly. He was no longer focused on building a core of strong lieutenants; he now shifted his recruitment from quality to quantity. He needed soldiers. Bodies to help execute his plan. His small group of five now expanded to over thirty.

***

Terrence held special meetings with twelve individuals from his growing group. He chose the ones with particularly violent pasts, recruits that had a history of using firearms or excessive battery. Any formal training, such as the military or MMA was also given priority to join his top twelve. He and his soldiers needed to find more information about whatever this thing was and then act boldly and swiftly to take it.

He overheard bits and pieces of comments about the Ark of the Covenant while eavesdropping on Zech, J, and Matthew in their offices. Maybe this power was related. Some sort of relic related to the Ark. Terrence envisioned harnessing the power of God here on Earth.

He knew of God's wrath, the "Old Testament God," as most phrased it, and the story of Uzzah. If this was indeed the lost Ark of the Covenant, Terrence could imagine himself as King David in the story of Uzzah, except he would not worry with compassion and argue with God. He would embrace the decision God made to take Uzzah's life and would apply it to everyone.

As the group of current and former criminals came together over a series of meetings in a backroom of one of the halfway houses, Terrence rallied them to action with speeches and guided instructions.

They started with a short chat and fist pounding table, "G-I-P!

"Men. We have an opportunity to do something the world will not forget. An opportunity to answer the call of God. To show the world. To open their eyes and let the scales fall.

"There is an item of great power that we must obtain to accelerate our plan. Many of you are not yet aware of the grand plan, but in time, you will know. For now, know that it is God inspired, and that you can become a greater man than you have ever imagined by doing your part. You each are a valuable member of this global organization and we will show the world. How often were you pushed aside, having to fend for yourself? How often were you misunderstood and blamed for others' incompetence? No more. God is speaking to us, empowering us to act. He chose you for this moment. He has been preparing you for this moment. For you to show what you, what *YOU*, can do."

Terrence pointed at each person in the room, softly and sternly mouthing the words, "what *YOU* can do" before continuing.

"If *HE* is for us, who could be against us?!"

Ignace gave a loud "Yes!" that startled two members. He then pumped his fist and it seemed to strengthen the entire group's resolve.

Terrence nodded and continued.

"This world is not for us. Not in its current form. We are different and we must shape this world for what is to come. We must bend it to our will, God's will.

"I want everyone to stop a moment and think of a major situation in your life. Whether good or bad, it doesn't matter. Close your eyes and think of your life-changing moment," Terrence paused and breathed deep.

"One of those life-changing moments was very recent for a fellow follower of ours. Open your eyes and look at his hand." Terrence turned and pointed to the disfigured extremity as Ignace held it up.

"God transformed him in order to show us what he can do. And with that power, we will do that to the world. To this nation. To this city. To anyone in our way.

"Somewhere in the local church, run by the Light family, is an artifact that holds this power. The power that did this to Ignace's hand.

"They lock it away. They seek to hide the power of God. The same power they hide and shy away from, this is the same power that we will embrace. They are preventing it from doing its duty. From humbling and teaching this world." Terrence paused another moment and emphasized his last statement, now in a more direct manner.

"We *WILL* humble and teach this world. Starting with the Lights and their church."

All of the men were on their feet now, with most shaking their clenched fists and nodding their head in agreement. Terrence took a step back and Ignace came in from the side to continue the speech.

"Six months ago, I was released after serving two years for aggravated battery. It was my second time in, and ever since I was released, I lived in this house. Anyone know how hard it is to find work after serving two stretches? Anyone remember how people look at you when you walk in asking for work, when they see your tattoos or realize you have done time?

"I got told to go be a bouncer, to go find a gym, to leave because I was making the customers uncomfortable.

"To leave. To LEAVE?! I have a kid, child support. If I don't pay it, I go back in.

"And I'll tell you what. I'm not going back in. No. No more. I'm not leaving until my work here is done. *THEY* can leave." as Ignace spoke Terrence pointed away from the crowd, separating this group from the rest of the world. "*THEY* can take a walk. Terrence was the only one who would talk to me like a human. Talk to me like

I had a purpose. And I am going to tell each of you that you also have a purpose.

"This guy paid for my groceries when I couldn't make ends meet. He helped me pay my child support. This group has money that can help us. This group has influence.

"This hand, THIS EXAMPLE." Ignace held up his disfigured hand. "This hand is proof of what we can do to the world. No more bending to its will. They will bend to ours. These are the gifts God gives us and we use them."

***

Terrence smiled as Ignace finished his portion of the rally. They went on to talk about assignments. Who would go where, ideas for what they were searching for, and what to do if they thought they found it. It was clear that whether they found something or not, the street-facing portion of the building should not be touched, but inside and the backside of the houses or churches were open for whatever was necessary to search and send a message.

They chose Sunday to be their operation, in particular, Sunday evening. Terrence knew they could hit the church before Zech and J's evening meeting, when the church was clear, and then move to individual houses as Zech and J came to the church. He also knew the police would be involved as soon as Zech arrived at the church.

To deal with the police, he made a phone call to his organizational support contact. His contact was like his handler or executive assistant. They were able to release a specific set of funds upon request and be able to do certain favors for Terrence as needed. It was not a service to be abused, as New Christian leadership monitored it closely. Terrence would be under strict scrutiny as the leading figure in the US plot.

Terrence had roughly $1.5 million budgeted for the two-year operation, with another $3.5 million as contingency. The money was for a three-year plan and included the cost of buying a modest house and car, in cash, as well as purchasing multiple lower cost condos or apartment rentals for key recruits. This also included funds for groceries and daily necessities for Terrence and the recruits he brought on, plus extra for firearms, explosives, bail, and bribes as needed.

Originally, Terrence balked at what he thought was a lowly sum. Over the years, his recruits, especially the ones from wealthy families, had contributed far more than a measly five million. There were times he thought the organization would have folded if it weren't for him. If the plan was to begin in New York or San Francisco, he would have requested triple the specified amount, but in the lower cost areas of Florida, there was no need to strong arm the organization. He would prove his value soon enough and have access to whatever he wanted.

Since he knew police involvement was inevitable, in his call to his contact to release funds, he also gave specific instructions for calls and reports to be made at a precise time on Sunday evening. One call was to be made to the power company and the others to the area police departments, starting with downtown and progressively extending towards the docks, near Paul's Storage Yard.

Now Terrence could better organize the search through the evening without having to deal with the authorities for a few hours. If he found what he was looking for, then no sweat, the police could use something to do anyway. If he did not, then he might have to use force, and the extra time without the police would be invaluable.

The time for gradual, long-term influence was over. He could smell his plan coming together and could envision the news casts. Videos of people joining his effort. He would remold society to his will, just as God molded back Ignace's hand. It was Terrence's God-given purpose, his gift.

As he loaded into the van and checked the time, he smiled. His memory flashed back to Micah grabbing him by the throat, picking him up and removing him against his will.

Never again.

He thought it then and he thought it now.

Never again.

The event felt like it was only moments ago. As if Micah placed him into the car as a boy, and with a swift turn, he rose up a man and began walking back to the original scene.

He was displeased that Micah was no longer around to see what he had become. To see what he was going to do. But Zech and J would have to do. He would keep them alive so they could witness it.

Anyone else, well...

They would be killing themselves by getting in his way.

Chapter Seventeen

Isaiah

I saiah had been watching for the New Christians ever since a young Terrence threatened him in front of Zech's house, nearly thirty years ago. In conversations with Zech, Isaiah would refer to them as the "Same Sinners," instead of using their "New Christian" name. He discussed with Zech how they were using the Lord's name for their own personal gain. It was the same old story, the same sin that kept rearing its ugly head in the world. Plus, he did not even like using the word "Christian" when referring to them, so "Same Sinners" became their name in his mind.

Terrence's story was a simple one to Isaiah. The man had twisted scripture in order to empower himself, effectively putting himself above God.

Isaiah had longed to preach to Terrence, to show him the error of his ways, to show him he could still come to Christ the right way. But Isaiah had also watched the struggle Micah went through trying to save the lost boy. Watching Micah wrestle with himself on how to save the one that got away brought up old memories for Isaiah. Memories from a lifetime ago when Isaiah and Rebecca moved their sprouting church into the local high school gym. The school principal was Isaiah's version of Terrence. A natural leader, smart, and capable, but unfortunately, misguided morally and spiritually.

As he looked back on the events that led him to leave the school gym and find their current property, Isaiah was heartbroken. He was happy with the outcome, and often thanked God for not answering his prayers from his younger days.

Seeing his grandchildren as they grew, watching the church expand, and long conversations with Jimmy were the life Isaiah now lived. He smiled more now than he did in his younger days. He felt God was allowing him to enjoy it. As if God was telling him that his time was coming to a close. Isaiah was certainly in no rush, but also now in his late eighties knew the time would come sooner than later. He prayed every day, asking God to allow him to see one more smile on his grandkids' and great grandkids' faces. The dozens of framed pictures covering his walls ensured that he would see all of his and Rebecca's offspring, at some of their cutest ages, every day of his life. The times he saw them in person was the closest thing he could imagine to heaven on Earth.

Seeing the generations beyond him, and the love it brought him, was the closest he felt to understanding God. A lifetime of preaching and studying the word. A lifetime of mentoring young leaders and coaching young people. When thinking of God's love, none of those things compared to two things: reading the Bible and watching the innocence of a smiling child. If he could be filled with this love, how the Lord must feel pouring out his love to all of his children across all generations.

Isaiah's experience helped him value the loved ones in his life and cherish the love of his late Rebecca, but it also showed him of the evils of the world. The wrecked lives of sin, of alcohol and drug abuse, of broken homes, of selfishness, of sexual aggression, and on and on. Sin always came back to pull down the world into the muck, to test morals and corrupt.

Many years ago, Isaiah wrestled with temptations, and he learned to see them as challenges, as a sign that he was doing God's work. A sign that he must be doing right if the enemy was tempting him so hard.

Demons come for us all, and if we are not careful, we are the demons that come for the world. Isaiah was old, but he was alert, he played brain games, read each day, and worked diligently to keep his mind sharp. If he was still alive, when so many of his peers had died, then God must have a reason, and Isaiah was going to be ready for it.

***

When Terrence showed up at Christmas Eve service, Isaiah knew Terrence was fulfilling his own prophecy from years before. Many hate-filled sinners threaten preachers, especially when those people are scared or at low points in their lives, but not many train in an extremist-style group for decades before returning to fulfill their threat. Isaiah saw when Terrence was first talking to J. He made note of it to speak with Zech, and later speak to J if needed.

After Christmas dinner at Zech and Mary's, Isaiah spoke to Zech, encouraging him to warn J at the right time, to use it as a coaching moment.

It was nearly a month later, when on a walk with Jimmy around the church, Isaiah saw J enter the church and rush out only moments later. J had overheard Zech telling Matthew about Micah's death. As J whipped out of the parking lot, trying to get away from Matthew and Zech, Isaiah had a hunch where he would go. He called Paul, and soon after J had arrived at the sports bar, Paul, Jimmy, and Isaiah entered as well.

J was in the back of the bar area, out of sight from most patrons, yet Isaiah sat in one of the few seats with line of sight to J. After ordering their drinks, Isaiah excused himself from his table and went to J.

J had just ordered, and he did not seem to notice that the young bartender with the tattoo stretching up her neck had lingered a few extra moments. She was trying to draw him into conversation, but his mind was elsewhere. He was imagining Zech shoving his father down a long flight of stairs, seeing in his mind an exaggerated version of what he overheard.

He felt the rage, like he needed to respond strongly, like he was seventeen years old and just saw someone cheap-shot Matthew. He was going to take that person out. No one would do that to his family.

Now he felt that same rage, but this time, it was against Zech. It surprised and confused him. To feel so angry over an incident thirty years ago, he had to leave the church and unconsciously found himself here, at the sports bar.

He was lost in his own mind, when Isaiah sat down.

J was surprised and it jolted him out of his thoughts.

Isaiah made a motion of "hello" but said nothing as he sat down smiling.

J started speaking first.

"Isaiah..." J said. But before Isaiah could respond, the bartender came back with his order.

"Here you go, big guy," the bartender said, looking to J and smiling, placing a full pitcher and basket of cheese fries in front of him. "Oh, I was wondering if you had someone else coming when you ordered a whole pitcher. Thought I might have to help you finish it." She raised her eyebrows on this last comment, adding a half-joking "eh, eh" before she left.

J was aghast. His normal confidence, his demeanor, his whole self was falling apart. With one story about his past, all the questions Terrence had been asking him about his father had spiraled into mental agony. What if he had finished the whole pitcher and then Isaiah showed up? He'd feel like such a fool. But not much more of a fool than he already felt.

J did have a glass of wine or beer every so often, but it was becoming more and more rare. Zech and he talked frequently about how church staff should not be seen drinking in public. Now Isaiah saw him, and he was obviously shaken by something, plus he was ordering a full pitcher for only himself.

J sat silently.

Isaiah did not reprimand or scold him. He just sat there with a slight smile on his face.

J could not take the silence any longer.

"I know what you're going to say, and no, I probably don't need to have all this. But come on, if you just found out that your dad's death was most likely caused by his best friend, and that that guy basically raised you, wouldn't you be feeling weird and want to escape as well?"

J continued without a word from Isaiah, "And, yes, I know Zech is a good guy, he basically is my dad. Yes, my mom was amazing, but I was at the Lights' house nearly every weekend and a couple nights per week. I mean, I admire him more than anyone. Look at what the church is doing under his leadership; it's never been better and still growing.

"But come on, he's talking to Matthew about shoving my dad, Micah, down metal steps, and he's never even brought it up to me? That's not right."

Isaiah said nothing as J kept on going, not giving much pause in the question.

"Shouldn't Zech have told me years ago? Why not tell me when I was a kid? Or at least when I started taking over more at the church. I am the one who will be leading the church when he retires, not any of his kids. Yet he never tells me?"

J stared off, through the steam rising from the hot fries and the melted cheese. Silence overtook the table.

After a few moments of silence, Isaiah spoke up.

"What would you have done? If you were in Zech's shoes," Isaiah said.

J shook his head and raised his shoulders, stating he did not know.

Isaiah soon continued, "Matthew's oldest, Beth, is now about the age you were when Micah went home to the Lord. What if you were involved in Matthew's death, would you tell her?"

J stopped and further considered the question. It was easy to say that he did not know when it was a situation from thirty years ago. Now Isaiah asked it in a way that hit close to home.

J imagined the little girl's face. He imagined her crying at her father's funeral. He took a deep breath and looked into Isaiah's eyes. Isaiah's skin was wrinkled heavily, but as J looked at his elder, Isaiah's soft smile and deep eyes seemed to hide all the wrinkles and pierce J's thoughts.

"No. No, I wouldn't tell her," J finally responded.

J sniffed as his eyes watered, his mind still on the idea of his best friend dying. Seeing the girl left without a father. With one question, Isaiah had put J in Zech's shoes.

They sat silent for over ten minutes, until Paul walked by the table, looking for Isaiah.

He said hi to J, but before a conversation could strike up, Isaiah stood up. J rose with him. He wanted to say thank you, to let him know the turnaround that Isaiah's presence had caused in J. His mouth moved, but no words came out.

Isaiah hugged him, then pulled back and asked, "You know, how's Ashley doing?"

"I... I don't know, it's been years."

"Hmmm, maybe you should find out," Isaiah said as he and Paul left J's booth.

J sat down and did not move again until Matthew showed up, over an hour later.

***

Isaiah and Jimmy had been taking walks around the lake behind church regularly for years now. They would talk about everything on their minds with no particular agenda. Both of them were grateful to get outside and move their legs without the help of a nurse. Many of their peers were confined to wheelchairs or round-the-clock nursing care, but not Isaiah and Jimmy. To thank the Lord, they kept moving.

They chose Sunday evening for their walks because outside of the occasional youth group or men's or women's events, the church was quiet that night. Zech and J came for their weekly meetings, but they were quiet. It was also nice that they sometimes waited in the parking lot for Isaiah and Jimmy. They would say hi and chat with the two sages. Isaiah cherished this time every week.

The small lake was a peaceful place to walk, especially before sunset, when the harsh Florida sun relented and a slight breeze blew across the lake. Isaiah was at peace here.

Lately, the peaceful Sundays were interrupted. First, seeing J leave the church so abruptly was a disruption to that normal peace. Another Sunday's peace was disturbed by Ignace's screams, after his hand was mutilated by the Ark.

Jimmy was in the middle of a story about his grandson when it was shattered by a deep, loud, and piercing scream. The sound was soon muffled by a van door rolling shut, and from their vantage point, the two men could see the van pull away.

Surprisingly, the two sages had not discussed the scream or gave it too much thought in the moment. They both instinctively had a "hope he is all right" thought combined with a "wonder if he had that coming" question in their minds. It would turn out to be the latter after Isaiah spoke with Zech.

As the van pulled out of view, Jimmy went back to talking about his grandson's new job. It was only when Jimmy mentioned that certain things seem to happen in threes did Isaiah link the van to Terrence and he grew concerned that there would be more to come.

It did not take long for their walk to be interrupted again; the following Sunday made three weeks in a row. The sages were on the far side of the lake and did not hear when the two vans pulled up to the church. They also could not discern the soft echoing noise that gave them pause. It turned out to be an axe cutting the incoming power lines and splitting the stucco and boards of the building.

They cautiously approached the church as the windows started crashing down. This noise was unmistakable and they shifted off the path to conceal themselves in the brush. They watched as the back windows were blown out one by one. Papers and debris flew about as the breeze from the lake now passed in and out of the offices.

There were at least a dozen people, maybe more, searching the various offices. Isaiah locked in on one person he recognized.

Terrence.

Terrence was leading the effort. Isaiah could see him as he hastily sorted through Zech's office, returning from the desk, to the shelves, then back again. Eventually, he took an axe and brought the sharp edge down swiftly on the thick wood desk. One blow did not split the desk, but after a few more rage-filled swings, the desk split in two.

Isaiah and Jimmy decided to wait it out instead of trying to sneak past to reach their car. Jimmy's phone was in his car, but there was no need to call the cops now. The security system should be alerting them. They said a prayer and before they knew it, the men were leaving the building.

The whole ordeal was roughly ten minutes. As they saw the group pulling out, they made way for Jimmy's car. Knowing the alarm system would alert authorities, but fearing the van was moving on to another target, Isaiah used Jimmy's phone to call Paul. He warned him to be ready. He said he did not have time to talk, but that someone might be coming to the Storage Yard with ill intent, and many guns.

As he hung up the phone, Isaiah nodded to Jimmy.

Jimmy nodded back.

It had been nearly sixty years since they fought side-by-side against the principal at the local high school. They might be elderly, but if they were still alive, then they could still fight evil.

They agreed to follow the vans.

***

The vans split up not long after leaving the church. Jimmy was a cautious driver, even in his younger days, and he made the split second decision to choose the van that required less lane changes to follow. The van was easy to follow from a safe distance, not only because it was so easy to see the oversized black van amongst the other cars, but because Jimmy seemed to know the exact route it was following. The van followed the same route Jimmy did after leaving the church. They were heading toward Jimmy's house.

As they entered the neighborhood, they wondered if this van was returning home, if the occupants lived mere houses away from Jimmy.

It was harder to remain inconspicuous in the low traffic neighborhood, but Jimmy knew the ins and outs of the roads well over his decades of living there. He could hang back in turns and speed up in straightaways to remain within sight.

They passed by Jimmy's street and continued deeper into the subdivision. The van came to a halt on the side of the road and they stopped roughly six houses away, just beyond a nearby stop sign. Isaiah thought the home the van stopped at looked familiar but could not place it. Jimmy knew it, though, as he sat on the HOA board and knew nearly every house in the neighborhood.

It was J's house.

The van door slid open and a group of men briskly walked to the back of the house, keeping their heads down and walking with a smooth purpose. They acted as if they belonged. Soon, another group stepped out of the van and followed just as smooth and brisk. They gave an appearance of belonging and purpose just like the first group. The only difference being one of the men scaring a young boy who nearly ran into him on his bike.

Isaiah wondered how many were in there. They counted eleven in all. It was most of the men they had seen at the church, but no Terrence. He must have been in the other van with only one or two of the others.

The men spent roughly ten minutes in the house, similar to the time spent in the church offices. Just before they watched the entire group reenter the van, the echo of smashing glass rang through the neighborhood. J's back windows must have been a parting gift as the men left his house.

Isaiah and Jimmy kept their heads down as the van passed by them.

They turned to follow them as Jimmy gave Isaiah his phone. He dialed 911. As they reached the front of the neighborhood, Jimmy hit the brakes as a basketball escaped a driveway and flew into the road. A young boy and girl dashed out, nearly falling as they saw the car and tried to stop themselves. The delay meant they lost the van. There were too many paths amongst the series of streetlights on the main road outside the neighborhood. Meanwhile, Isaiah kept trying 911. He was not getting through and thought Jimmy's network must be down.

Jimmy pulled back around into the neighborhood. Isaiah handed him the phone and Jimmy tried the call himself. This time, an operator picked up, took the details of the robbery, but Jimmy sensed something insincere in her voice as she said, "Someone will be out as soon as they can." He asked for the time estimate, but she did not give one. Upon asking further, Jimmy learned that the police in his area were all being diverted to handle an emergency situation. The operator let it slip how busy they were assembling nearly all on and off duty officers.

With a concerned look, he put the phone down and looked to Isaiah. Isaiah had overheard.

As the sun set, it was nearing time for Isaiah to return to his assisted living complex. He did not want Jimmy driving across town and then back again just to drop him off, especially since they were already in Jimmy's neighborhood. Jimmy agreed to loan Isaiah the car upon one condition, that Isaiah bring it back in the morning with fresh baked bagels and cream cheese.

Isaiah happily agreed.

***

Isaiah took the long way home so he could drive by Zech's house. If one van went to J's, maybe the other went to Zech's.

He was right. As he was pulling into Zech's neighborhood, the van was pulling out.

Isaiah turned around and followed it.

During the drive with Jimmy, Isaiah was trying to put the pieces together in his mind.

Why were they smashing into the church and now the pastors' houses?

Now following the van alone, it all fell into place.

Ignace's hand.

Terrence now knew about the Ark. But how much did he know? Zech was excellent at concealing the piece within his Bible.

If Terrence did know about the Ark, did he know about the crate at the Storage Yard? With the current smash and grab mentality of this group, Isaiah suspected Terrence did not know about the crate, but it was likely he knew about Zech's Bible.

He feared they would not stop until they found it. Isaiah witnessed Terrence's disappointment firsthand as it turned into rage that cut Zech's desk in half. The axe blade coming down sharply on the desk replayed in Isaiah's mind.

This group would destroy everything in their path as they searched for the Ark, even the lives of those in the way.

Isaiah slowed the car as he saw the van pull off into a small, rundown gas station on a side street. He couldn't believe it. Were they stopping for drinks and snacks in the middle of smashing windows and searching for an ancient artifact?

The van parked on the side of the store. As they unloaded, Isaiah parked in a far corner, away from the van but within close sight of it and the entrance. It seemed each of the eleven were getting out, as the door swung open, Isaiah caught a glimpse of numerous guns and sharp objects stored inside. This van was destruction on wheels, and Isaiah sensed it was hungry for more. Windows and desks were only the beginning of what it would eat.

Isaiah felt the urge to act. He knew he must do something. Before he could think, he felt himself getting up. The van was in between Isaiah and the entrance of the small store. He never thought about how he was an eighty-eight-year-old man. Or that he was walking toward eleven much stronger, younger men that seemed hell-bent on mayhem. He simply moved forward without a second thought.

As he approached the van, he saw the driver's side window down and heard the jingle of the keys swinging from the ignition. In a series of swift motions, Isaiah opened the door, stepped up the raised entrance, and took the keys. He kept walking, and in another motion just as smooth, he tossed the keys into the dumpster and walked toward the entrance. To anyone watching, it would have seemed the old man owned the van and was simply throwing out garbage. The keys quickly tumbled below the numerous garbage bags and smeared food remnants.

Isaiah kept going, now inside the store.

He saw three men arguing with a concerned clerk. The clerk was clearly not comfortable, now concerned with the large group active in his store. Another two men stood near the restroom and four walked around the store. Isaiah made his way through the aisles, His prior actions of effortlessly grabbing the keys and strolling into the store now dawned on him, realizing he walked straight into the lion's den.

He decided he would go toward the restroom. It had a line.

Once in line behind two large men, he overheard that one man was already in the men's room and another in the women's room. The men in line joked about the two in the restrooms. How both of them suddenly needed to go, an emergency or else "it's going to get messy in here," as one of them put it.

Isaiah thought that the sudden illness must have caused the unexpected pitstop to this tiny gas station. All eleven were in the store, with Isaiah and the clerk the only others. The clerk appeared to be the owner.

As Isaiah waited in line, one of the men walking around the store was opening up bags of chips and snacks, opening and tossing them at his leisure. He tried one thing, then tossed it aside to try another. As he turned the corner of an aisle, he was talking about their next location, "Next stop is up near the docks, that's the big one and last to search..." but he grew silent as his eyes found Isaiah's.

He stopped.

"Do I know you?" the man said as he approached closer.

Isaiah cleared his throat and smiled. He realized saying he was a retired preacher would alert them. These men just robbed a church and then the houses of its pastors.

Isaiah did not speak. He wasn't going to lie yet he struggled with what to say. While his mind raced, somehow he knew he could figure this situation out.

He decided to remain silent, smiling at the man and looking straight back into his eyes.

"You hear me, old man? I know you from somewhere."

Isaiah kept on smiling and tilted his ear toward the man, like he was trying to hear him better. Isaiah did not recognize the young man. He was good with faces, even after seeing thousands come through his church and ministries over his lifetime. Isaiah guessed the man had seen his picture in Zech's office. A portrait of the father and son, along with their "Temple Group," hung in Zech's office. In the picture, the group stood during the opening of the new church building. There was a flower-covered cross next to them symbolizing Micah's presence.

Isaiah wondered if this man had seen the picture, and if he smashed it like they had all the windows, desks, and drawers.

The man continued to get closer to Isaiah, but the questioning was interrupted. One of the men, who was previously hassling the store clerk, now shifted, antagonizing him into demanding cash from the register. As the man reached over, swiping at the clerk and the register, the man who was questioning Isaiah revealed himself as the leader of the ill-fated group.

"Hey, knock it off. If you are going to take the cash, just do it. It's time to leave."

The man in charge then turned as the bathroom doors opened, the two ill men walking out less pale than when they went in. He also looked to see Isaiah's back. The old man was now walking towards the door. Isaiah had used the distraction to get out of the store, and as he did, the man's eyes followed him. Through the window of the store, he saw Jimmy's car and he realized where he had seen Isaiah before.

"Hey! Old man! Stop!"

The commotion at the register distracted most of the group, giving Isaiah time to reach his car. As the man in charge moved toward the entrance, he shoved his peers, forcing them outside and ending the standoff at the register.

"Grab him! He's from the church!"

Isaiah was already pulling away as they ran toward his car.

The group piled into the van, and realized the keys were gone.

***

Isaiah drove around the corner and parked on the side of a nearby street. It had a view of the intersection ahead. He would see if the van headed north, toward the Storage Yard. The leader of this van had mentioned the docks.

Isaiah was right to warn Paul. Terrence must have worked it out that if he could not find the Ark at the church or Zech or J's house, he would go to the Storage Yard. Terrence might already be there. If the gas station stop was unexpected, then the van would head north, right through this intersection and the city's port area.

Isaiah took a deep breath. He began to feel his age. His body was tired and his mind weary.

He could turn the car around and return home.

He could also call the police again.

He did neither of the two options.

He sat and watched the traffic lights change colors in the intersection before him. He closed his aging eyes. The wrinkles filled his face.

He prayed for God's protection and wisdom.

He prayed for God to hold his Rebecca tight. He missed her, yet felt joyful that she had returned to Jesus, had returned home.

He prayed for God to be with Zech, with Luke, Mark, Matthew and their families. He prayed for J as he dealt the newly reopened wounds of his father's loss. For J to find his wife and to find a greater understanding of himself. For Matthew to continue helping the church in this time of need.

Finally, he prayed that God use him, Isaiah, for his Kingdom.

He prayed for strength. For wisdom. For courage.

As Isaiah opened his eyes, he saw the van continue north toward the Storage Yard. The men had figured out how to start the van. As it drove past Isaiah's line of sight, it seemed a darker black than it had before. As if the blackness of the paint was more than just physical, more than just pigment reflecting light.

It had a sense of death to it that pulsed from the van.

Isaiah no longer felt tired. In contrast to the van's blackness, he now had a soft, warm glow about himself.

He felt refreshed.

He was ready.

Chapter Eighteen

True Colors

Z ech arrived at the Storage Yard first and was greeted by Paul. Matthew was next. There was little conversation until Matthew started talking with Zech about the girls, how Liz and he planned to start potty-training their youngest, Lyn, soon. It was easy for him to shift the downtime in conversation to the girls; they were on his mind and he was with his father and father-in-law. Nearly every conversation they had was of their granddaughters.

As J arrived, the conversation shifted to the matter at hand.

The van.

The damage it was doing, who was in it, and when they thought it would arrive there.

J first apologized for being the last one to arrive. He had spent time calling the police about his house, but to no avail. He called the dispatcher back twice, and she would not say what was going on, but alluded to something "more important than a few broken windows" as she put it. J was a little ticked off by the comment, but he relented, knowing something was up in their city tonight.

They all agreed it was Terrence behind the break-ins, looking for Zech's Bible and smashing everything in his sight until he got it. Zech strongly believed Terrence was on his way to them next, to the Storage Yard. Paul mentioned the call from Isaiah earlier in the day, warning him of the van.

Paul had layers of defense built into his business. First, he never talked or advertised about all the valuables he had stored on location. A mere passerby would have no idea of the priceless items on-site, such as a crate that held parts of the original Ark of the Covenant.

On the outside, the yard looked like ordinary offices outside a small shipping port. Chain link fences and storage containers spread throughout behind the offices and close to the docks. The entrance had the same bordering chain link fence. An entrance gate was controlled by a manned security gate. Paul always had two guards on location. One at the entrance and one viewing and patrolling the storage areas, primarily through security cameras but also through walks to physically inspect at certain times. Those would not stop a major attack, but they were good for appearances and kept away most that needed to be kept honest.

The office building was flat, only appearing to have one story, and it was particularly wide. The normal visitor could not tell from the construction, but the structure was not only wide but significantly deep as well. It went back well further than expected and had basement layers. The subfloor level was not easy to construct, being near to the water, and was a costly addition, but Paul thought it valuable and worth the investment as the business grew.

The entrance of the building was similar to a lobby of a car dealership. The open floor plan had many windows in the wide space with couches and desks spread throughout. The back wall held numerous doors to offices and conference rooms. Zech remembered these doors well. Each time he came to see Paul, he was reminded of the first time Isaiah brought him and Micah here, when he learned the secret his family kept for generations.

The office doors and conference rooms behind the lobby were where the real security layers kicked in. These doors had heavy deadbolts and bulletproof windows. They were not impenetrable but would slow down many attacks, and gave the occupants inside time to call the authorities.

The final layer, which most people had no idea existed, was behind the offices and was the vault portion of the Storage Yard. To get to the vault portion, a visitor would have to enter the offices, then go through another door, which was typically hidden or blocked by design, before then coming to the corridor of the vault area. This area held the maximum security rooms, which lay on the sides of a long hallway that wrapped in a circle. Two staircases, one on each end of the circle, lead to a similar circular hallway within a sublevel. Every room had a fingerprint scanner and a number pad. Paul had upgraded to digital years ago and also reinforced the doors. The doors resembled undersized bank vaults, with a cold steel the size of a typical house's front door.

Paul looked over the lobby as the four men discussed the church and other household break-ins. He listened as the others mentioned aspects of the earlier break-ins. If the same people who broke into the church came to the Storage Yard tonight, would they employ the same strategy? Three things jumped out to him.

First, they did it when no one was around. Paul had security guards and cameras.

Second, they left the street-facing portions of the buildings alone but smashed through the back of the buildings. The Storage Yard was out of sight and had water behind it. Plus, there were no available entry points on the backside of the building. The invaders would need to come head-on and would be visible through the lobby.

Third, they clearly had weapons, such as axes and bats. But how many were there, and did they have firearms? Zech, Matthew, and J talked about only two people, Terrence and Ignace. If that was it, then four of them plus the security guards would be enough to dissuade any sort of attack and call the police as needed.

To be proactive, he decided to make a call to the police. He had friends on the force that he could inform of their suspicions. At least they could potentially go around the dispatcher that J had not had luck with.

However, when he called the local precinct, there was no answer. That couldn't be right. He called again. And again. Finally, on the third attempt, a lady short on breath answered.

"Hello, I'd like to speak with Sergeant Wallace."

"He's unavailable. If you have an emergency, call 911; otherwise, please call back later."

"What about Detective Li? Can you please connect me to him?"

"No one can talk now. Sir, I must go. If you have an emergency, call 911; otherwise, we can't help you."

"Wait, wait, but I want to talk to someone about something that might be happening tonight."

"Do you have information on the bombing? Or the other threats!?"

"What? No, I run a secure location and I suspect an attempted robbery is going to..." Paul quit talking, realizing what she had said. "Bombing?"

"Sir, if you have any information on the school incident that happened, it is your duty to inform us." The lady on the phone took a direct and forceful tone.

"What school?"

"It may be all of them. We are working to find out. So if you know something, tell me now or get off the line!"

Paul was silent and he went over to the lobby TV and switched it on. The others took note and walked up behind him.

"Sir. What do you know? Is this an emergency?"

"Sorry. Not an emergency. Good luck, ma'am." Paul hung up the phone. He could not find anything on the local news as he skimmed channels. As he kept flipping, he asked the others to search for school bombings. Their anticipation grew as they pulled out their phones and began searching.

J was the first to find something.

"Here. Megan Rodriguez just posted a video. She goes to our church and has three girls." He held the small screen so they could all huddle around. The video was posted twenty minutes ago. The woman's voice was hard to understand as she moved while recording. A large smoke cloud came into view as she turned past a corner house, in what appeared to be her neighborhood. The area on the screen widened and the video showed an elementary school parking lot. A corner of the center building was on fire, with hungry flames flowing out of two windows and reaching to the roof.

"Call 911! Call the fire department! CALL 911!" the woman screamed wildly in the short video. Paul looked up as the recording looped back to the beginning and the billowing smoke above a series of houses restarted.

"The police asked me if I knew anything about a bombing. That could be what she was asking about. But she said..." Paul paused as he shuddered at the thought. "She said it could be all of them."

J pressed the link in the comments to a local news station. The home page played a breaking news report.

The young broadcaster looked solemn as she quickly spoke.

"Hello. We have just learned of a school bombing in the Twin Lakes area. We also have reason to believe that more schools will be targeted tomorrow. Thankfully, no injuries or fatalities have been reported at this time from the one reported incident. The school offices that were impacted were believed to be empty at the time of the incident.

"The authorities ask you to please stay calm as they verify these claims and investigate the Twin Lakes incident.

"Please stay tuned and we will continue to be your first in coverage for your First Coast news." J exited the message. Paul picked up his phone and called his security guards.

Neither of them answered.

Matthew stepped close to Paul as he put down his phone.

Paul looked to Matthew. "We have company."

***

The black van pulled up slowly and stopped in the middle of the parking lot. The lot was small and flowed straight from the long two-lane road. The entrance road looped around from the other dock areas in the large port. The Storage Yard was the last on this side of the long road.

Matthew took note of how they parked. It was not in a single spot marked by the white lines in the black asphalt, but over the lines and covering four different spots. For some reason, this bugged Matthew and it stuck out in his head. Terrence was now showing his true colors. He was portraying that he was in charge.

Terrence got out of the van and smiled as he looked through the lobby windows. The lobby area was well-lit in the nighttime darkness. Terrence stood patiently, not moving, but smiling and looking in at the four men. His expression was eerie, as if he knew something they did not, and he was enjoying not telling them.

Ignace soon stepped out and walked to the front of the van. If events of the night and Terrence's eerie smile did not reflect their intentions, then Ignace did. He was not smiling but held a stern glare as he took his place next to Terrence. In his remaining good hand, he held a large shotgun, a modified Mossberg 590 that held extra rounds. He had straps with more ammunition crossed around his large chest. On his back, two wooden handles stuck out above his shoulder, one was another shotgun and the other a long axe.

Ignace handed the 590 to Terrence and then withdrew the other shotgun.

A long silence hung in the air.

Zech, J, Matthew, and Paul looked out the lobby windows. Any debate over the culprits from the break-ins was now put to rest.

Paul spoke first, quietly mouthing the words and knowing the lobby glass would conceal his sound from the outside.

"There is a gun safe in my office. It has two pistols, one shotgun, and two rifles. The code is 98625."

As soon as Paul finished speaking, the power in the building was cut.

Darkness.

***

Emergency lighting slowly kicked in as their eyes adjusted. Paul heard the building's generator kick in. It was propane-fueled and sized to sustain the emergency systems. It was also the building's third defense in the event of a power outage. The main line had a separate backup that was modeled after hospital power systems. If the generator kicked on, that meant the backup was not working. Paul knew this meant the feed from the power company was cut off completely.

Paul spoke quickly as he put the pieces together of the attack. He was the only one with any real security training and he spoke with the intent of empowering the others.

"They cut the power at the other places, and most likely, they did something to my security guards. Just like you all said, they were looking for something when they trashed the church and your houses. We can bet they'll do as much damage as they can. At least until they find it. But be sure, no one is getting into your secure room unless we want them to. Security systems are still active and default to locked during power outages."

Matthew thought the default locking mechanism was great, but it did nothing to deal with the two men carrying guns. Terrence and Ignace were now slowly walking toward the front door.

Zech stepped forward, mirroring Terrence in the windows. Matthew was about to run for Paul's office. They could hole up there and have their own guns for self-defense.

As Matthew thought, he was shocked to hear his father praying.

"Lord, we thank you for the chance to advance your kingdom. To protect your kingdom. Be with us tonight, Lord, as you work without us knowing. Be in us tonight just as you have saved us each and every day."

As Zech prayed, J stepped up and put a hand on Zech's shoulder. Paul did the same. As Matthew was ready to run for cover, he held his composure and walked to his father, putting a hand on his shoulder.

The prayer strengthened their resolve. It wiped out the impact of Terrence's fear tactics.

The cops were not coming.

The power was out.

Evil was approaching.

And now they stood. Together. Confident in God. Ready to act.

***

A confidence filled the four men, a strong and alert, yet peaceful, feeling.

Zech motioned Paul toward his office.

"Let's get the guns ready."

J and Matthew moved forward as Zech and Paul moved back toward the offices.

J locked the lobby door as he and Matthew took position just inside the door, near the first furniture section of the open lobby.

Terrence had reached the door only moments after J locked it. Upon seeing the locked door, gave a "really?" look towards J as he tilted his head. He motioned to Ignace, who fired a round at the locked door, blowing through the lock and shattering the glass on both of the double doors of the main entrance.

"I just want to talk," Terrence said as he stepped through the now hollow door frame, shards of glass cracking at his feet, shotgun at his side.

"There is nothing for you here," J spoke firmly.

Terrence took his time before responding. Ignace walked slowly through the empty door frame behind him.

"I think there is. In fact, you all being here reassures me that there is."

J and Matthew stood firm and silent, a cool breeze now coming through the broken door. Terrence grew impatient and tapped the gun against his leg.

He looked toward J.

"You can still realize your potential. You can still join," Terrence said, locking eyes with J. "Help the cause, tell me where it is."

J did not respond.

"You want to know about your dad. I would if I were you. I can tell you more. You trust the man that killed him, yet you hesitate with me? I have done nothing but try to help you. It is now your turn to help yourself. Are you going to follow in the footsteps of your father's killer or step up and become your own man?"

J's fists were clenched. He wanted to run at Terrence. To attack him. To hit him in the face over and over and over and over. J began taking a step toward Terrence. His sights were tunnel vision; he saw no shotgun.

He also did not see Ignace's smile break out as he raised his shotgun toward J. As J stepped forward, Ignace knew at least one of them was expendable and would be a good example to the others. He began feeling the soft pressure of the trigger.

In an instant, Matthew stepped forward and grabbed J's shoulder, simultaneously pulling him back a step and propelling himself in the forefront.

"J isn't lying. There is nothing here for you," Matthew spoke.

"Why are you even here?" Terrence snapped back quickly, irritated. "Trying to help your friend? Trying to be there for Daddy? You're not in the church, you don't know the history. If there is someone here that I would get rid of, I point to you."

Matthew deflected the insults. He doubted himself long enough in the past, but now he had the inner feeling. It was as if Zech was pressing the Bible against his chest at that very moment. He would not be brought down by these words. No more.

Matthew ignored the comments and took the offensive with his own line of questioning. J took notice of Matthew's demeanor and he shook the rage that was overpowering him. As Matthew began to question Terrence, J lost his tunnel vision and took notice of Ignace. J gradually edged closer to him as Ignace still held the gun, ready to fire, sights now set on Matthew.

"What is it that you think we have?" Matthew spoke as he stepped slowly forward.

"I am asking the questions here," Terrence replied, with irritation still filling his voice.

"You're the smart one. The clever one who has returned from the Middle East, ready to make glory for the New Christians in America. Right? It seems odd that you would risk whatever plan you had on coming here, with your guns drawn, and not even knowing what it is you are looking for."

"Are you not aware of who HOLDS THE POWER in this situation?" Terrence slowly raised his shotgun. Matthew ignored it, now locking eyes with Terrence and quickly closing the gap between them.

"Oh, but you didn't really risk much, did you? You are smarter than all of us. Too smart to risk it all tonight on whatever you think you overheard. You planted the bomb in that school and started the police on a wild goose chase. You had the power cut to the building and dealt with the security guards. I bet you've even thought of how to take care of the security footage from the cameras on this property and back at the church."

"You may be more observant than I previously thought—" but Terrence could not finish the sentence as Matthew interrupted him. It noticeably upset Terrence.

"But how did you convince your masters this was a good idea? You don't even know what you are after."

"I HAVE NO MASTERS!" Terrence blurted back. "This ends now. Hand it over or be a mere speed bump on my path to bring Revelation to this world."

Matthew was now less than a foot from the end of Terrence's shotgun. Terrence held both hands on the weapon pointing directly at Matthew's chest, but he was clearly rattled by the line of questioning, the way Matthew ignored the gun, the way Matthew ignored *him*.

Terrence was too rattled to fire, but Ignace was not.

Tension filled the air, as Matthew and Terrence held their eye contact, neither breaking free in their battle of wills.

Ignace's finger started closing on the trigger.

The sound of an opening door across the lobby broke the tension.

J lunged at Ignace's shotgun, his hand pushing the barrel upwards as his forearm swept the gun further toward the ceiling as Ignace fired.

The round aimed at Matthew's back now let loose but J's effort redirected it skyward. Matthew was spared but J was too close to avoid damage. The buckshot and heat of the round ripped past J's arm, taking the skin of his forearm and wrist off while blowing off his pinky and ring finger.

With Ignace's shot fired, Terrence cocked his weapon and fired towards Matthew's chest, but Matthew had rolled away in time, moving toward J, behind the tables and chairs that dotted the entrance of the lobby.

Zech and Paul came out of the office quickly. Each fired a round above Terrence, causing him and Ignace to fall back and take cover near the entrance. Zech and Paul slid down, taking cover behind another set of scattered furniture.

J left a trail of blood as he slid across the floor, taking a spot next to Matthew. Matthew flipped a large wooden table on its side for cover as Paul and Zech did the same on the other side of the lobby.

The three pairs formed a triangle across the large open lobby. Terrence and Ignace were near the entrance behind a desk. Matthew and J sheltered behind a table on the parking lot side of the lobby, while Zech and Paul hid behind a table on the office side of the lobby.

Paul peered over the table, only to have wood bits spray the side of his head as Terrence's shot came mere inches away.

Terrence and Ignace were outnumbered but still held the advantage. They had more coverage of the situation with better lines of sight on both parties. Plus, they knew Matthew and J had no weapons and the least amount of furniture to hide behind.

The time for talking was over and the younger two were expendable.

"Kill them," Terrence instructed Ignace as he pointed towards Matthew and J's area. "I will keep them down." He shifted his gaze, indicating Zech and Paul.

"Then we both close on them and get what we came for. Keep the old preacher alive; everyone else dies tonight."

Ignace nodded and both of them pounded the ground three times as they said "G-I-P!"

Keeping cover fire on Zech and Paul was easier said than done. Paul had seen the disadvantage and had crawled out from the table and shielded himself behind two fallen chairs. He could now safely keep Ignace at bay for at least as long as his ammunition lasted.

Paul's view of Ignace was rivaled by Ignace being in sight of Matthew and J. Their part of the lobby was more open and had less furniture for shelter. Ignace had them pinned down.

Matthew and J couldn't move because of Ignace, while Ignace couldn't advance because of Paul.

A stalemate was building, with Zech and Terrence left to determine the balance of power.

They each fired a volley of shots back and forth. Zech's six-round shotgun ran out first. Terrence's larger magazine now shifted the standoff and his impatience took over. He reloaded and began to move out of his position, keeping his barrel focused on Zech's position.

If he could not get a clean shot, he'd blast through the table. If Zech died, so be it. He'd tear the place apart to get what he needed if he had to.

As Zech reloaded, Terrence moved in and opened fire.

Matthew looked on in horror as his father crouched behind the spray of splintered wood and the table giving way.

On the sixth shot, from a gradually closer range, the thick table gave way. It snapped as large sections sprayed out, catching Zech.

Zech slid back in a crumpled roll. Matthew's eyes followed Terrence as he rounded the table, and looked down on the motionless Zech. Matthew began to stand and Ignace fired on his position, keeping him down.

Terrence smirked as he brought his foot back, preparing to kick Matthew's father. Zech lay motionless, but Terrence would test if any life was left in the man.

But Terrence paused.

His foot came down slowly as his eyes looked in between him and Zech.

Matthew could see Terrence's face look on with a puzzled expression. A glow now came upon Terrence, as if he were looking down on a lamp, the warm glow gently rising up to his face.

Terrence seemed frozen, and he moved back slightly, then a few more steps.

Matthew knew Terrence felt it. He found what he was looking for and now the sin inside of him was retreating, doing everything it could to escape the physical presence of God that was shining off the Ark.

Terrence was torn, his mind desperately trying to move his body closer, to grab the priceless artifact, but his body was being forced away, resisting more and more every second.

Zech's body twitched slightly. Then he began to move. As he brought himself up, Matthew could see the worn green Bible. It had taken the brunt of the blow. The green leather case of the Ark was now split and ripped pages shown through.

Zech had it tucked into his belt, near his back, and covered by his jacket. Now exposed, two heavenly golden feathers sat on the floor. It was the feathers of a wing portion, previously encased in the spine of the Bible, now shining brightly in the dark room.

***

Zech stood up and faced Terrence, who was still stunned and on his heels, ready to fall back. Zech picked up the Bible and held it in one hand, with his gun in the other.

The rest of the room remained in their stalemate, and were now looking to Terrence and Zech.

"Give it to me," Terrence said as he appeared to refocus his eyes and regain his prior state, still fighting the resistance of the Ark, urging to possess it.

"There is nothing for you here," Zech said loudly and firmly.

Zech's confidence overshadowed the fact that they were still outgunned. Even with a four to two advantage in their favor, the ammunition, firepower, and positioning tilted the advantage squarely back to Terrence and Ignace.

As each man desperately tried to think of what he could do to better the situation, of what they might do to take back the advantage, they heard a car approach.

Matthew looked past J, who had ripped off part of his shirt during the commotion and tied off his arm above his biceps to limit blood loss. As Matthew looked into the parking lot. He saw a large black van pull up next to the first van. They were identical.

That was how they covered so much ground without anyone seeing them. They had two vans.

"It's about time," Terrence said under his breath from across the room.

Eleven men piled out and stood next to the two vans. Each had at least one gun, additional ammunition, and some other type of weapon as well: a knife, crowbar, or axe stored in a holster on their back or leg. Ignace walked out to greet them, still keeping his gun positioned on Matthew and J through the lobby windows. Now all twelve stood and readied their advance to quickly end this situation.

The prize was at Terrence's feet.

Matthew looked to his father, Zech, and met his eyes, then to his father-in-law, Paul. And finally, to his best friend, Jeremiah, next to him. He looked each in the eyes. He had no options. He did not know what to do.

They were outplanned, outgunned, and now out-manned.

Matthew began to stand up as he closed his eyes.

He opened them as he started saying a prayer.

"Lord..."

But he never made it past the first word, the world seemed to stop before Matthew and he saw the next moment in slow motion.

A car came racing down the soft bend of the long road leading to the Storage Yard. It was moving fast and still picking up speed.

Most of the twelve did not hear it. The ones who did were not able to turn their heads in time to see it coming.

The car broke ninety miles per hour as it collided with the van and twelve men.

It tore through flesh and metal.

The front corner of the car hit Ignace first, as it cut through six men and then smashed into the first van. The remaining six were caught in between the two vans, instantly crushed as the first van left the ground and knocked over the second.

Both vans lay on their side as oil and blood filled the parking lot.

The car rested fifty yards away, smeared with the remains of the lives it took and the deep cuts of metal and glass from the collision.

As the slow-motion scene turned back to normal speed, it all happened in a blink of an eye. The men inside the lobby stood in silence, looking in disbelief over the carnage spread across the parking lot.

Matthew looked to the car.

It was Jimmy's car. The one he saw every Sunday at the church.

Matthew looked closer at the car, through the broken glass to the bloodied body within.

Isaiah was in the driver's seat. He looked peaceful.

He was dead.

Chapter Nineteen

The Aftermath

I saiah's funeral was a mix of somber and joyful emotions. Over a thousand people from the church and community came to pay their respects. The service was extended two hours in order for everyone to be able to walk by the casket. After service, only family and close friends proceeded to the burial at the family plot.

Zech had talked with Jimmy and found out how they followed the van to J's house and how Isaiah was supposed to go home. Neither was surprised by Isaiah's continuation to track the van.

All the Light family had returned to Zech and Mary's house for the funeral. Luke and his family came in from Georgia while Mark and his flew in from Eastern Europe. Looking back on the chaotic night at the Storage Yard, Matthew felt peace being with his close family.

Matthew's house was never hit by Terrence or the other van, but with the church, Zech's house, and J's all tossed and heavily damaged, Liz's concern grew immensely. Matthew had told her about Terrence, and everything that happened at the Storage Yard. He could tell it stressed her out, but just as the family being together helped Matthew, he could tell that Liz was beginning to settle as well. Liz also found joy in helping Mary redecorate the house after all the prior damage.

After Terrence smashed the mailbox and stared down Matthew, Matthew knew he was involved with Terrence to the end, whatever that might be.

Terrence would be back. Matthew was sure of it.

For Matthew, it was not just about helping his dad and his best friend run the church. He also felt closer to God, now more than ever before. This was about knowing there was evil in the world. Knowing his place against it. And knowing it was out there, waiting for him and his family.

Matthew also knew that Terrence would not stop. Terrence was coming for his church, for all his family had built through the generations. Matthew thought he must be there to protect it, not only what his family had built, but for all that was yet to come.

He looked at his two young girls, knowing that men like Terrence were out there. He also knew there were people out there like himself, ready to oppose evil and defend the good.

Matthew wondered if his girls would ever be involved, at least in the way he was.

Not if he could help it.

Regardless, he sighed in relief, knowing that would be a long, long time away.

He was going to work to keep the evil at bay, for his church, for his family, for himself. He would be the example of the man he wanted his daughters to marry.

He was so close to being killed by Terrence. He had walked right up to the barrel of his gun and survived. He trembled when he thought of it now, but in the moment, there was no fear; he knew he was protected. God had watched over him and stopped Terrence from pulling the trigger. And God also helped J reach Ignace's gun in time, to stop it from blowing a hole in Matthew's back.

If God had saved him, Matthew knew it was for a reason.

The Ark, the church, his family, more?

He did not know, but he would keep working to find out.

He would keep going.

***

Zech and Matthew picked up J and all three went to the Storage Yard together to meet with Paul. They had talked to the cops plenty in the past weeks, but this visit was not about the cops. Zech wanted to show them more about the crate.

After Micah's death, Zech had returned to the crate with Isaiah and pulled the piece of the Ark out. He had it securely in his Bible ever since.

Matthew had still felt confused about the situation with the Ark. He defaulted back to understanding it the best way he knew how, through a process engineering approach.

That God kept pursuing man.

That God kept providing ways to help man get closer to him.

The entirety of the Bible began unfolding in Matthew's mind like a simulation, a sort of repeated trial and error. God keeps nudging us along, and right when he lines it all up for us, we falter.

But no matter!

God lines it all up for us again and loves us unconditionally in the meantime.

Adam and Eve. Apple. Fail.

Moses and Aaron. Golden Calf. Fail.

Israelites. Naming Kings. Fail.

The Laws and the Pharisees. Well, God had had enough and shattered that one. It was time to upgrade the system. God knew if we were going to be with him forever, he was going to have to help us out.

Salvation is not reserved for one type of person.

It is not dependent on set rituals to cleanse and remove sin.

That has all been consolidated.

Now, it is all through Jesus.

And the best part, it is there for anyone who accepts *him*.

In Matthew's mind, this was like redesigning a system by incorporating crowdsourcing. Just as Wikipedia, a distributed network of people working for free, had trounced Microsoft's multi-million dollar Encyclopedia effort. Now we did not have to make a pilgrimage to the Temple, to one place. Now each person was their own temple. Each person could be reached individually by God and have God inside of them. No longer dependent on one system, but God in each person.

Matthew thought of these things on the drive to the Storage Yard. He had no idea if that was the right way to think of it, but it helped him relate to God.

***

The lobby of the Storage Yard was full of tarps. They were covering the blown-out windows and doors from the scene of the prior week. Paul was thankful none of the offices and back security areas were impacted. His security system was safe, especially the top priority item. The crate.

As they moved through the building and passed the series of security doors, into their particular vault, they felt the same feeling of confidence, security, love, and strength that they felt deep within themselves during the battle with Terrence and Ignace.

The crate sat in the far end of the secured room. A map hung on one wall. Matthew and J had never seen the map before.

It was a map of the globe, laid out with approximately a dozen pins. Most of the pins were in the US, but a few were across Europe, Israel, and the Philippines.

As Matthew and J looked across the map, Zech led them to the crate. Paul waited near the entrance of the room.

The same intense dichotomy of feelings grew in both Matthew and J as they approached the crate. A sense of love and welcoming, but also a sense of repulsion. Needles of pain reverberated through parts of their body, trying to escape, to run away. However, it was a little less than each of them had remembered before. It was still present, as they learned from Zech that it would never fully leave. It held them, a reminder of the potential darkness inside.

Zech held his Bible in one hand, as the duct-tape-repaired spine emanated the warm glow. With his other hand, he opened the crate.

Just as before, an intricately carved gold piece in the shape of feathers from a wing lay waiting, shining with the same warm glow as Zech's Bible.

"Pick it up," Zech said, motioning to J.

"What?" J was taken aback. He never expected any of them to touch the holy artifact.

"It's okay. It's your time." Zech held up his Bible as he spoke, with the spine facing J, reminding J of the piece he carried with himself.

J nodded and slowly moved closer. The feelings of warm love grew stronger in him, yet the painful points seem to be pushing harder. The love overtook the hurt as he picked up the priceless artifact. He held it up, examining it close to his face. The glow lit up his features and he squinted, as if the soft glow was a much brighter light to his eyes.

Zech spoke to J in an affirming tone, "A piece of the Ark of the Covenant is now yours. I believe God rests in these physical pieces and they are meant to remind and guide us. They are a link between the Old and New Testaments and I believe demonstrate that God is with us, supporting the case for Jesus Christ through the prophecies of the Old Testament. Jesus is the spiritual hot coal that cleanses the darkness, the sin, away from us, and I believe this is a physical representation of that process. The hurt you feel when you get close to it, let it be your guide. It will never go away, just as sin is within all men. But let the love you feel overtake you, to be the light that shines through the darkness. If you falter in your ways, slide from Jesus' and the Bible's moral code and teachings, this will tell you. I can tell you that from experience."

J had not realized it, but this visit to the Storage Yard was his indoctrination to being a keeper of the Ark. Zech was outlining what he had learned, to help guide J in his future decisions.

Zech continued, "Also, it is up to you how you use this. Many in the world are not ready for this, and you saw what it can do to those filled with more sin, more death, than they are filled with light. The light truly cuts right through death, and the sin can only retreat."

J held the piece tightly and nodded in an accepting manner to Zech. They embraced with a hug. J walked away from the crate holding his small piece of God. He walked toward a smiling Matthew, who congratulated him, and then over to Paul, who hugged him as well. Matthew had begun to follow J as he walked toward the entrance but noticed Zech was still at the crate, looking at Matthew.

"Now it's your turn."

"Whaaa... but, Dad. I'm not a preacher."

"That doesn't matter. It's your turn... If you choose to take it."

"But you said one person is in charge of it and another person is aware. Two people, one piece."

"Correct. That is *normally* how it works. One piece at a time, usually by generation." Zech paused before repeating and emphasizing "*Normally*, that is how it works, but not always."

"I don't understand. I have not gone to seminary, or studied the Bible. Dad, I don't mean to be rude, but until a couple months ago, I didn't even really like church. This is not for me."

Matthew was taken aback by his own bluntness and honestly, but it was how he felt. Either way, it did not seem to faze his father.

Zech responded, "So what happened over the past couple months?"

"Well, J and Terrence, then all this with the Ark. I mean, I read my Bible every day, but I also talk to the cat a lot more, so there's that..." Matthew stopped his rambling, noticing Zech smile on the "reading my Bible" comment.

Matthew looked back to J and then to his father with a confused look on his face, unsure. In contrast, Zech never looked more sure, more proud in all his life. Even J was now smiling after showing an initial confusion. J knew they would do this better together.

"Dad. This isn't for me..." Matthew said, beginning to be convinced. "Is it?"

He had acted with boldness and confidence in the face of Terrence's evil, but now that he was outside of the action, within his own mind, he doubted himself. Not seeing the path he was on.

Zech looked directly into his son's eyes.

"God doesn't call the qualified. He qualifies the called."

Matthew stood, silent, considering what his father said.

After a long moment, Matthew's posture straightened as he turned, now directly facing his father, showing his acceptance.

Zech opened the crate and a glowing piece sat, waiting patiently to be picked up. It looked nearly identical to the one J had picked up.

Matthew had not realized it earlier, as J took his piece, but Zech held up his Bible, which had a piece of the Ark in it. If J had just picked up one as well, that made two pieces. But even more concerning, he could have sworn the crate was empty after J took his. Yet as Zech opened the crate, a new holy piece was all alone in the crate, waiting for him.

Matthew's confused look returned to normal as he accepted what his dad was telling him. The supernatural that was exposing itself, was now trusting in him, and it was his turn to return that trust. To have faith.

Matthew knew he would be involved in the church going forward, but he had no idea the depths of what lay ahead of him.

The joy.

The challenges.

The heartache.

The pain.

Matthew picked up the Ark. He held it tight.

Chapter Twenty

Next

J opened his eyes and found himself on a train. It was nighttime and darkness lay outside the windows like a thick blanket. He could hardly see anything outside, only a blurred view of the horizon with no stars in the sky.

He squinted his eyes and tried to look ahead. Slowly approaching on his side of the train appeared to be a person. They were lit with a bright light, standing out in the darkness.

As the train roared forward, the person rapidly approached J. All his attention focused on seeing this one bright spot in the night.

The speed of the train gave only a split-second view of the person's face as J zoomed by.

It was his father, Micah.

J was speechless.

His father had just shot past, standing on a platform, with nothing else around him in the night air.

Micah was staring directly at J, somehow making eye contact as the train passed. He seemed to peer straight into J's soul while showing no emotion. A blank stare deep into his grown son.

J tried to speak. Tried to yell out for the train to stop, to go outside and talk to his father.

His legs felt like cement as he tried to get out of his seat, but he could not rise. He stopped struggling as he saw another bright spot approaching, another person, waiting outside on a platform in the night. The approaching light recaptured his full attention. This time, it was a woman. Waiting. Watching him. J sensed that whoever it was, they would be looking directly at him, even now as they were too far off to make out.

His eyes peered through the window as the figure approached. It was his mother, Ruth. She shot past as quickly as she arrived, and held the same blank, emotionless stare that Micah had pierced through J.

Before J could speak, before he could move his cement legs, she was gone to the distance, now out of sight behind him as the train moved on. He could now see more lights, more figures. Many more. Approaching faster. Faster.

Isaiah.

Zech.

Luke.

Mark.

All shot by his window in the dark, still night air. All staring at him without movement or a word. Lit up on a platform in the dark night.

J looked ahead.

An eerie sense overtook him as his point of view seemed to rise above the train. He could now see ahead of the train, and view both sides of the track in the approaching darkness. The tracks seemed to disappear, now a part of the growing darkness that the train was heading into, faster and faster. The blackness of the night seemed to pulse, to grow, and overtake the upcoming horizon.

Now two figures approached, one male on the same side as J's family passed by. One female on the other.

He could see the bodies but not the faces. The woman approached first. She wore the clean pressed white coat of a doctor with a stethoscope around her neck.

Her face materialized as she came into view.

It was Ashley.

She also stared at J, no emotion on her face. Staring straight through the train and piercing his eyes with hers. But she didn't pass by. Her rapid approach stopped instantly as she became parallel with J. She now stayed even with him as he and the train hurtled forward, as if she was connected to it, moving at the same quickening pace.

The other figure materialized an instant after Ashley.

It was Matthew.

He held the same look as all the others, and his approach also stopped abruptly, just like Ashley's. He stayed with J as the trio went faster into the darkness, picking up speed as they went.

J could sense their eyes on him. He looked at Ashley, and she stared at him emotionlessly. He tried to call out, but no words came.

He turned to Matthew, who held the same blank stare. As J tried to speak, he saw his friend's head turn.

Still moving, as if connected to the train, Matthew turned his head toward the oncoming darkness. He raised his hand and pointed. With his arm fully extended, he looked back at J.

J looked at Matthew and then followed his finger and looked ahead, where the tracks would have been, directly ahead.

There was a small creature in the distance.

A tiny snake-like creature. It was approaching rapidly, quicker than the others, and not on the side of the train, but coming directly at J.

J realized it was not only approaching fast, but it appeared to be growing, to be evolving and changing form.

The snake grew from the size of a small worm, into being over a foot long.

It kept growing.

Now it was as big as a man and picking up its head like a cobra ready to strike.

It kept growing.

Now as big as a building, with two large fangs the size of tree trunks growing out of its mouth.

It kept growing.

Arms and legs sprouted with sharp claws.

The fangs, the claws, were all pointed at J.

The head, now larger than a school bus, opened its wide jaws and showed rows of razor sharp teeth.

It bellowed a deep roar that seemed to shake the air with fear instead of noise.

The dragon snake was now right in front of J and the others.

It lunged forward, opening its jaws and snapping them shut.

Devouring J.

Devouring them all.

***

J had the same dream every night since the night at the Storage Yard. The night he lost two fingers from the shotgun blast meant for Matthew. The same night Isaiah sacrificed his own life to save them.

It took him three nights of having the recurring dream before he told Zech. He did not know what it meant, but he felt called to action somehow. It felt like a warning.

Ever since Terrence came to the church on Christmas Eve, J had felt uneasy in the church for some reason. He still felt welcome and like a contributing member, but no longer like he was home. As a child might feel returning to their parents home after growing up and moving out. It was home, but it wasn't.

He no longer felt like he was fulfilling his ultimate purpose within those walls.

He felt like he had a journey ahead of him.

Zech had helped him work through the dreams, trying to understand them and pray on them. To think of it as a message, a puzzle to decode and utilize.

Zech also recommended J talk to Mark about the dream. With Mark in town for Isaiah's funeral, the two had spoken at length about the dream as well as the differences and similarities in pastoring a church versus missionary work. They also talked about tips and tricks for international travel, and even into the finances and retirement plans for religious workers overseas.

The night before Zech took Matthew and J to the Storage Yard. J told Zech he would be leaving the church for an unknown period of time. If his mission was no longer within the church's walls, it was somewhere else, and he was going to find it.

"Well, it's about time you left, I can't stand you moping around here much longer," Zech had joked. Even in jest, Zech could not finish the wisecrack without laughing. The laughter was followed by a heartfelt hug and best wishes. Zech tried desperately to not overthink the dream, and warned J not to either. He thought J was going into a battle, into the belly of the beast. A battle he needed to be ready for. A battle where he needed the full armor of God.

***

Matthew and J had lunch together at the church after visiting the Storage Yard together and parting with Zech. They both held pieces of a priceless artifact. An artifact with supernatural powers, handed down generations and entrusted to them by the creator of the universe. They kept their pieces close, each within the new gift from Zech and Paul. A dark green Bible with a secret compartment in the spine.

Zech and Paul had given them the gifts before they left the Storage Yard. They could carry their piece of the Ark with them anywhere they went, in secrecy yet always at arm's length, just as Zech had done. The priceless treasure within the bindings of the Bible.

During lunch, J told Matthew about the dreams and they theorized what it meant and why he was having the same one over and over.

As lunch was wrapping up, J pulled out a map; it was a large, folded page of the globe, but zoomed in from the east coast of the US on one side to the Middle East on the other.

There were numerous markings and arrows on the map in the Mediterranean area, from areas around

Greece and into Turkey as well as down through Jerusalem.

It was a route. A travel agenda.

"So what's this," Matthew said.

"It's a compilation of Paul's three journeys."

"You using it in a sermon?" Matthew asked.

"Nope. I'm going to follow it."

Matthew stared at his friend, realizing he was leaving. It hit him like a ton of bricks. A deep sadness overtook Matthew, but as he looked at J, he was ultimately happy for him.

"How long?"

"No idea."

"When?"

"This week."

They sat in silence looking at the map. Matthew finally nodded. He smiled at his friend and broke the silence.

"Who is going to take over for you at the church?"

"Well, I know this one guy who is close to the head pastor. He has heard nearly every sermon imaginable, and rumors have it, he even has a piece of the original Ark of the Covenant."

"Funny," Matthew replied, not realizing that J's joke was more truth than humor.

They packed up their things, cleaned up lunch, and walked to their cars. They stopped, and without a word, they turned and gave each other a long, heartfelt hug.

As they broke off and began to turn, Matthew spoke, "I saw New England circled on your map. When did Paul pass through that area?

"Or did I miss the 'Letter to the Bostonians'?"

J smiled and drove away.

***

The story continues in **Book 2, *Shadows of the Ark.***

***

Reviews are a Gift

Thank you for reading. I hope you enjoyed reading it as much as I did writing it. **As an independent author, your word of mouth and reviews make all the difference.**

Please consider leaving a review.

***

Next Up - Free Preview!

Finally, before you go, I'd like to thank you for reading by giving you the first chapter of Shadows of the Ark, the next book in the Light of the Ark series.

Matthew Light discovered his family's holy secret. But now that he is an Ark holder, dark forces have him marked.

Evil knows no boundaries, coming for Matthew at his home, in the workplace, and in the church halls. With his best friend, Jeremiah, facing his own demons in Europe and his family's church locked in a legal battle, Matthew fights to survive the torturous attacks that pull him into a spiritual abyss.

Matthew, J, and their entire church face destruction as evil forces strike. If they don't internalize the power they've recently discovered, they will suffer a fate worse than death.

Please continue on to see the full first chapter.
I hope you enjoy it.

JAMES BONK

SHADOWS OF THE
ARK

BOOK 2 OF LIGHT OF THE ARK SERIES

Tidal Wave

M atthew watched Jeremiah drive away as his heart filled with bittersweet feelings. He would miss J, but he was happy for him. He admired J's action, considering the horrible recurring dream that flooded his friend's mind every night. As Matthew thought about it, maybe it was the dream that was driving J toward action more than all the other recent events.

Matthew got into his car and stared at the steering wheel, keys still in his hand. J's dream replayed in his mind. The introduction was creepy enough, the empty train with emotionless family and friends staring at him as he raced past, let alone the worm growing into a snake, then the snake into a dragon, and finally, the beast slamming its giant, horrible jaws on J, Matthew, and Ashley in one fluid motion.

Matthew felt a shiver down his spine as J described the dripping teeth that bit right through them, like a fork piercing tender sausage.

Besides the adventure of seeing Europe, J was going after his long-lost love, and Matthew admired that as well. It was a romantic addition to the impromptu trip to Europe that Matthew couldn't imagine himself doing. Liz's heart seemed to flutter at the thought when Matthew told her. No hotels booked, a one-way ticket, and minimal routes scouted beforehand. But J was a confident man. He was going to Boston to see Ashley and win her heart, and then off to Europe. With a map of Paul's New Testament journeys stuffed into his only piece of luggage, his backpack, J was going to show up, then let God guide his path.

Matthew stopped looking off in the distance and started the car. He felt the vibration of his truck underneath him as he pulled out of the parking lot. His mind backtracked from J's departure and the description of his dream. He thought back to Isaiah's funeral. Matthew had surprised himself by not breaking down into tears for the entire service. He was watery-eyed the whole morning before the service, and had broken down at the viewing the night before when he hugged his mother. But as he led his two daughters and wife Liz into their family's church for the open casket service, he held it together. He held his copy of the family Bible, and the ancient artifact hidden within, on his lap as they took their seat.

Matthew felt at peace as his father, Zechariah, the lead pastor in their family's church, led the service.

Zech gave an emotional eulogy and asked if anyone wanted to come to the front and share a story, a memory, of Isaiah. This was Matthew's cue.

Liz leaned over their two daughters and looked at Matthew.

"You okay?" she said. "You don't have to go up. Your brothers can handle it."

"I'm fine," Matthew nodded. "And if they're going, yes, I have to go up." He smiled at Liz.

Luke, Mark, and Matthew, along with J, had all agreed beforehand that they would be the first ones to speak. They all stood in unison and walked toward the front of the church. Each would discuss the most memorable time with their grandfather. They agreed nothing too dragged out, nothing too sappy, but heartfelt, clear, and concise. Exactly the way Isaiah would have given it.

Matthew wasn't sure he could communicate his memory without breaking down into tears, but there was no way he'd leave his brothers and J up there without him. He never felt overly emotional, but weddings and funerals hit him right in his tear ducts. And being the last of the four in their predetermined order, by age, gave him plenty of time to think of his watery eyes.

Luke took the stage first, and Matthew knew he would be fine. Matthew's oldest brother was the owner of a regional chain of vehicle repair shops through the Atlanta metro area. His leadership during the early stages of funding, recruiting, and then rehiring labor had embedded extraordinary confidence in different situations. He spoke like a seasoned speaker, giving pauses in all the right spots as he addressed the congregation directly and connected with the audience.

"I got into a lot of trouble in my teenage years," Luke led off, "and I know my parents were praying for me every night. But... for whatever reason... my dad just couldn't get through to me. It was like God had hardened my heart." Luke smiled as he looked to the side of the platform, toward his father. A small laugh came from the audience as Zech shook his head with a mocking stare of an angry father.

"But it was Isaiah who finally broke through to me. I had moved out, was on my own for years, and he began coming over, asking me to go on walks and telling me stories of when he and Grandma started their church. I couldn't believe those stories. He was like an action hero with a Bible. I hung on every word. Totally captivated."

Luke nodded as his eyes watered. "But it was his stories of dedication that stuck with me. The sermons he prepared for and gave with all his heart, even though only the same poor crowd showed up. I was turning wrenches every day, taking no accountability for my life, and here was my grandfather, sharing similar details, except he had a purpose. God was leading his life, and he was doing everything he could to help. All those sermons, all those empty pews, but he stuck with it, and he showed me what a little effort, applied every day, can grow into."

Luke stepped back as Mark stepped forward. Mark hugged his older brother and took the microphone.

Matthew knew Mark would cry, but somehow, he was still coherent. The former financial guru who handled all the biggest Silicon Valley IPOs had turned missionary years ago. All the acclaim and financial success only led to situations that pushed Mark away, leading to his calling for international missions.

Mark used his emotions when he spoke. He could connect with people on a deep level, and Matthew admired him for it, yet couldn't help but feel like an inadequate speaker as his brother began his memorial.

"Grandpa was always so consistent, so steady. He seemed to grow stronger when challenged, like he knew it was his purpose to run toward a fight instead of away. I had friends who thought he was a former Marine instead of a pastor all his life."

Mark wiped his eyes, smiled before he sniffed, and continued.

"There was a point in my life where I was looking away from what I knew was right. I started taking the easy road and was prospering financially because of it. I talked with Grandpa, and he told me the story of how he once carried a young man in need, on his back, for miles through thick woods over unsteady ground. He said he could have left the boy, and he probably would have been fine. He would have woken up the next day and figured out how to get home. But Grandpa knew the right thing to do was TO DO THE RIGHT THING! He hoisted the young man on his back and eventually got him home to safety. Grandpa helped me do the right thing, even when it wasn't easy."

Mark paused and wiped his eyes again. Tears rolling down his face but breathing steady, he turned to J.

J stepped forward on the podium. The funeral attendees knew Pastor Jeremiah well. He was the second in command to Zechariah for years, as well as Matthew's best friend and, for all intents and purposes, the fourth Light boy. After his father Micah died when J was a young age, he spent more time at the Lights' house than at his own.

"I became a pastor because of my late father and Pastor Zechariah Light." J motioned to Zech off to the side of the main stage. "And they wouldn't be pastors if it wasn't for Pastor... I mean, Grandpa Light. He held firm to his convictions and turned the key that unlocked this church and, eventually, my new family. I owe this family more than I could ever repay and I'd give my life for this church..." J looked down at his bandaged hand. The arm that only weeks earlier pushed up Ignace's shotgun and saved Matthew's life. The shell spray that took a swath of J's forearm and two fingers with it. J turned back to Matthew and smiled. "I'd give my life for this family because I know they would do the same for me, and because Isaiah gave his life protecting us."

Without looking back at the crowd, J stepped toward Matthew, and the two hugged. J handed him the microphone and Matthew stepped forward.

Luke was a business leader, Mark was an international missionary, and J was a pastor. Matthew was simply an engineering director at a local firm. He had practiced his speech and watched intently as the others gave theirs, trying to learn anything else he could in the last seconds.

Matthew gulped as he stepped up and faced the crowd.

"I don't have a... a specific memory of Grandpa..." Matthew stopped and blinked many times. He was trying to hold back the tears, to stay with his thoughts. He swallowed and imagined pushing the emotions back down as he looked at Liz and the girls. Beth and Lyn were red-eyed and sniffing as Liz held a tissue at the ready to wipe their noses. Liz was calm and collected. She never cried. Matthew joked with her that God formed her tear ducts from steel.

She smiled at Matthew as he looked deep into her eyes and continued, as if he was talking to her alone and not to the hundreds of families, friends, and church members in attendance.

"There isn't one specific memory I have of Grandpa, because they all seem to blend into one image, one persona that I remember him as. He seemed to see everything, whether in this church or at home. A new believer that was drifting, he'd know, and he would go find them before they left the building. He didn't want to take the chance that they'd never come back. At home, even when Grandma was still alive, he was the one who always, ALWAYS, knew you took some candy from their jar." He laughed to himself. "As kids, we figured out how to silence the glass jar by wrapping a towel around it, but he always still seemed to know.

"He ran a growing church, was deeply involved in the community. He usually hosted the entire family for holidays or whatever family event. He had so much going on, so many people to talk to, but even though I was the smallest grandkid he had, he always noticed me. I would look up at this figure, my grandfather, that was larger than life, with such history and stories and all that you heard from my brothers before me. But it never failed, whether mid-conversation or taking a turkey out of the oven. He'd see me and he'd wink. He'd wink at me and smile. I always knew that no matter what, I was important to him. He saw me. The man who saw everything, saw the smallest kid there who was just trying to survive." Matthew paused and swallowed. He wasn't worried about crying anymore. He was speaking from the heart and the spirit was guiding him.

"I pray that I have the same sight that Isaiah had. That I don't miss what is right in front of me."

Matthew thanked the crowd and caught his two daughters' eyes as he walked off the stage, winking at each of them. He handed his father the microphone and hugged him tight. Matthew's mother, Mary, stepped up from the first pew and gave him a hug, just as she did to the other boys. The four men all made their ways back to their pews and their individual families.

The memory of the funeral faded as Matthew continued his long drive back home, his eyes on the road ahead and his mind on the past.

He reached over to the passenger seat and laid his hand on the Bible. The harsh flicker of pain shot through him, followed by a loving and welcoming feeling that flowed through his body. He closed his eyes with a long blink and took it in as he sped down the long two-lane road that tunneled into the woods. The radio was off, and the sound of the engine filled his ears with a peaceful hum.

He opened his eyes and noticed dark clouds building on the horizon. The forecast was clear that day, but the humid North Florida air of early summer unleashed near-daily thunderstorms.

He dismissed it and drove along. Glancing in his rear-view mirror, the empty road rested beneath another set of angry storm clouds.

"Inland and the coast?" he said to himself as he pushed on the radio. Searching for a weather report, he skimmed his presets, but only various Christian, country, and pop songs played along.

As the clouds grew in front of him and behind, the sounds from the radio faded into static. The building storm grew darker, blacker, and seemed to eat everything in the atmosphere: the light, the radio waves, even the tops of tall pine trees seemed to disappear behind the thick mud in the sky.

Matthew leaned over his steering wheel, looking above him where the furious clouds met. They converged directly over him as he sped along. Wind gusts pushed the truck, at first gently, then more ferociously. He gripped the steering wheel tight, centering the four-door truck on the narrow two-lane road.

Looking to see if a tornado was cresting, he saw the clouds roll like waves. They reminded him more of an upside-down ocean, a black sea filled with fury, as if it would spit out a squall or launch into a hurricane at any moment.

White-knuckled on the wheel, he fought against the winds as they grew stronger and stronger. He pushed the gas pedal, hoping to get ahead of the worst of it. "Eyes forward, get through, come on Lord, let's get through," he repeated to himself. His arms tired as he tensed on the wheel, fighting the wind. Sweat beaded on his forehead.

Then, looking ahead, he eased off the gas and felt like a toothpick in the ocean as the storm clouds were on the ground. An opaque cloud rushed toward him like a black tidal wave. The trees bent under the wave's force, flexing their trunks and snapping off branches.

He slammed his foot on the brake and spun the wheel, forcing the truck into a 180-degree turn. The wind sideswiped the truck, forcing it from the road and off the shoulder. Grass and dirt flew up like water from a fountain as his tires dug into the earth.

He took his foot off the brake and stomped the gas, trying to get the truck out of the heavy roadside grass and driving the other direction. The spinning tires sank into the loose earth, spewing clumps of earth into the nearby forest as they failed to get traction.

Matthew turned his eyes away from the oncoming tidal wave and looked down the road previously behind him, where he was attempting to flee. His heart sank and his foot lifted off the pedal when he saw it.

Another wave barreled toward him from behind.

He looked through the trees on the sides of the road and saw them shake in the distance as the thick cloud of darkness rushed toward him. The wave came from not only the front and back, but now from the sides as well. It closed in all around him like pool water after a playful cannonball, except the opaque cloud of darkness, the mud, and the blackness seemed to swallow hope as it closed in.

In the instant before the collision, he grabbed his phone and pressed Liz's number, but before he saw if the signal caught, the waves crashed down on him.

He felt himself pushed and pulled in all directions. His truck was like a rubber duck in a splashing bathtub as giant hands made waves for the enjoyment of his misery.

Within his truck, he remained strapped to his seatbelt, the rushing waves flooding the cab. He felt the water latch on to him, putting pressure against him as if gripping tight and trying to rip him apart. It pushed and pulled on him, stealing the air from his lungs. It rushed his nostrils and forced his eyelids open. A deep blackness flooded his vision and wrapped his entire body with extreme pressure. He felt like a rag doll in a rinse cycle, thrown back and forth and forced to witness his own torturous method of death.

Before he lost consciousness, two red spots formed in front of him. They stayed with him as he thrashed in his truck and the rushing waves tossed the vehicle.

They were eyes.

Deep red, sinister eyes.

Thank You!

I hope you enjoyed the preview.

- Find it at https://store.jamesbonk.com/and enjoy a 15% discount with the code BESTSELLER when you buy directly from the author.

Acknowledgements

T hank you, Lord. None of this is possible without you.

My wife and daughters, for dealing with the extra time my mind spent in this world.

Leonard Petracci, for coaching me along this journey (*and for anyone who likes the Young Adult Sci-Fi / Urban Fantasy Genre, check out his work, especially the Star Child series*).

To Pastor Russ and my Life Group brothers at Southpoint Community Church, for helping me think through these topics via sermons and weekly discussions.

Photographer, Author Picture and Cover Model: Alicia Bonk (https://aliciabonk.com/)

Cover Art Designer: Jelena Gajic (zelengajic@gmail.com)

Editing (Proofing): Beth Lynne (https://www.bzhercules.com/index.html)

The Author

J ames Bonk writes Christian Fiction to develop his own faith and as a ministry. He lives in the North Atlanta area with his wife, two daughters, and fluffy Chartreux cat, Porkchop. When he's not writing, he's usually swimming or building forts with his girls!

His Light of the Ark book was the #1 New Release in its category upon release, with multiple five star reviews from adults and young adults alike.

Besides writing, parenting, and being a husband, James Bonk is a supply chain leader and business intelligence professional. He has a BS in Mechanical Engineering, MS in Industrial Engineering, and an MBA. He previously head his Professional Engineering license in Industrial Engineering.

Find out more at and get access to all his books at: https://store.jamesbonk.com/

You can also find James by searching James Bonk Author on your favorite platform or following the below links:

- Goodreads (https://www.goodreads.com/author/list /21997660.James_Bonk)

- Facebook (search *'James Bonk Author'* or go here: https://www.facebook.com/people/James-Bonk -Author/100092204034685/)
- BookBub (https://www.bookbub.com/profile/james -bonk)

The Author - James Bonk

Made in the USA
Columbia, SC
21 June 2024

37351452R00176